Dizzy Z

Matthew Holland

Published by
Soho Press Inc.
853 Broadway
New York, NY 10003

Library of Congress Cataloging-in-Publication Data

Holland, Matthew
    Dizzy Z: a novel / Matthew Holland.
      p.   cm.
    ISBN 1-56947-074-X
    I. Title.
PS3558.034956D59   1998
813'.54—dc21   97-29610
                                          CIP

Designed by Kathleen Lake

Manufactured in the United States
10 9 8 7 6 5 4 3 2 1

Read this book LOUD!

Contents

for Dan and for Mike

Part

1

1 Rant

ICK IT!!!

The problem is that the more famous my success as a musician makes me, the more it fucks up my ability to produce decent music. I get so god-damn, mother-fucking, son-of-a-bitching sick of touring, riding from town to town, playing the same goddamn, fucking songs night after night to idiots and morons who'd probably lick my asshole if I screamed at them, that that's all I want to do—scream, or pull stupid shit, like I do tonight.

I drink an entire bottle of Crown Royal right after the show. I couldn't even explain why, except that the band is getting along so horribly right now, which stresses me out about as much as having my fingernails ripped off with a pair of vice grips. Then Murph, our goddamn manager, lets someone cue up a couple of songs from the live Springsteen 1975–1985 collection in the dressing room. Not that Murph has ever understood me.

"Hey, Murph, any chance of you turning that *down* a little?" I yell. The rest of the band is there in the dressing room, but at this point there are only four or five groupies milling around, plus a couple of roadies who come in to ask Grover a question about his drum set. This is still too many people for what I'd really like to do, which is drop my jeans and air out my sweaty crotch.

"What's the matter?" Murph sneers. His face is normally so red that if you didn't know him, you'd assume he was almost as big a booze hound as I am. And right now it's even brighter than that. "Isn't this good enough for you?" he says.

"Actually it's too good."

"What?"

"I'm an insecure bastard, you know that. Don't play live shit for us ten minutes after we've come off the stage ourselves."

The moment freezes. He's staring at me intently. His eyes are small and focused; his brow is furrowed. He has no idea what I'm talking about. Drunk as I am, this is a revelation which pisses me off just as fully as the realization, only a moment earlier, that Springsteen's songs are so goddamn good I may never match them. That's what really pissed me off. Before I have time to think about what I'm doing, I cross the room, stab buttons on the stereo console until the CD player opens, and hurl the entire cartridge across the room. It strikes the wall, pieces of plastic snapping off, and falls to the floor. As I storm out, my second bottle of Crown Royal in hand, everyone else falls silent, even Jay. I can hear the wheels churning, their puny minds spinning, searching for an appropriate wisecrack.

"You're paying for that, asshole," Jay finally shouts. "It doesn't belong to us—it belongs to the guy who owns the stadium."

" 'It belongs to the guy who owns the stadium . . . ' " I mimic, a high falsetto. "Fuck off."

The band is Blood Cheetah, sometimes shortened to just Cheetah. What's in a name? Goddamn, I couldn't begin to say, except for starting with the huge paradox about success; that a new group can hardly hack itself a finger-hold without a good name, something that's hip and innovative, reflecting their musical style without being a cliché of that style. But once a band has developed a a reputation, all of the work they've done—their music, their videos and publicity stunts and love lives—becomes their name's legacy, overwhelms and stands for their name, makes it cooler than it was to begin with.

When Blood Cheetah is on tour, the tiny battle is to avoid negative reviews in the media, the larger battle is to stay out of jail, and the huge battle is to keep from killing each other or ourselves. Just the way Jay is always bringing up my offenses—past and present, real or perceived—is indicative of all the bullshit we put ourselves through, the same way my behavior illustrates how I always fall apart on our tours, until I'm strung out for weeks at a time without time budging, the hours a slug's slime trail, crackling in the desert noon heat, and me drunk and hung over at the same time . . . Aaaaargh!

Jay's our lead singer. Millions of teenagers across the country think he's a very cool guy. Except that he doesn't have brains enough to shave his head, or at least hack his golden-dyed locks back ninety percent with a heavy-duty weed eater. Nothing looks worse than a guy who's losing his hair, but tries to wear it long and hide losing it. Image is important in the music business (although Michael Stipe has proven that once you reach a certain level of success, you don't need all your teeth, let alone all of your hair). Ironically, all the primping, dyeing, combing, untangling, debugging, curling, ponytailing-at-dinnertime, and other hair maintenance is making Jay bald even faster. My own hair is fairly full, but sometime in the spring—maybe right after the Oklahoma City bombing and as a subconscious rebellion against how totally psychopathic the world has become—I quit trying to make it appear studly and hip, which has naturally made it very interesting and hip. By refusing to comb it, cut it, or condition it, I've allowed it to weave itself into a single huge dreadlock, my beavertail I call it. Gardener's shears would go dull trying to lop it off.

We're all from Dorchester, south of South Boston, and pronounced with the proper sneer by just about everyone except local news anchors; nose in the air, spittle out the side of the mouth: fuck'n Dohchesta, man. We may be dopes, dope fiends, drunks, perverts, scumbags, assholes, white trash, whatever you want to call us, but the five of us knew there was more to life than a dead-end factory job and a mortgage we'd be lucky to pay off by the time we retired. All it took for me was a picture of Cheryl Ladd on a late-seventies *TV Guide* cover. Her absolutely scorching period on *Charlie's Angels*, when she oozed sex and one glance of her, soaking wet in a bikini, gave me an instant baseball-bat erection. Dorchester is still with us, and maybe that's the biggest reason we're still together as a band; it's the type of blue-collar neighborhood you have to be from to understand. There's an underlying fear that if we ever break up, the rest of the world will see us as the punks we once were. Every band is a gang, don't let them fool you.

K Dot is totally lethargic and tragic these days, often as drunk as me, can't walk a hundred yards without huffing and puffing, but he goes about six-one, two twenty, and could kick the rest of our asses put together if push came to shove, even Grover's, no matter how many sit-ups Grover does or how many boxes of Wheaties he eats, because K Dot's always been tougher than anyone, and isn't that the one thing about the old stomping grounds that never fucking leaves you?

K Dot plays bass, Alex plays the other guitar position— which is a constant source of frustration and would take about three hours to explain, the way he's supposed to play rhythm only, but how he and I end up dickering over the juicy lead material, like a pair of twins fighting for their parents' affection.

Jay sings. And Grover is the drummer, only one of the reasons he's the group's resident fitness nut. Drumming takes a shitload of energy, so his arms were muscular long before he started working out with weights. Me, I could just about be encased in cement and still play, as long as my hands and wrists were free.

I suppose I've known K Dot the longest (I could even tell you what his real name is), and I should admit he's the glue that holds us together, both musically and emotionally. But in such an intense, intensive, inescapable relationship as being on this goddamn spring-and-summer-long stadium tour, our loyalties and friendships are constantly in flux. (*You were my best friend while you were a friend . . .*) To misquote Lionel Richie, "When young guys are starting out together and it's them against the world, nothing can tear them apart, but once they're successful, it's like slicing butter with a hot knife."

Tubbs follows me outside and then onto the bus, probably to protect me from myself as much as to make sure overzealous fans don't get at me. Blood Cheetah has sold almost nineteen million albums in the last ten years, which makes us pretty big goddamn stars, but the real danger is still our own unpredictable and irrational tendencies.

"You all right, Mac?" he asks.

"Yeah, I'm fine."

"You sure?"

I open the door to my berth and collapse on the bed, trying not to spill any of the Crown Royal. Tubbs pokes his massive black head in the door. His concern is getting ridiculous.

"Tubbs? Can it be? Is it really you, Tubbs? I heard they'd wiped your battalion out back in Carson City. Say it ain't so, Tubbs. *Say it ain't so, Tubbs, please say it ain't so. . . .* We'll show those bastards. Is it really you, Tubbs?"

"Seriously, Mac, you gonna be all right in there?"

"Well, I'm still alive. Might have a concussion, though."

"A what? What are you talking about?"

I start giggling, painful as any motion might be. "I ran into a pretty big ego tonight."

"What the hell are you talking about?"

"It was my own, Tubbs, get it?"

"Lift your right arm," he commands.

I comply.

"Now your left."

"This is how you see what shape I'm in?"

He squeezes into the berth and cracks the window slightly. "Roll over in case you puke, and don't you dare take anything else tonight except for maybe some water. Got it, Mac?"

7

"Sure," I say, shielding the Crown Royal with my body.

"You got any drugs in here you wanna give me to get rid of so you won't take 'em?"

"No."

"You sure?"

"I'm sure, Tubbs."

He turns to leave. "You better not. 'Night, Mac."

My name isn't Mac. I'd suspect the lard-assed bastard was trying to get back at me for nicknaming him Tubbs, except he calls everybody Mac. My given name is David Dillinger Zimmerman. I think my parents threw the Dillinger in because they knew I'd be a wild one, and it would give reporters a kick every time I got arrested. DZ, Zimm, Zimmster, DDZ, DDT, Doc Z, Dillinger, and Double D. I prefer either Dizzy or just Z.

8

It's nights like this when I wonder what's the goddamn point anymore and why *not* check out early, except that maybe I haven't done everything I can. . . . *What are you gonna do when the insects stand still?* . . . But maybe with one more album I could say it all and not have anyone else want to make any more music either, because they were too intimidated and jealous, just overwhelmed, too goddamn scared, chickenshit, worthless, embarrassed by their own feeble efforts, atonal, tone-deaf, unmelodious, crass, bullied, and insignificant. *Drop to your knees, it's you the world kills* . . . That's how I felt when they put Springsteen on the system tonight. His songs aren't really that much better than mine—at least if album sales indicate anything—but it's been so long since I wrote any new material that that's how I felt when they put him on.

Maybe it's not even the perfect album I need, maybe it's just the perfect song, right up there in self-righteousness, rebellion, and slashed power chords with whatever you choose for your own personal favorite rock 'n' roll classics. I know I've already written a few tunes that are considered such, but I don't even think they're my best material, they're just the ones that got incessantly and stupidly overplayed on FM greatest hits

"Real Rock" stations, damn it, or worst of all got popular because they were the videos that were foisted on the public, huckstered, watered down, and fed like gruel—*gruel, glorious gruel*—to the disc-buying public, the target demographic of bored, frustrated, alienated, and pissed-off teenagers. None of which even mentions the perfect note, the perfect musical sound, the Grail of even the heaviest heavy metal bands.

Pretty soon it's two thirty in the morning. I sit up, back against the glass of the window, cool through my T-shirt. The bus is silent, but I can hear a car or two leaving the stadium outside. In the distance, a siren blares, then fades away. The other guys are off partying somewhere. I resume drinking the Crown Royal, and the more I drink, the darker my thoughts get.

Can't I start again? Can't I redo, redux, Dippity Doo? What's the rock 'n' roll equivalent of a James Earl Jones howl of joyous laughter, David Lee Roth when Van Halen was young and didn't care about anything except whether the sun was shining every California day? Jay and I used to be like that, a long time ago. It's what I want again, not to piss and moan constantly, bitch about this, bitch about that, bitch because I'm drunk so often, occasionally boosted with various recreational drugs. Hell, I wish I had a big fat fucking doobie joint right now. Nothing works right, no work is done except playing Blood Cheetah's goddamn shows, and what fun is that anymore? Can't it be better than a warped production line, another factory job, with a hallucinatory punch clock, the foreman a million people all demanding my fucking time and attention and sobriety: management, sound check guys, lighting guys, all our various roadies, the fucking press, which is tearing us new assholes every day because so much is going wrong this time, and last but most importantly, the goddamn fans.

Sometimes I get so goddamned, motherfucking, God-mother-damn-fucking shit piss fuck sick of even thinking about music, *especially* rock 'n' roll; who's hot, who's next to be, who's already embittered, who gets what type of publicity,

9

who wrote what, who I have to worry about being better than me, when I myself have met literally hundreds of guys who can play a guitar as well as I can, at least technically . . .

I get so sick of worrying about all this shit that, even when I'm sober for two or three days straight, and beginning to dream about thinking issues through—it's about as pleasant as puking sand, broken glass or rose thorns, the type of puking where the synapse below your balls clenches so tight it's almost an autocastration and you wake up with sore stomach muscles. Flashbacks aren't even a phenomenon anymore, nothing surprising, nothing terrifying; when it's late at night or early in the morning, whenever I'm calmest, I slip from the present into certain parts of the past as easily as most people breathe, or post a note to pick up milk on the way home. I could enjoy it if I had more time, if there wasn't the goddamn, motherfucking crush of people, places, faces (*ha, him rhyme good!*), and travel . . . Aaaaaargh!

Even my obscenities are clichés, every time I scream "Goddamn, motherfucking shit piss fuck!" And this fucking pisses me off to no end. I'm nasty and gnarly and only give a shit about anything at the end of everything, in the absolute, final, on-your-knees-praying-for-your-holy-God-motherfucking-soul second, or whatever description of the universe-about-to-end you personally prefer. Feel free to kick words into my gaping, epiglottal hole of a mouth, everybody else does. Feel free to criticize me, make fun of me, try to steal my money, point out my arrogance, stupid mistakes, my personal crises, my hypocrisies; even to commit the worst sins of all, telling me my music sucks or perverting my work into things I myself never intended, which is so fucking shit piss fuck easy, because all I ever intended it to be was just that, simply that—music.

Cunt is the only word I can even begin to find offensive anymore, and that's because it's about women, meant to degrade, abuse, and subjugate them, and women have at some points played important roles in my life, my fucking measly existence of sucking in equal parts whiskey, drugs, and oxygen, a bloated corpse of a luminescent white carp, eyes bulging, gills rasping for breath, half-dead, rolling and unable to leave the surface, the minnows nibbling at my flank, my scales flaking off. *Cunt* is probably the only taboo word left in movies, as well. *Bitch* lost its ability to shock anyone after J. R. Ewing used it on television—though it's incredibly typical of me that that probably wasn't the first time the censors let it by, just the first one I can remember. Cunts may be what some of the other guys in the band, or even in the crew, call the young chicks who are so tempting, and sometimes worth the effort, but who the hell could I call that and really mean it but myself? Little Miss hot-ass, hot-legs, tight-box, blowjob-lips, wasp-waisted blond Clipper?

She's been my girlfriend, off and on, for about four years. She's modeling down in L.A. right now, and I'm dying to call her, if for no other reason than that I promised I wouldn't call until this tour was over and we'd both had time to work out our feelings. We've been telling ourselves it's over for three of the four years we've been together, and that we should move on to other relationships. Then we end up back together. We'll see what happens this time. I guess she's got some pretty good reasons to be pissed off at me.

There it is, fuck fuck fuck (*fuck this and fuck that, fuck it . . .*), so here I am, this is reality; wretched, painful, useless—MY LIFE IS HELL—and just admitting this much is only the beginning of the huge shit that needs to launch from my anus for life to ever be good again. Taxi! Waiter! Fire! It's almost time for me to go. It's almost time for me to pass out again. I take a few final swigs to put me over the precipice. The taste spreads fragrantly as it warms in my mouth, then burns as I swallow slowly. I can't believe this is my second bottle tonight and I can't believe I haven't finished it either.

The mattress is calling. I should have come back to the bus and tried to write some music. I guess I've only been ranting roller-coaster lunatic psychotic poisoned thoughts. My mind is the only place I'm at home anymore. But at least tonight won't be when I check out.

2 | Hangover Number 4287

I COME TO FOUR HOURS LATER. WHY CAN'T PEOPLE WITH RE-
pressed memories realize they're the lucky ones? Although
a lot of my sordid past is permanently blacked out and
irretrievable, there's even more I wish I could erase. The way
I acted after tonight's show is just the latest sound bite.

The bus is rolling along the highway smoothly, but I turned
my radio on at some point, maybe in my sleep, and I am forced
to endure thirty or forty seconds of harsh static, since whatever
station I tuned in is now hundreds of miles away, out of range.
When I stretch across my mattress for the power switch, I realize I'm alone, which is a relief. Having sex with fans and
groupies is one thing, but dragging them from city to city is absolutely crazy—borders on kidnapping. Everyone in the band
has been threatened with arrest for statutory rape at least once.
Even if the girl is old enough, even if she's in her early to mid
twenties and going through an experimental phase—remaining otherwise docile, understanding, nonexpectant, and cling-
free—you still end up feeling incredibly guilty.

At least I do, and usually drop them off at a bus stop or a

cab company, a couple of hundred-dollar bills balled in their fist. Once as we were traveling through Georgia, I freaked out on a bad combination of heat and poison mushrooms, a hangover, and killer hot chili. I ran up and down the aisle screaming, flailing my arms, and was about to get fresh air by ramming my head through the windshield, when Tubbs got the bus to the side of the road. That's his official job, driving, though he ends up being a bodyguard, too. I dragged a girl out by the arm, sprinted in front of oncoming traffic, threw five hundred dollars into the first car that stopped, and told the driver to take the girl wherever she wanted to go. Which unfortunately doesn't even rate as the worst thing I've done in the last few years. *I am a reprobate, I'm the ideal date . . .*

The fire burning in my gut could fuel an F16 jet fighter right now. *Right Now!* Who isn't obsessed with himself? It gives me something to concentrate on besides how terrible I feel. It's only because my wiring is haywire that I've been able to get any work done at all in life. When I'm fired up, I picture my brain as a huge mass of electrical connections, zapping each other just this side of total meltdown. Blue sparks, flashes, a lightning bolt echoing endlessly around a fishbowl, all mixed somehow with rhythm and ecstasy and a crazy, beautiful beat.

Unfortunately, reality for me is a hangover so severe I don't think I'll be able to get rid of it by taking a drink. The egg-shaped decanter bottle is lying in the bed next to me, with about half of the pale burnished liquor left, so I make sure the top is on securely and drop it onto the carpeted floor. Then I kneel on the bed, slide the window open, and puke into the wind, splattering the side of the bus.

Tubbs will have heard me, or seen me in the rearview mirror, or maybe he's been expecting this moment ever since he helped me earlier; might even be flashing his high beams at Earl the Pearl to prove he's won a bet.

I head up to the front of the bus to talk to him, because he's one of the few people who never lies to me. And because he's awake.

"Hey, Mac, I guess you made it after all. You know what time of night it is?" he asks, though he's wearing a genuine Rolex which Grover gave him.

"No know, no wanna know, no care." I plunk down on the top step by the door, one of my favorite places to hang out, except that the bus's motion is making me sick, so I put my elbows on my knees and my head in my hands. Both of the band's buses have giant murals of sprinting cheetahs painted on the sides, over jet black backgrounds, which is about the dumbest thing you can do if you don't want everyone in the goddamn country to recognize you. I can't begin to say how embarrassed I am that we spent six hundred fucking Gs on each of the buses, but what really killed me was the two-week session of our Cheetah Congress (also a pun on *cheater*, especially in Boston where they're pronounced the same) that it took us to argue out every amenity we wanted on the buses, which is why they cost so much, from the simple question of whether we needed one bus or two, to asinine details like how much it would cost to make it look like the cheetahs were actually running down the highway as the buses moved. Way too much, although maybe R.E.M. buses would be cool with schizoid, freaked-out, blinking, four-foot diameter eyes on the back panel, scaring the Blue Blockers off the cotton-toppers they blew past.

"Some show tonight, eh?" I say.

"I wouldn't know. I was out here watching the vehicles for most of it, remember?"

"Oh, yeah. Well, let me tell you, it was some show tonight."

"Yeah, I guess it was."

"That obvious? We sucked."

"Maybe I'm just getting used to some things."

"Sorry about the side of the bus."

"Aw, that ain't nothing. Little water next time we stop will take care of that."

"Wake me up and make me clean it," I insist, but I know he won't. He has no idea what self-flagellation does for idiots like me, which is one of the reasons I dig him. We picked him up at a truckstop in Dallas after one of our previous drivers got arrested for waving a gun at a cop. I'd be lying if I said the fact that he's huge and black and intimidating wasn't the real reason we chose him, or if I argued that the nickname Tubbs was an allusion to Tubbs from Miami Vice. Even blind men can see he's bloated and strong as an elephant, all six-four, three hundred pounds of him. But he's had a hard enough life to not be judgmental about too many of my flaws, which keeps our relationship easy—so what if he and Earl the Pearl occasionally stop for fast food late at night (*not linguine fettucine, or bulgur wheat, but a big warm bun and a huge chunk of meat . . .*), leaving the buses idling and undefended when they think everyone else is passed out?

"Don't you worry about anything," he assures me.

"You're too good to us," I say, sounding like a total femme. "Hey, do you have any water? I'm kind of parched right now."

He knows several gallons of obscenely expensive bottled water are sitting in the refrigerator just behind the first seats, along with the vitamins, fruit, fruit juices, vegetables, leftover Chinese take-out, instant burritos, and luncheon meats Annie stocks in her ever-vigilant, ever-futile battle to keep our frail, toxic bodies alive and functioning, but he passes me the half-gallon plastic bottle resting by his feet. Annie is part of our management team, Murph's right-hand man, so to speak. She's like a surrogate mom to us. It kind of surprised me that Tubbs was the one to escort me out to the bus earlier, not her.

Tequila, whisky, brandy, vodka, gin, wine, beer; any alcohol you name, I've leapt onto tables at parties—from intimate family gatherings to sardine-packed football stadiums pulsing with sweat-soaked fans—and screamed, "The Elixir of the Gods!" (*One Bourbon, One Scotch, and One Beer . . .*) Ten thousand times, a million. But now for the million-and-first time I know water is the true elixir, which is why the Indians were wise enough to dance for rain. I myself would kneel down and puke out prayers of gratitude if I didn't feel like hell just sitting motionless, and if Tubbs wouldn't think I'm crazier than he already does.

15

"Where are we?" I ask.

"Not too far from Sacramento. It'll be light pretty soon. You should get some more sleep. Take the bottle with you."

When I pull another mouthful of the water, swishing it around to clear my residual puke taste, I realize that I haven't brushed my teeth since the previous morning. The plaque buildup has the texture of aging, wet sandpaper. I try to clear some of it with my finger. I know I smell, too. Tubbs is probably getting high from breathing the chemicals seeping out of my pores. "Maybe I'll just sit here for another minute, huh?"

Tubbs chuckles. "Sure, take your time."

"Thanks."

"Ain't nothing but a thang."

"Where's everybody else?" I ask.

"Most of 'em are on the other bus."

"How about Jay?"

Tubbs gestures over his shoulder with his thumb. "Naw, he's in the back."

"Wonderful."

I go numb for maybe ten minutes, then the word *zing* pops into my head, though nothing about the bus's motion qualifies as zinging, remaining, instead, rhythmic and enchanting, the highway deserted, not offering cars for us to zigzag past, let alone traffic to zing through. I start to feel self-conscious, sitting here not talking to Tubbs, but I don't feel quite so horrendous that all I can do is moan out loud, writhe on my side clutching my stomach, and wish I was dead, either. (*From the clashes of disaster spring the posies of distress . . .*) So I try to force conversation again, however awkward.

"God, it was some show tonight," I say.

"Hmm? How's that?"

"We sucked."

"Aw, I'm sure it wasn't that bad."

"Well . . . I mean . . . it was just interminable. Some shows you do and it's like, 'This show is going great, but maybe if we catch a buzz, it'll go even better and things will flow.' But tonight it was more like, 'We better play the show and wait till it's over to get drunk, or something bad might happen.' Which just made us play worse than we already were, I guess. It felt like I was walking a tightrope, though I knew it was only a few inches off the ground."

Tubbs just kind of grunts.

"I mean . . . I don't know. Where's Dodge City, anyhow? I don't even care what state it's in, who cares how fucking big it is? Just once I'd like to say, 'Let's get the hell out of Dodge!' and really mean it. Do you have any clue where it is?"

"Unless I'm supposed to be takin' you there, I'm sure I don't know where it is, Mac."

"You know what's really sick? That I understand exactly what you mean. No know, no wanna know, no care. Life's a crock of shit and I'm the fly who thinks he's showing off by diving in the deepest."

Tubbs keeps the bus moving at a perfectly steady speed; the engine noise is consistent as a flat-line EKG. Murph could be paying Tubbs by the hour and he wouldn't be any happier. "Oh, don't say things like that. That's talking smack. Ain't none of this business I've seen that's that bad. A few minutes ago you said you enjoyed the show."

"I didn't say I enjoyed it, I said it was some show."

"Well . . . ?"

"Well what?"

"Well, did anything good happen or not? Not two minutes ago you said the audience was out of control."

"I didn't say they were out of control, I said I felt like I was gonna fall into the audience. It was . . . I don't know. They were there to see us, of course, which usually makes people happy, but there was something weird in the air, like if we disappeared, things would get ugly in a hurry. The party was on edge. I just wanted it to be over. I wanted someone to save us. What's the best movie comparison? Maybe when the *Millennium Falcon* comes swooping in at the end of the original *Star Wars*. You know . . . *Dum de dum dum* . . . That's how it should have felt. It was just a weird vibe."

Tubbs doesn't respond; probably he's thinking what a crazy honky I am. My first mistake is always laying my soul bare to the types of guys who really just care if I got laid or not, or who wonder if they can get hazardous duty pay for talking to me. But I've started this, so I've got to find a way to end it, too. Conversation is an unexpected visitor whose face I can't slam the door in.

"Any good side shows?" Tubbs asks.

"Just the usual assortment of chicks flashing their tits, chicks flashing their asses, chicks making obscene gestures about themselves, stroking themselves suggestively, sucking their fingers every time you catch their eye, a few chicks holding up Blood Cheetah signs they probably made as a favor to their damn boyfriends, plus chicks screaming every time I played a solo. I swear I don't know why women ever wear anything besides torn-up Levi's or super-short miniskirts."

"Any real lookers?"

"Let me tell you, one blonde, in the second row. I could've blown a load into her mouth from the back of the stage."

Tubbs's laughter is masculine and conspiratorial. "Heh, heh, now isn't that what it's all about?"

"I guess it is."

Why ruin Tubbs's crazy rock star fantasies or hopscotch past the basic line of understanding and camaraderie we've established? I'm free to go back to bed now but I sit hunched over a little while longer, still miserable, my head in my trembling hands, as if my fingers were positive and negative terminals, zapping my brain back to a pure state of energy, zinging me, for shit's sake.

I know he imagines himself with some sort of charm, intelligence or looks, the power to seduce any woman, every guy does, so it would be incredibly douchey to tell him that the second-row blonde was with a man she obviously wasn't going to get more than three feet from—though I have busted exactly this type of couple up once or twice in the past—or point out that the young girl K Dot decided to put his drunken energies into backstage was subtly refusing to even sip a beer, never a sign you're about to get laid. Tubbs isn't the kind of guy to understand that I don't give two shits about any of it anymore: money, babes, or drugs, so long as I have a bottle at hand and a pillow under my head when it's time for some down time. Maybe we could duct tape one in place.

I grab the water bottle and stand up. "Good night, Tubbs."

" 'Night, Mac. Just remember to use the toilet from now on."

"I'm on my way there right now."

Before I pull my Levi's off and climb back into bed, I slide my lucky coin, a 1795 half eagle, from the fifth pocket, and then from its protective velvet sheath, and lie awake in the dark, twirling it around my fingers the way Grover spins a drumstick. Eventually I grab my twelve-string acoustic as well, the only guitar I keep in my berth these days, and lay fingering the strings, trying to clear my mind and actually come up with something new, just as I'd wanted to when I bolted from the dressing room earlier. But all I can manage is to pluck the long, drawn-out intro to "Hallelujah Blues" over and over, not even getting it quite right, missing half the notes.

I'm totally naked, exhausted, unable to get to sleep, and pissed off at myself again. The only part of my body that doesn't ache is my sternum, where I've placed the cool weight of the half eagle. I can picture it as a stake, two hundred years old, driven straight through my body and out the bottom of the bus, kicking up sparks. But a lucky piece can't make good things happen, all it can do is prevent really bad things, or remind you how much worse life could be, how you could be horribly mangled in a car wreck, bones and guts hanging out obscenely, or a life prison sentence for shooting a clerk in a Store 24 robbery gone wrong, or how you could be dead. And since I'm still alive, I guess I've got nothing to fucking complain about.

3 | Fuzz

HENEVER I WATCH *COPS* OR *REAL ADVENTURES OF THE Highway Patrol*, they bust some poor young clod for possession and I groan to myself, not only feeling sorry for the guy because he's a tiny random cog about to be tossed into the vast, archaic, imponderable, self-defeating legal system, but also because we live in such a psychotic world that most of the reasons people want to keep certain drugs illegal seem to make sense, whereas in a perfect world they wouldn't. Mostly it's just a case of drugs-are-illegal-now-and-look-how-many-problems-they-already-cause. Sometimes I think the best option would not only be to legalize drugs, but to purposely addict society's most criminal element (MOCRE-LEM) to synthetic narcotics designed to pacify them enough that they'd be overjoyed to do the jobs politicians really mean nobody wants when they thump on the podium and shout, "We need more education!" Like sewer cleaners, McDonald's minimum wage earners etcetera.

I wake up when I hear Tubbs talking with someone at the front of the bus. Before I can roll over and even pretend to hide—never mind that I can never hide—that same someone is knocking on the door to my berth. "David Zimmerman?" His voice is stern and official, as if just intimidating me will make me answer. "We would like to speak with you for a moment."

"Do you have a warrant for either me or the bus?" I call out. The reply comes in a more moderate tone. "Aren't you smart enough to realize how much more of a hassle we'll give you if you make us go and get one?"

Touché. *I Fought the Law* . . . Another goddamn round of police intimidation, questioning, and maneuvering begins, except that this time, there aren't quite as many threats as normal. The flatfoots seem more interested in gathering information than in making a headline-grabbing bust on charges they know will be dropped later. Several perfunctory questions establish that I was on stage with the band during the hours of last night's show. Then they get to the heart of the matter.

"Did you say anything out of the ordinary to the crowd last night?" the older of the two cops asks. He has tucked his hat under his arm, but he still has his sunglasses on. I wish I had a pair of shades myself. The only reason he doesn't look like a total robot is the gray hair peppering his black crewcut. I can't imagine what having someone like this for a father would be like.

"What do you mean?"

"For instance, in between songs. Do you try to get the crowd riled up, or do you just concentrate on playing?"

"We have a pretty strict play list, and only change around two or three songs each night, so that we don't always jam on the same ones, but I guess the whole show is kind of designed to get people pumped at certain times. Build it up to a crescendo. That sort of thing, sure."

"Do you personally encourage the crowd?" he asks.

"Me?"

"Yes, you, not the band."

"I'm not sure I follow."

"Yeah, right."

My parrying is subtle, but he seems to realize he's getting

nowhere with the informal, buddy-buddy routine. He strokes his jaw as if he had a beard. "Mr. Zimmerman, have you ever told an audience to get up and dance, or to sing along with a song?"

"Yeah, sure, every band does that, although it's not my personal favorite trick. Jay, our singer, he loves that stuff."

The younger cop interrupts. "We'll be speaking with him in due time."

"Mr. Zimmerman, do you recall egging the crowd on last night?"

Now I see, for the first time, really, what their angle is, and who they might be trying to pin something on, me, if not the other guys as well. Now I know what types of accusations to deny, but simply figuring this out ends the game for me. The two replies I'd like to make—and might make if I was still drinking on last night's rampage—are both wise-ass; that I don't recall anything longer than ten minutes ago, and that I probably screamed something like, "Smoke the fattest joint you can find, drive a hundred miles an hour, and drop acid till it pours out your ears!" But I'm too hungover for that crap now. I want to end this ordeal as quickly as possible, if only so I can crawl back into my bed.

"I don't recall saying or doing anything that was in any way different from hundreds of other shows we've played without a problem."

Old Salt-and-Pepper grins. He knows that was a good answer. He pulls a small spiral notebook from his breast pocket. "Do you remember saying, 'Come on, come on, come on, everybody get f-ing crazy. Are you gonna sit on your asses all night or do something?'"

"No, I don't."

"Do you remember shouting, 'You're gonna die someday, so why not die tonight?'"

"Not at all."

"Is it possible that any member of your band besides you made these comments last night?"

"Well, yeah, of course it's possible. Anything's possible, isn't it? Look at Michael Jackson taking a poke at Elvis's daughter. But I really don't remember anything specific like what you're talking about, although sometimes the show is pretty wild even on stage. It's crazy how hard some of the kids will try just to touch us: sprint at the security line full speed, try to dive over everybody, crowd surfing, whatever."

I try to act like I'm as amazed as anyone by the things that go on, though my short period of amazement turned into endless apathy years ago. My guess would be that someone in the crowd got hurt trying to climb onto the stage, or afterward, being not so gently taken care of by stadium security. (Everybody's paranoid about liability.) Blood Cheetah has never inspired much moshing—which I'm so old in rock 'n' roll years, I still call slamming—but the crush can get nasty at the front of even a small-size general admission section, and everyone still remembers the kid who ended up a quadriplegic after Lollapalooza '94.

23

"Do you remember shouting 'Go crazy!' into your microphone about two-thirds of the way through the show?"

I squint. "Did I do that? I honestly don't remember."

"Yes, you did," the younger cop snaps. He has been looking up and down the bus's aisle intently, but trying desperately to seem casual, sheer ill will not being sufficient reason to bust me. He's two or three intimidating inches taller than old Salt-and-Pepper, who was probably two or three intimidating inches taller than the old cops back when he was a rookie. They both look like they have to shave four times a day. "We have several witnesses who claim you said exactly that."

I only fidget a little, standing in the berth's doorway wearing nothing but my Levi's. "Well, 'Go crazy!' is chanted three times real quick at the beginning of our song 'Livewire,' the same way you might shout 'Kick it!' to start a song. It's even that way on the album."

Old Salt-and-Pepper jots down a few last items, then flips his notebook shut. "That's all the information we'll need for now. We may be interviewing you again, however."

"Our tour schedule is announced on every rock station this side of the Rockies."

"Don't worry, we know where you're headed," the younger cop says, his tone smug and demeaning.

This cracks me up. I can hardly stop laughing, but suddenly my head aches, my hands are shaky, and though my body is cold, a sheen of sweat breaks out on my forehead. I follow the cops down the bus's aisle. The younger cop keeps poking around, tapping on the overhead storage bins.

"Any chance of us finding narcotics if we brought a K9 unit in here?" he asks.

"Well, an awful lot of people come on and off the bus, some without our permission. Who knows what could have gotten left behind? Hell, seventy-five percent of the paper money in L.A. shows traces of coke in the fibers."

"You're one for the books, aren't you?"

"I believe I have the right not to answer that."

As the cops are stepping out of the bus, I finally get up the guts to ask exactly why they're investigating, what they'd hoped to find.

"You haven't figured it out?" the older cop asks.

"No, I really haven't. Usually it's drugs you guys are looking for."

"Did you happen to notice that there was a brawl going on while you were playing last night?"

"I guess I saw . . . something out by the soundboard, but it's tough to see from the stage, except for when all the house lights are on before and after the show."

Salt-and-Pepper puts his hat back on. "This is off the record, of course, but it appears that two fairly large groups of guys went after each other."

"You mean like gangs?"

"We're not exactly sure. Nobody was claiming any gang connections once security and the local police got everyone sorted out. Then again, if you were in a gang nowadays, would you brag about it to law enforcement officials? There were more fights outside afterward, but you probably missed that, too. Hopefully it was nothing more than young studs who'd been out in the sun too long, got drunk, and took their frustrations out the only way they knew how. The big problem was that at least four young women ended up in the hospital. Just got caught in the ruckus. One ended up with a concussion, a broken jaw, and probably a few scars on her face. Nice way to end a night out, eh?"

"Are you allowed to give me her name?"

Old Salt-and-Pepper steps down onto the pavement. A wall of heat blasts me in the chest and makes my eyes feel very dry. I'm blinking and squinting at the same time. I have to shade my eyes.

"Even if I was, I'm not sure I would," he says.

"So much for remaining an impartial instrument of the law," I say. Cops have an incredible amount of discretionary power, and most are willing to use it. But at least I'm not getting a free ride to the slammer. "What are the odds I'm going to be charged with anything, even though I didn't do anything? It would probably be inciting to riot, or something like that, right?"

"Let's call it fifty-fifty. High enough that you have something to worry about, for the next few days at least. It'll probably depend a lot on what you or other band members actually said."

I make a mental note to have Walker destroy any tapes he might have made last night, if the cops haven't already confiscated them. Then I say silent prayers that I didn't scream anything all that provocative during the show, and that any bootlegs taped by fans won't be widely available for five or ten years, let alone within the week. Blood Cheetah's official recording policy has always been "Don't ask, don't tell," which means that any kid who can tuck a tape recorder under his sweatshirt can make his own live albums (LIVE! DOUBLE LIVE PLATINUM NOT DEAD YET BUT ON THE DRUGS THAT MIGHT KILL THEM!), then trade them like baseball cards for other bootlegs, rides to shows, pot, a six-pack, laundry services, what have you. *Rhythm Nation . . .* If this was a Deadhead Nation, our

25

treasury notes would be tie-dyed swatches of hemp with Chunky Cherry Jerry Garcia's fat face grinning out.

The cops' cruiser is parked behind the bus, while the other Cheetah bus is waiting right in front of us. This doesn't faze me at the moment, though it will later, when I realize they made a specific point of chasing my bus down to interrogate me, albeit ineffectually and unprofessionally.

I step down onto the road surface and nearly pass out from the heat rising off the pavement. My feet feel instantly scorched.

"Hey, officer . . ."

Only Salt-and-Pepper turns around.

"Maybe you won't believe me, but I am sorry if anyone got hurt. I really am. Anyone who understands this band knows violence isn't our scene."

His frown is tight and superior. "Don't be sorry, change things. Both of us are just lucky that guns weren't involved. Don't let there be another incident."

Jay pretends to just be waking up and rolling out of his berth as I climb back onto the bus. I ignore him, because I'm totally fucking pissed off, and I want to sock him when he asks in a too-innocent, too-polite, too-James Spader voice, "What's up? Where are we? What's going on out there?" One of his defining characteristics (maybe a Mohawk 'do would make him one of the Jayhawks) is that he takes his shirt off about twenty minutes into every show, and twenty minutes into every cook-out, and twenty minutes into every party, so naturally he's bare-chested now. His body isn't all that bad (he's not nearly as gaunt and emaciated as me), but he's no Grover, either. He has tattoos on both forearms and both biceps: a dragon, a broadsword, the Harley Davidson logo and, of course, a sprinting Cheetah.

I'm pissed that my feet just got sizzled, I'm pissed that everything related to the conversation with the police is suddenly looming up in my face and won't go away any way resembling easily. One more fucking major hassle for me. And I'm pissed that pulling my sandals on to run up to the other bus is so much like showing up late for school when you know the principal is going to chew you out for his own personal, juvenile pleasure.

At least Grover is the first person I run into beside Earl the Pearl. Since he takes such sickeningly good care of himself and never drinks more than a beer or two after our shows, he's usually up at downright respectable hours, like a banker or a supermarket manager. *Our Grover, is a very, very, very fine Grover.* Once we even considered making a calendar of him, and calling it "Grover in Clover."

"What in the Sam Hell is a 'goin' on back there?!" he cackles, then throws his head back and howls with laughter. He's constantly quoting lines from movies or making comparisons to sports, but neither of these quirks bothers me, as long as he remains optimistic, and sticks with action flicks for material, not Monty Python. One of my three rules in life is that anybody who quotes Monty Python is a dork.

"Little trouble with the police," I say.

"Well, they obviously haven't slapped you into a roadside set of stocks, where kids on vacation can toss soda cans at your head, so it can't be all that bad."

I plunk down into one of the bus's front seats. "Sure, it can. But I guess if it can always be worse, it can always be worse than worse, too."

"So, what's the scoop?"

"Let's just wait thirty seconds. I only want to tell the story once."

Sure enough, K Dot and Alex both stagger out of bed when they hear Grover and me talking. Each of the buses has four small berths, with the original theory being that we'd switch around at random anytime we needed to sleep and weren't staying in a hotel, or maybe we'd designate one bus for carrying contraband, then spend most of our time riding the other. But what's actually happened is that I've customized and

27

claimed one berth, while the other guys float around a little more freely. Who hangs out where tends to mirror where our loyalties currently lie.

"Exactly what the fuck is wrong now?" K Dot yells. He turns out to be more hung over than Alex is, and subsequently more surly, accusative . . . imposing. He's wearing cut-off jean shorts and a necklace with a silver cross. His stomach is pretty fat now, but at least the skin around his belly button isn't wrinkled yet.

"The police are investigating whether or not we said anything that stoked a big fight in the audience last night."

"Of course we didn't!" Alex exclaims. He has a scar on the left side of his forehead from where his ex-wife hit him with a beer bottle a few years ago, and though it's been healed over for a long time, right now it looks like it might start oozing.

K Dot is already trying to take charge. "You can drive, Earl. Fuck Jay if he isn't up here to talk about this yet. Let him rot and worry about what we're plotting behind his back. What went down, Z?"

Relating my conversation with the cops back to the guys in the band is worse than the conversation itself. Not only do they demand details I can't remember, they each let me know, with varying degrees of subtlety, that they'd have handled the situation entirely differently, the bastards. Ten years ago, they'd have had the balls to admit that in the same situation, they'd have been scared and intimidated, too. The more specific K Dot's questions are, the more stupid my answers sound, and while I know he's already positioning himself not to get blamed for whatever trouble we may be in later, I'm currently too vulnerable to accuse him of it. He might not even be aware that that's what he's doing.

"So they were only looking for you?" he says.

"They said they'd talk to the rest of you, too."

"When's that gonna happen? Why did they take off?"

"I certainly don't know."

Grover tries to placate K Dot. "Maybe they got some sort of

call. Maybe they were just trying to fire a warning shot across our bow. Hell, maybe it was just a couple of local-yokel cops who saw the buses and decided to play a joke on the infamous outlaw, David Dillinger Zimmerman."

"No, they knew too much about last night's show," Alex says.

K Dot looks annoyed. He's sitting so close that I can see the spaces between his dark facial hairs. "Shit, can you at least tell us their badge numbers, or their names? Or where they were from?"

"Excuse me?"

"California state cops? Reno city detectives? Nevada sheriffs? Feds? What?"

My face turns redder than it already was. I'm embarrassed to have let him down again. I move toward the bus's refrigerator for a chilled bottle of Absolut.

"Your guess is as good as mine." 29

4 | A Girl of Eighteen

 TAKE MY SECOND AND THEN THIRD SWIGS OF THE ABSOLUT. "Where the fuck is Murph through all this?" I ask the other guys. It's like asking a couple of kindergarten kids where Santa is hiding. Alex laughs, K Dot snorts. "He's the one who's supposed to take care of this shit for us."

Goddamn son of a bitch. Murph isn't even his real name, just a tag someone in high school gave him because he reminded them of a guy named Murphy. He's as big a bastard as any small-town sheriff or crooked politician, and it's all on our money. Sometimes I wish doctors could insert a chip into my brain that would let me keep all of Blood Cheetah's endless figures, calculations, debts, and credits perfectly straight, so we wouldn't need him. You've got to really trust someone to hand him the reins of a large, complicated, and potentially shady operation like a rock 'n' roll stadium tour, but the people you've known all your life and are most likely to trust probably don't have the proper managerial skills. And even if they do, they still think it should be their prerogative to manipulate all the different types of deals—from T-shirt sales to the rare unsold ticket—for their own benefit, not just take a steady salary or a small percentage of the gross. What we should probably do is hire two or three young snotnoses right out of Harvard Business School, threaten their lives daily, never let them drink, make sure they're married, never let them meet each other, give them each total access to all of our financial information, and then see what numbers they each come up with. Of course, this is what we hired Murph for, to clean up our business details—which K Dot had previously done a world-class job of screwing up—only to find out, over the years, that the larger your operation gets, the more support is needed by the people you hired, until even thinking about logistics makes you reach for the bottle. Never blame yourself for your drinking.

My only solace is that Walker and his boys have been granted absolute, irrevocable, unarguable authority over all of our sound equipment and sound production. He's the type of guy you'd see pawing through a magazine rack in your hometown public library and say, 'They really shouldn't let the homeless use city buildings as afternoon country clubs,' because it's tough to see past his ragged appearance and realize he's a genius and should be worth more money than all of us put together. If, during a sound check, I suggest, "Maybe there's a tiny tear vibrating everything wrong in the top speaker of bass monitor number two," he'll literally come sprinting from the sound board with a handful of tools, or he'll dash out to the truck he calls The Sound Semi to fetch a replacement part. After a month or so of touring, only the actual instruments feel like they're ours.

"Hey, Earl, hand me the phone," I say. "Anybody remember what Murph's number is in the car?"

Grover knows the number, but when I call, nobody answers, which makes me want to throw the goddamn phone right through the bus windshield. What good is having cell phones on both the buses if our fucking manager won't even answer when we call him? His office's answering machine, back in Boston, claims his business is something called "client relations services," but that's just because he's the type of guy who thinks using big words every now and then makes him sound more intelligent. Even Annie is invisible, so we can't enjoy the quick high of her endlessly optimistic and rational I'll-get-the-details-of-whatever-trouble-you-boys-are-in-now-and-see-how-we-can-take-care-of-it routine. Since she's a woman, she's pretty effective with police. They aren't threatened by her, so they don't have to prove how tough they are. Sometimes she'll ride on one of the buses for a day or two, then go back to riding in Murph's Mercedes, along with Murph, his girlfriend Geena, and sometimes Murph's brother, Eddie, who's really just another leech, though I guess if he's a professional, the term is *sycophant*. They circle around the band's travels not like a mosquito, which lands anywhere it can find flesh, making itself easy to swat, but like a dragonfly, which is untouchable even if it perches on the tip of your nose.

I swear, I hate touring if for no other reason than that there are so many people in charge of so many things, so many people to answer questions for and ask questions of—details, details, details—and I hardly remember who does what for me, not even the names of the two or three guys who work most closely with Walker, all of whom I just address as Bud these days, the same way Tubbs calls everyone Mac. I'd call Walker and see if he knew where Murph was, but I doubt he would. He probably worked until dawn disassembling all of our gear, and now he's following in our path, catching a quick cat nap in The Sound Semi. We have three other semis as well, but The Sound Semi is the one that carries our most valuable gear, which Walker wants to supervise personally. A stadium tour is an incredibly ponderous operation. By the time we get into a town and pick up whatever temporary labor is necessary, the crew can swell to over two hundred workers.

Ironically, Tubbs and Earl the Pearl are probably as vital as anyone in the whole ridiculous fucking process in terms of concerts coming off anywhere near on time, and who knows what promises, exhortation, bribes, secret pacts, and negotiations either Murph, Walker, Annie, or any of our record company's executives have made to get them to keep up their end

of things. Maybe I poured my heart and guts into writing Blood
Cheetah's songs over the last decade, but once a tour starts,
I'm as much a pawn as anyone else, an astronaut who everyone thinks is brave, but really just flicks the switches Mission
Control tells him to, and wonders if a chimpanzee could be
trained to replace him. *Shock the Monkey*... Even when the
record company sends its perfect young yuppie punks to catch
up with us, their attitude is, ask K Dot and Jay how the tour
is going, assure me my royalties are being deposited back in
Boston and ask me how I'm doing, then slyly ask K Dot and
Jay how long it'll be until I implode. Or explode. *Burning
through the night.*

Neither K Dot, Alex, or Grover is about to build my confidence back up right now, though they would have in the old
days, the traitorous bastards, not even a game of cards as we
wait to reach Sacramento. That loser Murph is probably
perched at a blackjack table somewhere back in Nevada this
very second. K Dot shakes his head a couple of times, grum-
bles, then heads back to bed, while Alex starts fishing around
the pantry for some breakfast and Grover pulls out the latest
edition of *Sports Illustrated.*

I have Earl pull over and let me run back to the other bus,
the Absolut bottle in tow. Jay proceeds to question me about
what the cops had to say, standing cross-armed and cocky in
front of me, massaging the tattoos on his forearms like they're
some sort of magic lanterns. But even when I'm done with
him, pissing him off just a little bit more because I don't feel
like going into every goddamn detail again, especially the
ones I can't remember, and maybe pushing him that much
closer to finally decking me, I'm just thinking, What the hell
does any of this mean? Not only the superweird police visit,
or the fact that I'm not getting any support from guys who've
been my best buddies since high school, or even the essential
strangeness of being on the West Coast, riding in the morning
sunshine, through withered brown hills gradually more pop-
ulated—until it's obvious we're coming into a major city—but
also what does this morning mean on an eternal scale, what

33

does it mean in relation to the centuries and the eons? What does everything I've ever thought and felt, seen, heard, or touched mean to anyone but me, everyone else absolutely involved with what they themselves are seeing and feeling, with their own crises and doubts and revelations?

Traffic is heavier now. The way cars blow past the buses on the left, then cut back over to exit on the right makes me realize they're mostly commuters who're late for work. They're probably glancing at the giant cheetahs on the sides of the buses, and the 99.99 percent who aren't devout Blood Cheetah fans and so eager for our next concert that they can't have a bowel movement, wonder, Who the hell is riding in those? But they forget the buses the instant they get cut off by another vehicle or when they walk into their office buildings and get hit with the first problem of the morning before their asses are even behind their desks. There are, thank God, movie stars who're about a zillion times more famous than everyone in our band put together, and I often find myself wondering what they're doing at exactly that moment: driving to the bank to cash a huge check, or making love to someone equally gorgeous. But I know the truth is probably that they're doing something incredibly boring, like taking the dog for a walk, or waiting for someone, anyone, to call. I mean, does Tom Hanks get up as late as I do when he doesn't have a project to work on?

As many hallucinogens as I've experimented with in my day, I've never found one that truly made me believe I was another person, another mind. Even my God and Jesus trips have primarily been freaked-out expansions of my own consciousness, attempts to expand my soul into what I thought was the soul of the universe, to reach a beautiful and peaceful and effortless union. I tend to either think I'm God and can understand everything about time, reality, space, and human nature, or to suddenly see that my face is a torn and desperate Jesus, right down to my beavertail of dark, tangled hair, which is probably closer to what his actually looked like on the cross than the flaxen, groomed brunette most statues and paintings depict. Very little effort is required for me to close my eyes and flash back to the night in Dorchester I dropped some mushrooms this black cat-woman gave me at a Halloween party gone wrong. I stood in front of a mirror and saw blood pour out of my eyes, my upraised hands become candles, my chest hairs turn into worms.

You want to really scare yourself? At exactly midnight on a Friday the thirteenth, walk backwards up a flight of thirteen steps thirteen times, repeating the Lord's Prayer backwards once each flight, with no lights on, other than a candle you're holding, then at the top, the last ascent, turn around and see the Devil. And you have to be alone. SEE THE DEVIL! (*Shout At the Devil!* . . .) Or at least that's what several people have told me would happen, some of them while we shared various drugs. The point is that being alone gives you time to do an enormous head job on yourself, whether you intended to or not. But why not admit that I can be absolutely terrified of the dark? Sometimes I let myself get so scared, sitting alone in my apartment in Boston, which is about as secure as Fort Knox, that the fear is a drug, a mind trip I can relax and let myself sink into, until I'm at the point where either my door buzzer or my phone ringing would give me a heart attack. Heart attacks could be what I'm paranoid of at any such moment, the most obvious of the hundred ways my abused body might surge before suddenly kicking, but so could random violence, intentional violence, or drug overdoses. If you can't freak yourself out by imagining all of the horrific and horrible fates a person can meet at random, then you're not very creative, sign of an inferior mind, although if you can't forget them, there's trouble as well.

I sit cross-legged on my bed for forty-five minutes or so, really working myself into a sort of tranced-out groove. While I do take a couple more quick swigs of vodka, I also eat handfuls of raisin bran and a banana, so I'm not getting wasted, per se, I'm just enjoying the happy moment. Sometimes after a rough night of partying (what a brilliant euphemism for drugs and drinking), I'll wake up and feel pretty good for an hour or two, even when it's not residual drunkenness. Sometimes I feel so good, especially when there's an activity going on, like bickering with the cops, that I'm lulled into believing I won't be very hungover. Then, an hour or two later, I feel like total lethargic crap, and won't recover until I get totally smashed again, or until enough time has passed for my bloodstream to clean out. Two or three days, max. My only problem is that I never wait two or three days.

I should probably pick up my twelve-string and see if playing helps me forget about all the shit that's going on right now, but I'm too comfortable to move, my legs crossed into a position which will make them ache when I do move later, my back against the window again. I'm trying to remember exactly what the cops said about the women who got hurt last night. Are women as enraged and revenge-minded by reports of women and children being killed in this fucked-up world's war zones as men usually are—a call to arms, action, retaliation—or is their reaction just dismay? Plenty of credible reports have accused the Bosnian Serbs of setting up rape camps in their obscene little ethnic cleansing campaign, perhaps proving that Hitler wasn't qualitatively worse than the rest of us, but just posted bigger numbers, as Grover would say. That almost nobody talks about something like this proves how easily men can make women ashamed of being vulnerable, as well as how rarely men want to admit to their own destructive, domineering urges.

Maybe the woman whose jaw was broken was dating one of the assholes who started the brawl. I'm always amazed at how many guys get into fights even when they're getting laid on a regular schedule. Maybe she was an innocent bystander. Maybe she was even old Salt-and-Pepper's daughter, which was why he didn't want to give out her name. His vendetta might be directed against me personally, my pasty white, withered (as opposed to weathered), unshaven face, my bloodshot eyes. Righteous anger always needs a concrete enemy. I try to imagine what the woman's face looked like, what everything about her looked like, but I know that not only am I guessing, I'm turning her into the girl I'd love to meet. *She's been coming for years but leaves before I meet her . . . if I met her right now I'd learn too much about her . . .* If her hair is blond, she's the sort of blonde who has no idea how blessed and graceful she seems to other people; if she's a brunette, her hair looks better after being out in the sun and wind and rain all day than it does when she leaves a salon. She loves going without a bra, her breasts small but pert and well-formed. She's shy when talking in front of more than a couple close friends, yet determined when she wants to get somewhere or finish a project. She won't disobey her parents, but since they were ultraliberal hippies, they don't lay down too many rules. She's about five foot four, maximum, and weighs just over a hundred pounds. When she's glad to see you, she says hello instead of just hi. She isn't really a woman yet, just a girl, maybe eighteen or nineteen years old. And best of all, the bruises she got at a Blood Cheetah concert, where I encouraged the goddamn crowd to riot, don't make her look like a female Frankenstein, they actually make her more attractive, enhance the effect of a shy, beautiful girl. You can fall in love with her as you stroke her skin, gently, lovingly. You can fall in love with the way she flinches, but doesn't break the touch of your fingertips on her cheekbone.

Clipper was probably like that when she was eighteen, except totally different, with a larger frame, larger breasts, a larger mouth, and an incredible ability never to shut up, even when she had no idea what the hell she was talking about. *Yackety yackety yackety . . .* She's the most ambitious woman anyone ever met, but she's never had any clue where to aim her ambition, other than yearning for fame (or notoriety), fortune (or outrageously expensive digs), and adventure (or parties where men fall all over her). So naturally she became a model, which has no job requirements besides beauty and enough restraint to not go postal with a mascara pencil when photographers and makeup people are in her face all day. Our relationship, such as it is, has always been based on our mutual hope that dating one another would make us both more popular and more happy; that our popularity as a celebrity couple would somehow ensure our happiness.

Los Angeles was where we first met, back in the early nineties, when I was even crazier than I am now and thought that living there instead of Boston made brilliant sense. A bad kind of start. Driving into Nevada on the bus the other day made me nostalgic for some of the times we've had together, especially a trip we took to Vegas once (*Viva! . . . Viva! . . . Viva! . . .*) just as leaving the state now and entering California, her state, makes me want to call her on the bus's cellular phone. Apologize for all the mistakes I've made in the past. I also want to call her because I can't call the girl who was hurt at our concert, although I'm too lazy to even bother with the idiot leads like dialing hospitals and newspapers in Reno, to see if anyone there would tell me anything. Besides Annie, the only women I'm in touch with on a regular basis are groupies as stupid as grapes, dying to repeat back any phrases I use. I suppose there are also a few women stuck in Boston I could call, but they're all either pissed off at me for stupid shit I've done in the past, or they're never home because they're slaving away at some crappy job, and are too busy changing diapers in their spare time to endure another drunken, whiny diatribe from the one guy in the high-school class who made more money than God, but is never happy.

Clipper might make me happy someday, but right now she's too busy trying to get her career jump-started again. Or maybe to meet someone she likes better than me. L.A. is a wild town. Who knows who she's hanging out with? We both have a pretty big history of dating other people when we're mad at each other. The truth is that I'm probably too much of an introspective headcase to ever be satisfied with her, while she's probably too gregarious, carefree, and attractive to be satisfied with me. If we had both been born in the same small town, but not used our respective talents to escape, we never would've ended up together. She would have married an ex-high-school football star, while I would have been a bachelor until I was about fifty. Little girls don't say, 'When I grow up I want to marry a scrawny guy who's two inches shorter than me.'

I'm not sure whether I'm the luckiest goddamn guy in the world, or a total idiot, but I realize now that the gorgeous women I wanted to become famous for and meet are usually the ones who have the hardest time understanding *why* I wanted to get famous and meet them. The only good news is that I didn't have to suffer through a divorce to learn this, the way Alex did. And I'm not sure he even learned his lesson. A lot of nights, he drinks even more than I do. The scar on his forehead was the easy one to get over. It's the emotional scars that still affect him. Probably the only type of woman I'd have any chance at all of being happy with would be one from Dorchester, who knew both me and my family. Which is also why I may die single.

5 | Hotel California

'M THE ONLY ONE TO STAY ON EITHER OF THE BUSES WHEN WE get to our hotel in Sacramento. Even Tubbs and Earl get a room, then take shifts guarding the buses. Bands have become a lot more savvy over the years about how to avoid crowds. Despite the incredibly stupid idea of having the giant cheetah murals on the sides of the buses, we can maintain anonymity pretty well (as long as the word *party* doesn't flash through K Dot's brain). The common scenario: Grover heads for the health club and weight machines, while Alex, K Dot, and Jay get off on room service, hot tubs, or masseuses, if only to prove they've earned themselves some amenities. This joint seems fairly classy, which everybody except me loves these days. Staying in expensive hotels reinforces the idea that they've made it, that, as K Dot might roar, "We have a *RRIVED*, motherfucker!" But it just makes me feel guilty. Why spend two hundred dollars a night on a place to either be asleep, take a shower, or murder a couple of hours watching useless cable TV infomercials?

I've heard that in Japan they rent rooms literally the size of large coffins, which sounds pretty practical and efficient to me.

Staying in my berth is the same concept, with all sorts of other advantages; having the same mattress and pillow hardness and the same sheet smell every night makes it easier to sleep when I'm having trouble sleeping, and I never have to pretend I'm still asleep when maids come around. Also, Tubbs knows more about reeling me in and protecting me from myself or from fans when I'm wasted than any old candy-ass, self-appointedly superior doorman. Fans and groupies never guess I'm on the bus at five in the morning. I never have to haul any luggage around—maybe just a clean T-shirt when I duck into one of the guys' rooms for a quick shower—plus I know the best spots to lean my twelve-string or a bottle of booze, and can reach for any of the dozen items on my bed's headboard ledge without looking—usually picks, a butterfly knife, some hundred-dollar bills, four cut-off Budweiser cans, for pennies, nickels, dimes, and quarters, condoms, a couple of books and magazines, pencils, lined paper, three or four types of vitamins, a bottle of Listerine (Scope doesn't give you that antiseptic alcohol clean), sometimes a bottle of water, a deck of cards . . . The only problem is that *The Bed's Too Big Without You* . . . I had a picture of Clipper on one of the walls for a while, but I got drunk and tore it up right at the beginning of this tour. God, can we both be resolute. The photo was actually a magazine cover, and it killed me to think that her smile, no matter how seductive, wasn't for me, but for men all over the country, to make them feel she was theirs, too.

Another quirk which a lot of people have a hard time understanding, and which can cause friction with the guys, especially Jay and K Dot, is that I hate eating in restaurants, even though I eat most of my meals in restaurants, the exceptions being whatever I get from the bus's refrigerator or the small pantry next to it, like this raisin bran. The nicer the restaurant is, the more I hate it. Not only does having someone wait on me make me feel totally self-conscious and obtrusive, when a buffet would be less hassle for everyone involved, but I'm also reminded of how much goddamn food people in this country waste, and of the terrifying fact that I don't know a single

41

farmer. *Rain On the Scarecrow* . . . I don't know any farmers, and I wouldn't have any idea how to survive if I couldn't buy food at a store, besides pinching pigeons in Faneuil Hall, then not knowing how to clean them any more than I'd know how to launch the space shuttle. I mean, how many farmers would it take getting pissed-off and refusing to sell their crops to shut down the humongous fucking grid of humanity and garbage containers that is New York City?

If you are what you eat, I'm a chunk of dead meat. The documentaries on the rain forest tribe in South America which sends the men hunting for two weeks, then feasts on rotting meat and primitive beer, hit home. That's how my gut feels some mornings. I could live on cereal, chocolate, and frozen pizza if I had to, but what ends up happening when we're traveling is huge double-cheeseburger-weighted-down-with-grease-type scarfing. Two Whoppers will last me twenty-four hours. What happens at home is me sneaking into one of the tiny Italian restaurants near my apartment in the North End, for a plate of linguine with calamari—the family-run holes in the wall where they put up with my idiosyncrasies not because I'm famous, but because after eleven or twelve years, they're finally convinced I'm not a spy. *A bottle of red vino, a bottle of white* . . . Even the catered buffets that get set up to feed the roadie crews seem wastefully extravagant in comparison. So obviously *my* utopian paradise would include large, centrally located feeding centers, like campus dining commons, very efficiently run, with no stigma attached to showing up for a free meal. The problem with this country isn't that too many people are on food stamps, but that too few are.

I sprawl in my bunk for most of the day, or sit on the edge of the bed, strumming the twelve-string but not really working it the way I need to to get new material out. Then I walk up and down the bus's aisle a few times, fetching another bottle of water. My hangover isn't as focused now as it was earlier in the morning (*Oh, say can you see* . . .) but it's set in deeper, like Levi's after you've washed them a few times and see what color they're really going to be. Tubbs rousts me from a nap eventually and I go into the hotel, which is decorated to look like a medieval castle, right down to bellmen in Beefeater's Gin outfits. I take a shower and pinch a nubbly, constipated shit in Jay's bathroom, then we all climb onto the other bus for a quick shuttle to the stadium, where we'll go through a sound check in preparation for tomorrow night's show. When we get to the stadium, the hassles begin immediately, if only because none of the sound equipment is ready yet.

"Hey, Dizzy Zimmerman! God, I'm your biggest fan. God, I've got at least two copies of everything you've ever recorded!"

"Really? I made a tape of myself puking once, and swearing that I'd never, never, *never* drink again if I made it through the night, but I didn't know it had been released. How high did it chart?"

43

"Hey, we've got all kinds of beer over here, if you want one."

"Sure, why not . . ."

It turns out that the guy is the lead guitarist for the Sacramento shows' opening band, the Cali Coptors. He was just leaving the cement-and-girder public bathroom as we showed up. And one of my three rules in life is still right; anyone who tells you his life story in the first five minutes you know him is probably a loser. His name is Joe Arnold. After a quick, disgusted shrug from Walker, who's still got his guys rewiring just about every circuit, I head for the long table where the caterers have set food out behind the stage, because a plate of chow will at least give me an excuse to ignore this guy. He's already following me around like a lost puppy. The sight of a security guard reminds me instantly of my trouble with the cops back in Nevada.

Joe gets wound up pretty fast. "Yeah, we've put out one album, and I think we're gonna change the spelling of our name to one word for our next album, so the first one's like a collector's item if it does any good. Hey, want another beer?

We should really move to L.A. if we're gonna go big-time, but we haven't been able to save enough money because my mom's in the hospital right now and our drummer, he's around here somewhere, he had to pay for all these drunk driving classes, though he only blew point one-one. God, I can't believe I finally got to meet you. I've wanted to be able to play like you since I was about fourteen. I almost crapped my pants when we got the call and found out we'd be opening for you. My mom said she'd make the show if she has to steal a nurse's uniform and sneak out of the hospital. Something's wrong with her balance. She keeps getting headaches and bumping into things. Hey, hopefully I'm not too drunk here, I'm just nervous, meeting you and all."

"I only have that problem when I meet famous women."

"What?"

"I said, as long as you sober up in time for the show tomorrow."

"Hey, would you sign my forehead for me?"

"No."

"I promise not to wash it off until after the concert."

"Then definitely no."

"How about my guitar?"

"Sure, why not . . ."

He runs off to find it, and comes back with a beautiful Martin and a thick black magic marker, which he probably scammed from Walker. I'm less perturbed by him now, some beer and potato salad in my stomach, so I don't write anything wise-ass, just: *Thanks a lot for all the help & good luck—Dizzy.*

The temperature is still high and the sun has dropped out of sight, which improves my mood immeasurably. We haven't seen any rain in the last three weeks. We haven't seen anything but hot, bright sunlight and hot, bright spotlights. Grover and Jay both love cultivating tans in the summer, spending as much time lying out as possible. Jay follows Grover around like he had a set of muscles, too, not just tattoos. K Dot likes warm weather primarily because women wear less clothing. Myself, I'm a vampire. Besides Boston, dreary, overcast Seattle would be about the best city for me to live in, or Portland, Maine, where there's a fairly high tolerance for drunks and junkies. It wouldn't bother me at all if we played our concerts entirely in the dark, using glow-in-the-dark instruments. It would save me from seeing Alex scowl at me every time he thinks I've switched guitar parts with him or am showing off.

Joe can't be any more than twenty-two or twenty-three, but then, Springsteen was only twenty-three when he made the *Born to Run* album. Joe has long black hair and red acne marks on his forehead, which the heat hasn't helped any. If he was cockier, and if he plays as well as the demo the Cali Copters sent us indicates, he might intimidate the shit out of me, especially if there were a few local babes around who were more interested in his group than in Blood Cheetah. After a few minutes, the rest of his band wanders over, their plates heaped with more food than they probably eat in a week. They're all about the same age, the same rock demographic. Luckily none of them uses the word *gig*, which would make me gag.

"So why did you choose us to open for you, anyway?" the drummer asks. "Why not somebody bigger?"

"Same reason I took a fat chick to my prom; you were available." This cracks them all up, maybe a bit too much. "No, really it's because we like to give younger bands a chance. There are also advantages. If you suck, we look all that much better. Plus new groups don't get as much of an attitude about details like whether to use their own equipment or some of ours, which makes it easier to do the stage change-over. But mostly it's a philosophical ideal about playing with different bands and mixing the lineup around a little. And you guys work cheap, don't you?"

"Not for long," one of them snaps. Then, realizing how cocky he sounds, he adds, "I mean, hopefully playing shows like this will kind of snowball, so we'll get a good reputation and even more opportunities."

I don't know which instrument (which "position," Grover would say, like it was baseball) this ugly little puke plays, and

I certainly don't care, but it bums me out that he decided to be nice to me, to waffle, almost apologize, after he'd shown how he really felt, especially since he only changed his tone when he realized who he was talking to, me, David Dillinger Zimmerman, DDZ, Dizzy, the one guy in this goddamn world who'd be embarrassed to death to admit he was once just as cocky, but who also understands, forever and truly, that if you're not the most arrogant son of a bitch in the world when it comes to your own ambition and commitment, you don't have a chance in hell of making it in rock 'n' roll. You might appear to the world to be the meekest, most gracious, quietest guy, probably this is even advantageous, but deep down, you've got to be screaming at the world, Come on, you fucking, motherfucking bastards, I'm gonna write the best goddamn songs anybody's ever heard, and if you don't like 'em, it's 'cause you're all fucking morons!

46   "Well," I say, "take your best shot."

The rest of the evening passes too slowly while we're at the stadium setting up, me trying to resist getting drunk, disablingly drunk at least—don't worry about the eager head buzz I catch with the Cali Copters as we eat, then goes too quickly when the entire crew, the two bands, a few groupies, and half a dozen hangers-on, including Murph, Annie, and their delegation, who show up at about nine o'clock, invade first a local biker bar, then Cheetah's row of hotel rooms, attracting momentary police attention at both venues.

Murph is apparently so pissed off at me that he isn't even talking to me. I'm not sure whether this is because he knows about the cops on the highway yet or not, but I assume he does. He wouldn't hold a grudge this long about the way I acted in the dressing room after the show the other night. At one point in the biker bar, I catch Annie's eye. She's usually more accessible than Murph, although part of that is an act. One of their best routines is that he gets furious at one of the guys in the band for something, then she buddies up to whoever he's mad at, and lets him pour his heart out, which is usually enough to solve whatever the problem is.

"So?" I ask.

"Things don't look so good right now, Dizzy," she says. She's wearing a pair of khaki shorts and a long-sleeved Blood Cheetah T-shirt. She always wears Blood Cheetah shirts when the band is on tour, like a Gap employee advertising the store's merchandise by wearing it to work. Her hair is fashionably cut, but short and practical. She's the only one in our immediate entourage who spent any time in college.

"How bad is it?" I ask. I'm smiling because I know she wants me to ask this question, if only so she can play her role and make me feel better.

"It's pretty bad," she says, looking down. Then she looks back up at me and gives me just the trace of a smile. "But don't worry. Murph and I will get the details ironed out. You can count on that. We always have before, haven't we? Things will work out in the end."

Our sound checks are where about half a dozen of Walker's serfs bob around like headless chickens (*Sue me, blew me, how can you screw me? . . .*), running wires under the stage, duct-taping cables into place, hanging lights, adjusting speaker levels, and double-checking the speakers, while the other guys and I sit bored and listless on the stage, plucking a string or two whenever Walker asks us to, ignoring how sick we are of one another by simply ignoring each other. Luckily the Cali Coptors are still too intimidated to ask to jam with us at any point in the evening.

We probably play the first thirty seconds of "Remote" twenty times, until Walker—God who he is—is certain every adjustment is perfect, though he'll re-review everything tomorrow morning. We can set up and play all in one day, but doing it sucks, which is why, plus travel and hangovers, we schedule at least one full free day between concerts. The only illegal drug I take is several hits of hashish, burning the hard powder on K Dot's glowing Swiss Army knife after he heats

47

the blade with a cigarette lighter, then trapping the smoke in a Dixie cup and sucking through a pinhole. But I'm still drunk and exhausted sooner than anyone else, so I stagger out to the bus and collapse into my bunk as soon as the security cops show up at the hotel. Alone.

6 | Fore!

'M FREE TO DO ALMOST ANYTHING I WANT BEFORE A CONCERT—
hopefully showing up relatively sober—so I get a good
jump on doing absolutely nothing before tonight's show
by staying in bed until one fifteen in the afternoon, then nurs-
ing a mild hangover for the next few hours, my primary medicine being fruit juice, which is supposedly more effective than
just water, and a couple of cold tacos Tubbs has brought back
from a Taco Bell. Waiting around like this always makes me
wonder how professional athletes spend the hours before a
championship game, especially if the game isn't scheduled
until early evening. What could Joe Montana have done before
any of his Super Bowls started that he wouldn't have worried
might put him off his game, like sucking down a few beers,
wrestling with his teammates, or having sex with his wife? (*the
marching band refused to yield . . .*)

Tubbs and Earl are ostensibly guarding the buses, but I
know there are about a dozen people, from Murph and Annie
to record executives I've never met, who've hinted that they
should keep an eye on me as well, an idea so goddamn insulting (even if it is defensible) that I feel like injecting a

syringe of heroin the size of a caulking tube into my ass, if only to see what'll happen. They do run off a couple of groups of teenagers who've figured out where the band is staying, but the kids must all have tickets to the show, because they're doing calm things like taking pictures of each other kissing the cheetah murals, not chaining themselves to the bus's axles. The kids obviously have no idea I'm anywhere in the vicinity, let alone staring out at them from behind a smoked window.

It wasn't all that long ago that I loved getting out and doing something before our shows—walking around the hipster section of whatever town we were in, talking with whoever happened to be around—reporters even—or showing up at the venue early and anticipating how many fans would flood in later, how a silent hall would boom with music and applause. Few places hold possibility open the way an empty stage does. But now I have trouble caring; can only care when my health is perfect and maybe I've written a new song, which is never the case. Maybe the song I haven't written won't appear on a Blood Cheetah disc for ten years, but the timing isn't important. All that matters is that I know I will write it, first proving to myself there's still music in me, then finishing off by perfecting and reworking every note, singing and howling and beating on whichever guitar I'm using, convinced I'm happier than anyone else has ever been.

Dusk. The heat of the day starts to dissipate, but the air remains warm and comfortable, so you know the women will still be wearing jean shorts and halter tops at ten o'clock, which happens maybe half a dozen nights each summer back in Boston. Dusk is also a time of hope and goodwill, the brilliant sunset making me think the world might survive, after all, though, for all I know, the brilliant shades of orange are caused by upper-atmosphere atomic bomb test particles. Hell, in California, dusk is a more satisfying time than even midnight, which is really only a portentous, exciting, it's-time-to-head-out hour in New York City, perfect for cross-dressers, junkies, and subway ghosts.

I'm feeling pretty good by the time Tubbs takes me to the

stadium; too good to worry about stupid shit like Tubbs arguing with the limo driver the record company has hired for the night over who actually drives the limo (Tubbs wins) or even about the insanity of showing up in a Nazi-length Mercedes limo in the first place, when a Jeep Cherokee would be anonymous, edging through a long stretch of parking lot where thousands of fans leap up from their tailgate parties and barbecues to cheer wildly. One guy bounces a Frisbee off the tinted windows, a token of affection which cracks me up so badly I want to pop my head through the sunroof and snag the disk in my teeth. The fucking record company probably tried some ridiculous stunt like parading all five of us in in limos exactly five minutes apart, the morons. Either way, K Dot, Grover, Alex, and Jay are already lounging around the dressing room, while the Cali Coptors are pacing around nervously, waiting to go on stage. Their drummer is so white he looks green. Naturally, K Dot and Alex are having some fun with him.

"Well, there're only about forty thousand people out there," K Dot says, swigging from a Sam Adams. We drink Boston beer whenever we can. "Maybe you should puke on purpose. Alex used to do that all the time, didn't you?"

"Sure did. Best thing for you. I've heard Flea does the same thing, from the Chili Peppers."

"I'll be all right." The drummer is working as hard to convince himself of this as he is to convince anyone else. "As soon as we start playing, I'll be fine. I'm just a little anxious to get started, that's all."

K Dot is draped sideways across a Baracalounger, his gut cradled like a medium-sized watermelon. He takes another tug of beer, then flips his hair back, the way a woman might. "First time we played a show this big, I fucked up so bad, the rest of the band shaved my head. I wonder if we'll have to do that to you."

"Naw, he'd look pretty terrible bald," Alex says.

"Rock 'n' roll's a tough business."

"Let's hope he's up to the challenge."

51

The kid is glancing around the room nervously. He can barely stand still. He probably spent an hour figuring out exactly which jeans to wear tonight. "I'll be fine. As soon as we start playing, I'll be fine. Should I have a beer?"

Alex guffaws. "I certainly would."

Murph is also agitated and impatient. I can tell he's still pissed off at me before he even says a word. "Nice of you to show up. Any chance you're so late because you were calling detox centers?"

"What the hell is that supposed to mean?"

"It's supposed to mean that you've been screwing up lately."

I stride slowly around the room, pretending to look for something. "Okay, guys, where's the portable TV hidden? Murph here must be angry because he saw something attached to my name on Court TV."

"Very funny."

Annie tries to calm us down. "Hey, listen, Dizzy, that's not what he meant to say. We're just worried about you. You have been hitting it kind of hard lately, haven't you? And that shows itself in the way the band's affairs work out, if you know what I mean."

"Sometimes I think I'm not hitting it hard enough."

Murph snorts. "That's exactly the type of attitude you need to lose, mister."

"We can talk about this all tomorrow," Annie suggests. She's the only one who's even remotely embarrassed that we're yelling at each other in front of about twenty-five people: the two bands, several well-dressed record company guys and their dates—for whom Murph may be overacting, considering that he didn't say squat to me at the party last night—as well as a handful of backstage personnel, caterers, and groupies, one of whom Jay is already putting serious moves on, not warming his voice up. In a lot of ways, Annie's the most practical person I know—it's only because she acts as a buffer between the guys in the band and Murph that she ends up taking abuse. Tonight she's wearing sneakers, bagged-out canvas shorts, and her standard Blood Cheetah T-shirt. She looks like she could climb up and hang a stage light with the best of Walker's crew.

"Hey, guess what, Murph," I say. "I really don't care if I play tonight or not, or if I ever play again, for that fucking matter. If you want me to walk back out the door and start hitchhiking home to Boston, just say the word."

"You wouldn't live a month without the band."

"I've got enough money for the rest of my life. It's all in percentages now, you know that."

Murph snorts again, "You're unbelievable," then turns away and joins Geena, his girlfriend, near the buffet table.

"Don't worry about him," Annie whispers to me, kind of taking my elbow and leading me into a neutral corner. "He's just nervous because of all the brass that's showing up tonight, and because of what happened out in Reno the other night."

"What did happen?" I ask.

"We were hoping to ask you exactly the same thing. The district attorney in Reno has contacted the record company. Plus they're coming down on the stadium owner pretty hard. It looks like a lot of parents are mad about what happened out there. Expect a good interrogation from the lawyers within the next day or two."

"Great. It would've been nice if you guys were around to meet the cops with me. Isn't that what we have managers for in the first place?"

"Dizzy, we'll talk about all this later."

I sit down on a doubled step that runs the width of the room on one side, my head in my hands, remembering that we played this same venue on tours in '89 and '92. Just the steps remind me of that, and as I calm down a little, I can flash back to those concerts, and to all the other shows we've done when I was exhausted before we even hit the stage; to every show when the music was so mechanical and I was so dazed that I'd forget which song we were playing. The good mood that I was working myself into as Tubbs drove me to the stadium has disappeared. The only trick that works in pulling myself out of

53

this nosedive is telling myself how satisfied and content I'd be if I really did quit the band tonight, then started hitchhiking across the country in the morning. Passing motorists tend to notice which thumbs are swaddled in hundred-dollar bills.

Hell, if I had any balls left I would quit, if only to piss off that motherfucker Murph. "You just stop being a rock 'n' roll star," is how John Lydon, a.k.a. Johnny Rotten, once described rejecting fame. It kills me to realize that most of today's teenagers couldn't identify him. I should quit, shave my head, undergo more plastic surgery than Michael Jackson, who's gone absolutely insane, change my name, dress some way besides a baggy T-shirt and scrungy jeans, maybe a thirties gangster slouch, then move to Nepal with my twelve-string and a burlap sack filled with assorted picks, a goatskin water bag over my shoulder. Under the stars I'd write songs that I'd forget in the morning. But even sitting here, cradling my head, is a pathetically public and self-conscious act, no matter how few of the people coming and going from the room are actually watching me. Or trying not to watch, then scoffing, like Jay.

At the same time, I don't feel nearly expressive or rebellious or individual enough. I can remember sitting in my classes nearly every day in high school, imagining myself doing something totally outrageous, anything outrageous, from plunking down on top of my desk with my legs crossed Indian-style to sprouting a second head, if only to see how the other kids would react, whether they'd notice at all. *If you don't see me it's 'cause I'm watching you . . .* I always pretended that instead of being mocked, I'd be greeted with something akin to admiration, the girls cooing devotedly, then wanting me to ravish them, the other guys—we never would have called ourselves boys—kicking back and saying, "Yeah, that Dizzy, he's cool, he's all right." Even then I knew I'd end up as a fucked-up rock star. The other mind game I'd play was to pretend the front of the room was straight down from me; that gravity was screwed up and my seat was suspended high against a wall, from where I could, with a precise, balletic dive, plummet past the teacher and out through the window into the infinite blue sky.

*   *   *

Eventually I wander out to the stage wings and catch some of the Cali Coptors' show. The drummer has responded to the pressure he was feeling earlier by setting six-packs of opened beers on each side of his stool. He's squinting so hard that he probably can't see the audience, let alone tell whether there are forty faces or forty thousand out there. Sweat is showing on both the front and the back of the Blood Cheetah T-shirt he's wearing, but he isn't slowing down any; he's playing every song so fast that the other guys are having trouble keeping up. This is a terrible way to ruin a song you've worked months to perfect—even a Ramones tune has a specific pace it sounds best at—and although the poor drummer is just nervous, and twitchy as antelope when lions (or cheetahs) show up at the watering hole, the other guys in the band may vent their own nerves and anxiety by screaming at him when they get off the stage. Their first big show, their first big fight; maybe they'll make it in this business after all.

A rock concert tends to be a launch-'em-and-leave-'em medium, but there are always a lot of people hiding in the wings when a band is playing, like sound guys, management, and assorted VIPs, as well as a few security people and stagehands, who're dying for a microphone stand to topple over so they can sprint helpfully out in front of the crowd. All of which makes it pretty tough for me to get focused and really experience the Coptors' music. Nobody tells me I'm in the way, exactly, but nobody's asking for my autograph, either, on body parts or CD liner notes. I find a canvas director's chair and set myself up just inside the stage-left offstage wall. A couple of the stagehands smirk sarcastically, probably assuming I'm already drunk. They probably also think that just because I don't react to them, I haven't seen their grimaces, like waiters who won't let themselves enjoy serving a fat, boisterous family in a posh restaurant. Lucky for them I'm too busy watching the Coptors' guitarist to give a shit what they think of me. And lucky for them, I'm not drunk yet.

A voice rings out behind me. "Why, hello, Mr. Zimmerman."

"What now?"

"Do you see yourself out there ten years back?"

"Longer than that."

He's one of the record company stiffs, artificially suntanned, dressed in a tan suit, probably subsidized by my songs, which is beginning to wrinkle. I should remember his name. I don't. The blonde standing behind him is equally overdressed for a rock concert, especially a Blood Cheetah show. They're both holding mixed drinks. Maybe there'll be a seriously swank party at the hotel for late night.

"This is Alicia."

"How are you?"

"Hi."

Neither of us knows whether to shake hands, but after an awkward pause, I stand up and she steps forward to give me a tiny, insincere hug, which is even more awkward for me, because I'm sober and I'm from Boston.

"So Dizzy . . . that's his nickname, Leesh . . . Dizzy, how ya feeling tonight?"

"No complaints so far, but if you give me a minute, maybe I can come up with some."

The blonde giggles at this. I could drop a half dollar into her cleavage.

"So, you're feeling all right?"

"Yeah, sure."

"Need anything? A beer maybe?"

"Sure, why not? . . ."

He smiles as he nods for the blonde to fetch me one, and I know his motive is more sinister than just trying to impress her. He motions me back to where it's a bit darker. The Cali Coptors are just finishing up their set. "So, uh ,do you need anything stronger, Dizzy?"

"Well, what exactly is available?" Now we're both smiling. Our shit-eating grins flick out at each other like rapiers. "Is it like an all-night pharmacy, where I can order at random?"

"I was thinking maybe something to blow you up into the right state of mind. Get you jacked up for playing."

"Couldn't hurt." The problem with hangovers is that once you've lived through them, your body feels so healthy and alive that you want to celebrate again, maybe have a drink or take a hit. "But, you know, it's still kind of early."

"What do you mean?"

I shrug, following him even farther into the catacomb of stage rafters, where fewer eyes can see what we're doing. It's like standing inside a skeleton. "I don't know, it's just that sometimes, starting a concert straight can be all right, then maybe taking a little something a quarter of the way in, so that I can still be gaining altitude when the show is peaking. It doesn't take a lot to get me playing my best. I hate coming back down at the wrong time."

"Why Dizzy, I'm shocked. It almost sounds like you're holding something back from the audience," the exec exclaims. His expression is probably exactly the same when he turns someone down for a raise. "Besides, we can refuel you in midflight if we need to."

I suck down the rest of my beer in one long gulp. "I didn't say I was saying no."

"No, of course not . . ."

"Besides, you don't want to be the first person I call a dumb motherfucker to his face all day, do you?"

He glances around quickly, then pulls a small plastic baggie out of his suit's inner breast pocket, unzips the seal carefully, and dumps several grams onto his left palm. Mirrors and straws are obviously too sophisticated for him. I laugh out loud, then grab his wrist, flip the powder into my own outstretched palm, and more or less throw it at my face, snorting back as much as possible. Quite a bit of the coke lands in my mouth, but I also get it all over my skin. I probably look like the flour-covered cliché of a husband taking over for the wife in a kitchen. I'm already walking away when he calls after me.

"Hey, Dizzy, have a good show!"

57

7 | Four, Three, Two, One

WHONG! WHANG! TCHANG! THE FIRST THREE CHORDS of "Howling." The first three notes of the first song of the thirty-sixth goddamn concert of this tour, pretty symmetrical mathematics, plus a distinctive start to a distinctive song. The rules to opening a rock 'n' roll show are to play something off your latest album; to play something the audience will recognize immediately; and to play something you hope will be one of your future classics, so that fifteen years down the road, your now-middle-aged fans will boast, "Yeah, well I saw them back when 'Howling' and the whole *Funk & Fugue* disc were brand new!" Also to play something that fucking rocks.

I'd windmill the chords, à la Pete Townshend, if that wasn't such a cliché. He was so good that most of what he innovated became the clichés. Instead, I knock my Stratocaster—the first of six guitars I'll play tonight, plus a Yamaha piano—against my crotch and hip, almost like I want to hump it. *Hua!* I once stood in an alley in Cambridge, Mass., baked out of my everlasting mind, and watched a street musician play an acoustic guitar while a drunk bum sat next to him, shouting out "*Hua!*"

for percussion, and I understood, once and forever, everything I'd ever need to know about rock music. *Hua!*

Here's where every goddamn, self-righteous politician is going to chew me up and spit me out, vilify me, revile me, defileth me. (Judge not, lest ye be judged. Rock not, lest ye be rocked.) Here's where every goddamn Republican, as well as most Democrats ("We're a moderate party now") flips over in the graves they've yet to fill; where every school principal, every parent—even those who have drug skeletons in their own closets—here's where even K Dot and Grover go ballistic on me for mentioning this, for reminding the country why "Just say no!" doesn't work: DRUGS ARE A BLAST!!! I'll be damned if snorting a faceful of coke doesn't make me feel like God, like I can play all night at two hundred decibels, with my heart ready to burst through my chest wall. I'm so wired that forty-five minutes after the record company exec cokes me up, I'm still swirling my tongue around, licking the roof of my mouth, the inside and outside of my lips, reaching up toward my nose, enjoying the exhilarating, numbing sensation, desperate to ingest every last grain of the powder, then find more powder. The fans in the first two dozen rows must think I've turned into Paul Stanley, from Kiss. DRUGS WILL BLOW YOUR FUCKING MIND! The reason the government can't stop people from taking them is that they make you the happiest person in the world. Every addict has had a hell of a good ride working himself into the addiction. We don't need time machines that can carry us forward into the future or back into the past, we need a way to stop time, to catch a perfect buzz and ride it blazing into eternity. Of course, God was probably wasted when he created mankind, and look how fucked up that project got. The government can't stop people from taking drugs, and since this country is better at revenge and violence than at admitting their programs don't work, we keep wasting billions and letting kids blow each other away in the ghettos. I'll never trust anyone who argues that drugs should be illegal, but has never smoked a joint themselves.

I only wish there was a way to leap from a peak of coke

to a cloud wisp of marijuana to a valley of morphine instantaneously, no worrying about side-effects, overdoses, canceled-effects, symbiotic effects, hangovers, suicidal rages, depressions, or DTs. Blood Cheetah's songs vary a lot in lots of ways, as do our albums, because every decent disc is a progression, just as our career has been a long fucking struggle of a musical progression, so one of my biggest problems is which buzz is ideal for which songs. The play list we run through is designed to make the concert an experience with some amount of coherence, although which tunes we extend into jams changes each night, sometimes without us expecting them to, so it only makes sense that the chemicals in your brain should be part of a progression as well. It's a coursing feeling if you're using coke, sifting if it's pot, and seeping if it's heroin. What's right for "Howling" or "D.C. Me" or "Livewire," where I'm basically slashing and banging an electric guitar, is wrong for "Hallelujah Blues" or even "Ludvig was Luvly," which we hardly ever play anymore.

The pause is perfect. The pause is forever and just a fraction of an instant, then Grover kicks in with his bitchin'-ass drum roll, not a roll really, but close enough that it would sound like a roll if K Dot didn't leap into the fray with his bass a split second later, then me and Alex with our guitars. One of the biggest things which keeps us so tight and intense as a band is that we're all paranoid about what the others might do if we simply didn't participate in a tune. Grover could beat his way to New Orleans if the rest of us gave him twenty seconds. *Hua!* Then Jay is howling—not screaming but howling—the difference is a matter of control. You can't be in control when you're screaming. He's howling with every ounce of energy he can muster, howling the way the beginning of a Blood Cheetah show demands and the way a song entitled "Howling" promises. His voice is a mid to high baritone, higher the harder and faster he tries to push the sound out, and it's just as much an instrument as any of our instruments, with enough of a rasp that people assume he smokes. When he's really letting loose, you'd swear he takes a breath midnote, but that's an auditory illusion. Your ears can be tricked just as easily as your eyes. Jay's wind is so good that if the whole band had a footrace, he'd be the only one besides Grover to last more than fifty yards.

He starts out standing on the extreme edge of the stage, head and hair flung back wildly, Tarzan with tattoos but emaciated muscles, cocky as hell, the only way a real rock star can be, ready to kneel on one of the security guy's heads or plunge over the precipice, if that's what the crowd wants. He probably doesn't know I've seen him practice standing so close to the edge of the stage, when he thought nobody else was around. He used to stage dive pretty often, too, but he got concussions once or twice when the crowd dropped him, plus assorted jabs, punches, shots to the head, the groin, and women ripping at his hair, so he didn't protest too much when we decided to use an eight-foot pit area at all our outdoor shows. The pit also makes security and safety issues easier, especially when there's a section of two or three thousand general admission tickets. Pulling exhausted, dehydrated, overheated fans out through the front instead of the back makes sense if only because struggling for hours to worm their way up to the front tends to be what exhausts and dehydrates them. That and booze, sunburns, day-long barbecues, and chasing the opposite sex. As Grover once said, "Unlike a football game, a Blood Cheetah show needs an equal number of ambulances for the stars and the fans." That Grover, he's such a wise-ass. He knows they stopped calling ambulances for me years ago.

"Under Worms" follows "Howling," then "Distraught," and "Washington Towers," all from *Funk & Fugue*. I'm feeling pretty good through each of them, Maybe it's the coke, maybe something deeper. Maybe even the sobriety and partially clean system I was approaching before the coke, which is good. I can look out at an audience sometimes and drive myself all kinds of crazy, from paranoid to pissed-off, though I know a cool sort of detachment is best: not concentrating on anything but the music and playing well, not letting myself get distracted.

Babes in the first few rows might distract me. Jay and K Dot love to single them out and look them in the eye for a song or two, then signal a stagehand exactly who they'd like to invite backstage after the show. Super-ugly, scrawny, geeky guys might mesmerize me, too. First I'm bummed out that losers and freaks dig Blood Cheetah, then I feel guilty, remembering that the reason we started the band was that we all felt like freaks and losers in high school ourselves, not because we were so popular we had nothing else to do.

I squint my eyes and imagine what would happen if the entire audience surged forward at the same time. I estimate how many tons of muscle that is. I picture the bodies as ants or as chia sprouts or all lined up for the world's longest tug o'war. I wonder how many of the world's historic turning-point battles were fought with fewer combatants than are bouncing up and down in front of me, waving their fists. Tonight I'm relaxed enough to enjoy the adulation and to dance around to the groove all-mightily. As fucked up as we can be, Blood Cheetah does have a boatload of musical talent, so if I'm playing behind, or too far ahead, or just can't control my fingers on the strings, I can take a second to get my head together, maybe even stop playing altogether, depending on the song. K Dot and Alex won't let the error be too apparent, though they'll chew me out after the show if I screw up often enough to throw them off their sets.

"I'd love to be so big a star that I could just stand up on stage and shake my ass and have thousands of chicks start screaming," I remember telling K Dot, when we were about eighteen or nineteen, perhaps our last year of high school. I probably said the same thing to hundreds of other people as well, none of whom had any faith in me and K Dot at all. We talked a lot about what life would be like once we were rock 'n' roll stars, partly because we wanted it to happen so badly and partly because not talking about it would have been the same as admitting it might not happen. "Just get up there and maybe if I moon 'em, they'd really go nuts."

"But if you're famous, you get arrested for mooning people," K Dot replied. "Look at how many times shit like that happened to Jim Morrison."

"Yeah. Wow. Well, it would still be pretty cool."

"I bet there was always someone to bail him out," K Dot said. "I bet there was one guy whose only job was getting him out of jail."

I tried to come up with something better than that. "I bet there were even chicks who would've paid to see him hang a moon."

We must've laughed for half an hour.

Now those days usually seem a million years ago, or the old cliché, "like they were a dream." But when they don't, when my memories are simply those of a thirty-five-year-old, financially-secure white male, smart enough to realize I'd never want to relive the days it took to get me here, I'm able to laugh about it. Hell, sometimes I'm even able to live up to my old idealism, my old righteous goals. So I step up closer to the edge of the stage, turn around, and shake my skinny ass for the crowd, playing the whole time.

They love it. They scream and shout and make piercing catcalls. They react so well that I keep wiggling for thirty or forty seconds. Jay's giving me a superior, embarrassed scowl, so is K Dot, but fuck them, the stupid motherfuckers, it's everything I can do to forgive them. I tell myself their memories of how we were as kids have just been eaten away by all the drugs they've shared with me and with other people over the years. Unfortunately, a lot of those other people are dead now. I don't even think dying on stage would be so bad, either. Imagine the headlines different types of publications would use if I backed up a few more feet, still shaking my ass, a dog scratching himself against the brick corner of a fireplace, and fell into the security pit, snapping my neck or impaling myself on my Stratocaster's neck: *Dropping Like a Rock Star*, or *Dizzying Heights* or whatever.

Not that I'd want to do it when I wasn't absolutely certain video cameras were recording every second, and not that the coke in my system would let me feel anything less than a fifty-foot fall right now. I could probably dive off head first and bounce to safety, my head a pencil's eraser, my body the tensile wooden shaft. Maybe Jay and I should have a kung fu fight on a narrow log far above a raging river someday, settle our differences, see who really leads this band. Rock concerts aren't Broadway musicals, even if the tickets are sometimes just as expensive; it's all right to have some rough edges, or to start half an hour late because one guy's getting laid, another's in the john, and a third is so drunk you have to duct-tape his drumsticks to his hands.

Hell, it's even cool to have a major breakdown in the middle of the show, especially if we come back from the interruption that much more pissed off, intense, and psyched to play hard. Rock fans are like car racing fans; their adrenaline flows from danger, from the possibility that there'll be a tremendous crash at any second. Who wouldn't want to be able to brag, "I was at the Blood Cheetah show the night Jay banged a groupie right on stage, Alex threw two thousand joints into the audience, K Dot wrestled seventy cops into submission, Grover took a bite out of a cymbal then quit the group in the middle of a song, and Dizzy dove off the stage?" And what sort of personal commentary would Kurt Loder give the story when he announced it on *MTV News?* Exactly how would he make me look like a total idiot?

K Dot comes strolling over. It's kind of a rock 'n' roll cliché (a Townshend) to have the bassist hanging out stage right, while the guitar players bounce around stage left, but that's the way it works with us, as important to me as always sleeping with women on my right flank, not my left. The only question is how bold I might be on a given night, lurking fifteen feet behind Alex or strutting forward, like I'm doing now.

"You hoping someone'll give you an enema?" K Dot shouts

into my ear. "Or you gonna drop your pants and use your underwear for a surrender flag?"

Then he wanders back to his part of the stage, smiling in self-satisfaction, I assume. The audience probably thinks he told me something technical, like, "Jay should be singing in a lower key," but Jay and Alex can see what's developing. I duckwalk a couple of steps across the stage, nearly falling, because that's a move you really have to concentrate on, even when you're not playing a guitar, then I kind of jog over to where K Dot is standing. His body smells like sweat, his breath like bad breath.

"I can remember when you couldn't fart and play, let alone walk and talk while you played!" I yell.

"What?!"

We keep the stage's monitor speakers set considerably lower than the P.A. system, as if that'll delay our inevitable hearing loss by more than six or seven minutes, but they're still pretty loud. Think about how deaf old people are now, then remember that the first generation of electric rockers hasn't hit their sixties yet; deafness is just another career move Townshend has beaten everybody to. So at first I think K Dot really didn't hear me. He gives me what he considers his choir-boy smile.

"I said, 'Don't confuse yourself by trying to play and think at the same time!'"

"What?!!"

"Huh!"

"What?"

I'm already boogying back to my side of the stage. "I said, 'FUCK YOU!!!'"

Which for some reason K Dot respects. He's grinning the way he usually reserves for when I admit he's right about something. Maybe he's happy that he can still get me riled, that there's anything at all I still care about. Or maybe he's just happy that the guys in the band still have the balls to tell him off, when nobody else dares to. Even someone like President

65

Clinton probably still has an old high-school buddy or two who swings by the Oval Office and says, "Nice desk, asswipe!" Which is a pretty good way to keep your perspective. I kneel near the edge of the stage and start ripping through the scales which serve as a lead for "The Vanguard." My fingers fly effortlessly over the notes, which in turn makes me want to play even more crisply. *You're always ahead of what's coming next . . . Avant . . . Savant . . . Fixed or flexed . . .*

8 The Railroad

ONIGHT THE MUSIC IS BEAUTIFUL. TONIGHT THE MUSIC IS pouring out of me like my soul itself. But this isn't always the case. Just the other night, in Reno, I felt like the world's king faker, although this might have been because my blood chemistry was so fucked up. A lot of times, the best parts of touring are catching an outrageously tasty buzz—which obviously isn't worth the pain it causes later—and fantasizing about when the tour will finally be over and I can finally stop needing a buzz just to get up in the morning. But what ranks next is playing shows in terms of its actually being a job, the one part of my day I get into a groove.

All the years I was in school I told anyone who'd listen that I hated school. In the first few years that followed school, I busted my ass at a factory job in Dorchester, considering myself little more than an indentured servant, unable to support myself through music alone. I'd roll over as my alarm rang at 6:15 A.M. and moan out loud. But maybe I was wrong. Maybe having a regular, solid work schedule is more important to human beings than it seems to those of us with idyllic images of hunter-gatherers kicking back whenever they damn well felt like it. Even when I showed up at the factory on two hours' sleep, exhausted and nastily hungover, or still drunk, work helped straighten me out, forced me to suffer, to endure, be a man when I'd have preferred lying on my couch all day, feeling sorry for myself.

These days, our shows fill the same function. No matter how wrecked I may be physically, and no matter how closely my bandmates resemble Vietcong snipers, or what legal controversies roil over our heads, we do have to go out and play in front of paying customers. And regardless of how much I bitch about being on this tour, the truth is that something incredibly drastic would have to happen for me to be the one to pull the corroded plug: terrorists kidnapping Tubbs and a busload of groupies, or one of the other guys dying, or me dying. Even when we go on forty-five minutes late, with various pharmaceuticals surging through my bloodstream, the job is the job is the job. So what if sprinting out onto the stage can be like leaping from a high diving board with only someone else's assurance there's water below?

I know the best thing would be for me to always perform totally sober, then get wasted afterward. Hell, a lot of nights I do go on sober. But there are also nights, like tonight, when there's more than just the pressure of having to play. A specific pressure someone might be putting on me, like that motherfucking, son-of-a-bitch record executive. I've got the balls to accuse him behind his back, but not to resist him to his face. Just the gleam in his eye and the cocky way he treated me when the blonde was around told me I'd better not embarrass him in front of her, any more than I should release solo singles under another label. I really was feeling peaceful when Tubbs brought me in to the stadium. My typical M.O. is to down a few beers right before we hit the stage, then take a bottle of hard alcohol out with me, disguised third-grade fashion from undercover, reasonable-suspicion seeking cops, as a two-liter soda bottle. I'm not so different from the Cali Coptors' drummer, after all. Sometimes I'll take a joint with me, too.

I try not to drink any of the booze until the show is well

under way, and I'm certain I can keep increasing my buzz until the performance ends. It's like someone who coordinates his moment of greatest inebriation with his natural bedtime. But on a night like tonight, I know I'll just keep ingesting substances until I pass out. The only question is whether this will happen before or after the concert ends.

The technical aspects are another reason concerts are a good time to be sober. One of Dizzy's basic rules of rock 'n' fucking roll is that as soon as a band stops growing with each new album, both emotionally and artistically, they're dead. Finito. So *Funk & Fugue* contains several songs which are still incredibly challenging for us to perform live. When we're playing perfectly, we can manage it, the music rolling out like ultimate apocalyptic thunder, but just as often we fall short. Sometimes we even think we've nailed these tunes, then realize later, when we review Walker's tapes, that the illusion was created by whatever high we were on. Half the time I'm not sure the fans notice—depending on which drugs they're on themselves. I mean, I know that the most devoted of our troops are incredibly perceptive about how well we're playing, how one show compares to the last few, everyone on tiptoe as we heat up, but when we're having a bad show, I don't care. It's easy to justify my indifference by telling myself there are literally tens of thousands of people in the audience who won't notice if we substitute a song like "Speaker's Cantata" for "Lust in D Minor," which is one of our older anthems, a staple on our play list for the last three tours, let alone minor variations within songs. *She turned away when she turned to you . . . I hung my head 'cause I always knew . . .*

If I'm having trouble fingering the notes of the lead quickly enough, for instance, I can always get Grover and K Dot to slow down a notch, or I can simply not play them all, skip every other of the overlying scales, the same way an ice skater can omit a tricky triple jump from his routine, then end up in the same place on the ice anyhow. Most of our songs are recognizable from the bass and drums alone, or from the rhythm guitar and the drums, so the additional instrumentation

69

just adds more layers to the sound (watch the Talking Heads' *Stop Making Sense* video of "Psycho Killer" for an excellently hip illustration of how this works), although there are quite a few of our songs where it's the voraciously electric leads which give the music its true structure and power, not the rhythm guitar. An old blues influence. On a great night, I feel like the devil himself, zapping my spellbound minions with beautifully torturous and melodic bolts. I can close my eyes for half an hour at a time, slip the shackles this fucked-up world slaps on everyone, and live entirely within the music. At moments like this, I'm not just playing a guitar, I'm transporting myself to the heart of the universe.

At the same time, we've had to make decisions about this tour which keep us from sound qualities we might have preferred under ideal circumstances. Professional horn players fit into this category, a whole sixty-piece orchestra does, as do a full-time keyboard player, a goddamn ukulele artist, and the delicious, high-heeled, scantily clothed, honey-voiced female backup singers we carried on our last major tour, two years ago. Ironically, K Dot and I were in a lot better shape to croon away then than we are now. At the moment, Grover and Alex are the reindeer pulling hardest behind Jay's Rudolph. Additional musicians cost a shitload of money, plus they make most aspects of planning, rehearsing, setting up, performing, and breaking down shows more difficult in a mechanical sense. The money shouldn't matter, except for the basic rule stating that the more something costs, the more bloated and phony it ends up being. Outside musicians can also throw the band's rhythm off. The truth of the matter is that having jammed together for the last fifteen years has made us all extraordinarily close musically.

The biggest challenge of this tour is how well I'll come through when we get to the tunes which I have to play piano on. I picture myself as a movie hero sometimes, a spaghetti western gunslinger, who appears to have ditched, then comes thundering slyly back at the crucial last second, pistols spinning like pinwheels and a shit-eating grin ear to ear. And sometimes I actually come through in such dramatic fashion. If it wasn't so goddamn loud on the stage, I'd swear there were nights when I can hear the guys hold their collective breath as I start plunking out the intro to "Remote," scared I'll need either a metronome or an instantaneous blood transfusion. The beginning of the song is actually pretty similar to the first forty-five seconds of "Hallelujah Blues," except that it's on the piano—which creates a fuller sound when the guitars finally kick in—and that the range of its complexity grows both more quickly and more dramatically. My mood should actually change as I claw my way through the notes. I can't get away with just pushing my fingers up and down on the old ivories. I have to get more aggressive, ready to rip someone's god-damn head off. Part of the guys' concern is justified, because piano isn't even close to being my first instrument, just as the harmonica isn't Jay's first instrument—humming to himself in a bathtub is.

As it turns out, having studied the piano over the last five or six years has also made me a better guitar player. I under-stand now how much more I have to learn, a knowledge I was too immature for when I was fifteen and could copy every Stones tune on a guitar. I'm no longer the brash kid who would tell people how great he was even while begging for their help, any tidbit they might fling in my direction. I know that a professional instructor can point out weaknesses in sec-onds which might take me weeks or even months to correct on my own, though I'm also a strong believer in the idea that the best musicians, those who're truly original, develop their own styles even as they learn music theory, if not before. Teaching a young kid how music works is better than just showing him which piano keys to press to get "Mary Had a Little Lamb," but maybe the way to discover the one genius in a million is to simply provide a backing beat, offer an in-strument, and see if what they teach themselves sounds right. Jimi Hendrix didn't learn how to pull his mind-fuck acid trips out of six strings by replicating other artists' songs. None of the great rock 'n' roll ax-men did. Hell, Hendrix didn't even know how to read music.

Sometimes I can tell how my first drink will taste while I'm still sober, or how a certain drug will hit me, while other times, I can predict exactly how wretchedly, disgustingly, painfully, regretfully . . . how unavoidably horrible I'll feel once a buzz comes crashing back to Earth. Luckily it's easier to reverse an approaching coke crash than a booze crash. With booze, you tend to plateau out, but with coke, you have to either get a lot higher, or let it go altogether, and prepare to suffer the consequences. I'm starting to get this sensation, plus sheer wired exhaustion, as we finish "Moby Box Culture." It's about an eight-minute song, but we jam it out tonight until it's nearly twice that. The piano and the rhythm guitar, which Alex does a pretty good job of transforming into a sort of sharp rhythm lead, play off of each other violently, then subside to the point where all you can hear is K Dot's bass thrumming along, which he hates, since it's only six notes, over and over again, until I ease back in. Then it builds slowly back up, almost like dueling banjos. The stage lights have been dimmed except for the one on K Dot, and now ease back on, until the ultimate catastrophic, orgiastic end, when we're all pounding on our instruments and Jay's screeching like army ants were chewing the wrinkles off his sac.

The ending is sudden; the reverberations rumble out over the audience and fade into the distance. Forty thousand fans are screaming their goddamn lungs out. As the lights go down again, this sound starts to spook me. I'm as drenched with sweat as if I'd been having sex in a steam room. My breathing is irregular, my sides are heaving. Even though I bend my fingers back and crack my knuckles, my hands start shaking.

"You all right?" Alex rushes over. He's sweating, too, but at least he doesn't give the impression that for him, Ping-Pong would be an endurance sport. His concern seems genuine.

"Yeah, I think so."

"Are you all right to keep playing?"

"I'll be fine in about fifteen seconds. Better than ever."

I stand up from the piano bench too quickly, the blood rushes out of my head, and my vision goes black. Luckily I'm smart enough to realize what's happening and sit back down before I fall over; am already prepared to defend myself with the argument that Grover has the same type of blackout when he leaps up from a chair too quickly, although with him, it's from having such low blood pressure.

One of Alex's hands is on my shoulder. "You sure you're okay?"

"Yeah, I'm fine." I'm ready to stand up again. "Just a little dizzy, that's all. That's a joke, son."

"Wicked funny."

I'd snort and oink for him, but I can't. I've always wondered whether playing solo shows would be a power trip or a royal pain in the ass. Usually I conclude that the pressure would incapacitate me within twenty or thirty seconds. But one of the disadvantages of being part of a band is that none of your mates wants to let you alone dictate the pace of a performance, whereas some entertainment demigod, say Michael Jackson, is backed by outside musicians who're paid extremely well to do whatever the fuck he says. At least ten or fifteen people, excluding stagehands, are hovering in the wing as I stride over, the stage still dark.

"What the hell is wrong with you?" Murph demands. His face is almost as sweaty as mine. His cheeks are crimson. "Are you all right? Get the hell back out there!"

Instantly I decide to piss him off. I plunk down in the folding metal chair Geena has been sitting in as she leaps up. "Water . . ."

Annie is already running over with a two-liter bottle.

"On head."

She dumps it all over me, then a large quantity down my throat.

"Fertilize beavertail."

"What?" Murph screams, his face inches from mine. He

could be a prizefighter's manager now. I purposely don't focus my eyes on him. "Get the hell back out there, you idiot!"

"Food."

"What? Don't fuck with me, Dizzy!"

"Coke."

Annie's lifting my arm, making me stand, and trying to support me, though I'm only pretending to need the assistance. For a woman, she has pretty strong shoulders. She could probably lift more weight than me. She's also whispering into my ear, trying to calm me down, not make a scene. But what the hell good is not making a scene? The easiest solution would have been to simply slide me a finger covered with coke, subtly, like dealing off the bottom of a deck, not make me ask for it in a robot voice. Everyone within thirty-five yards knows exactly what I'm getting now, so there isn't much sense in her and the record company exec pulling me into the scaffolding.

74

"We can kill all the witnesses if we have to," I say.

"Shut up and cover a nostril."

The audience is still screaming as I bounce back into view, the lights coming up. They have no idea anything is wrong, and the truth is, nothing is. Nothing-fucking-what-so-ever, except for fooling with Murph and the gang, and me really needing the lift. Yee ha! Arriba! The coke jumpstarts me immediately. I swill from beers throughout the rest of the show, but I also remind myself to drink water occasionally, from the bottles Grover keeps next to his drumset, or dump it on my head and wander over to one of the two large fans mounted on the side of the stage. And the next time I head over for a little vital stimulation, Murph and the exec are more accommodating.

"Pit stop," I yell. "New tires."

What else is there to say? For the rest of the show, I have to concentrate on something besides my own crumbling nerves in order to not start thinking of myself as already a skeleton, despite the coke. I glare over into the wings, or stare at the rest of the band, then glance out at the audience, trying to give some of the chicks in the front the only sort of winsome, smiling, seductive expression I can manage, the one which video directors try to frame appealingly, but which wears thin quickly in real life. There seem to be quite a few babes tonight, women who'd give me a hard-on the second I met them, even if I knew I'd regret them in the morning. Sometimes I literally stand on stage and think to myself, putting a twist on a George Carlin line, that if ten thousand women are watching me, half of them have to be better looking than average, which gives me five thousand to choose from.

I switch from piano back to guitar, from one guitar to another, depending on the song, and everything goes the way it should: the verses Jay always tries to get the audience to sing, Grover's drum solo, etcetera—all run through in an order designed to bring the entire show to a climax with our older anthems. The concert is almost finished before I remember the cops pulling the bus over back in Nevada. And by the time I scan the crowd to make sure there aren't any fights tonight, my attitude is essentially, "Oh well, fuck it, whatever happens happens." *Que sera, sera.*

We've always had a philosophical opposition to long, drawn-out breaks before our encore—as if we're so modest that the crowds surprise us with their gratitude and enthusiasm—and to playing other artists' songs. What are we going to do, be the ten millionth goddamn group to end with "Twist and Shout?" We dispense with the formalities, swig down a couple of quick shots backstage, where groupies, fans, and various sycophants are already milling around, then hit the stage again, finishing with a long jam on "Stout Billy," a silly song I wrote about thirteen years ago. Thirteen long years.

75

9 | Katherine the Great

MY IDEAL WAY TO SPEND THE SECONDS IMMEDIATELY FOL-
lowing the final note of our final song tonight would
be to stroll offstage, drop ten or fifteen feet into a jun-
gle-enclosed lagoon of wonderfully warm, reinvigoratingly
cool, crystal blue Hawaiian water, float for twenty minutes,
maybe paddle around a bit to release tension, then climb onto
a lush bank where the only other soul was a gorgeously shy
native girl, ready to serve my every whim, even if it's just a
hug.

But NO! What always happens happens: noise, people,
commotion, blah blah fucking blah, and it doesn't help to
make a scene about my privacy, because whatever leverage I
had before the show, like threatening to not go on, is gone
now. Tonight the record company decides to throw us a party.
A welcome to California. But instead of springing for anywhere halfway decent, they end up holding it in the dressing
room, and the passageways surrounding it, plus the backstage
and everywhere Walker's men are working. For the first half
hour I sit exactly where I did before the show, on the long,
shallow steps that divide the dressing room into two levels,

my head in my hands, remembering high school again and laughing to myself that behavior which would once have made me an outcast now identifies me as a troubled artiste, a genius so creative he can't remember to tie his own shoes, though I haven't done any real work in eight months.

The music on the sound system is the Black Crowes' first album, then three or four cuts from the Cali Coptors' album, and finally what sounds like a late seventies mega disco hits compilation, which is fine with me, being sick as a goddamn dog of rock 'n' roll, not wanting anything resembling our own musical style in my head right now, and also enjoying the old-time associations groups like the Brothers goddamn Gibb bring (*Stayin' Alive . . .*) I just wish they'd turn it down about eighty decibels, the stupid motherfuckers, at least until I get another snort of the record exec's fine, fine blow. None of the other guys are into the party yet, either; K Dot and Alex are slumped on a couch, looking dazed, Jay has disappeared, and Grover is probably out helping Walker. Hell, everybody's having a blast at the Blood Cheetah party except Blood Cheetah. I can feel the movement of legs passing me, an occasional pat on the back and quick words of congratulation; can pick out individual conversations from the background murmur. It's amazing how many people will talk about me in the third person when they're only a few feet away. Or address me while I'm ignoring them.

"DDZ, my man, great show!"

"You're the greatest!"

"Best show I ever saw. Really, I mean it."

Murph comes over and kind of nudges me with the side of his knee. K Dot has already left the couch. "Hey, Earth to Dizzy. Any time you want to rejoin the living would be fine with us."

"Fuck off!"

"Have it your own way, but it's my managerial duty to remind you there are some pretty influential people here, so you might not want to act like a chucklehead the whole night."

He's lucky I don't chomp down on one of his ankles. "Don't

77

even start with me about your so-called managerial duties right now, pal! You haven't exactly been saving the fleet lately." If Manager Murph had lost a single red blood cell for every dollar he's made off of us, his vapid corpse would crumple in on itself like a rotten fruit.

The strangest part of the entire night is that the police show up incredibly early, so early that I assume either Murph or someone smarter than him has complained about a trivial matter, in order to let them snoop around while affairs are still relatively calm. A state police lieutenant confers with one of his sergeants, the head of stadium security, and Annie. Four troopers sniff around casually, looking for underage groupies or stagehands smoking joints out in the open. I stay on the steps, but I'm smart enough to keep my eyes open and act alert, if only so none of the troopers will ask, "What the hell is wrong with him?"

78

My heart is pounding erratically, my mouth is dry, and my hands are shaking so badly I need to put them on my knees— all my typically paranoid, about-to-be-busted symptoms, the feeling your average scofflaw motorist gets when he's pulled over, times a hundred, because I'm still worried about the cops back in Nevada.

"How are you doing?" one of the troopers actually asks me. He doesn't act like he suspects me of anything in particular. Just being friendly. His voice and tone are surfer-innocent. True California.

"Better than usual, I guess," I quip.

The music is turned down while the cops are present, then back up when they depart and we're turned over to the stadium security guys, who I've always preferred to think of as substitute teachers, not rent-a-cops. That's about how much power they have. They're just happy if no bodies are left over in the morning. Soon there are about seventy people in the room, aged from perhaps seventeen to forty-five, dressed every way from expensive silk suits and tiny black dresses to cut-off jean shorts and tank tops stitched out of bandannas. *They're dancing in the stalls, they're dancing in the halls...*

Three young girls wearing cut-offs and floral tank tops start dancing on a table, barefoot, totally unselfconscious, which is more than I can say for the goddamn suits, though the suits may sink enough drinks to put moves on the girls later.

Songs that came out in '75 or '76 are probably older than the girls, and the list of guys who could have fathered them in a desperate lull on a desperate tour (like this one) runs from Peter Frampton to Johnny Rotten, but the girls are too young to care about any of that bullshit. They just want to dance, they just want to bounce around, meet some rock stars. I assume this experience is new for them, since I don't recognize them from among the obsessed groupies who follow us show to show. There are quite a few of these in the room right now, though gratefully, Blood Cheetah is no Grateful Dead. But who knows, in the last year, maybe these girls have partied with every band to roll within several hundred miles of here, San Francisco included, which is kind of a dream city for all the hoping-to-be-cool young people stuck growing up in Sacramento.

All three of them have tan, cellulite-free legs, even the stocky one, who'll begin to look downright chubby as soon as winter comes and her tan fades. They all have long hair, and none of them wears much makeup. Their smiles are the size of a small bay, as they laugh at each other and shout jokes over the music, then take turns jumping down to chug from a gallon jug of wine. How could I, how could anyone, not love them instantly, even knowing from long experience that despite how easy they'd be to bed, their type of innocence is a huge pain in the ass? And how come when women sweat, the liquid is like a nectar, but when I sweat, cow afterbirth sludge oozes out of my pores? After a few minutes, Grover appears and leaps up to dance with them, a beer in one hand. But he's not the one they should look out for, Jay is, or I am.

I could almost crash now, and I probably would if I either knew where an appropriately private and chilly catwalk was or if Tubbs slung me over his massive shoulder and hauled me forcibly back to the bus. Instead, I find my old friend the record company exec, tugging his sleeve until he follows me into a bathroom, where I snort another handful of coke. He tries to make himself feel better about the whole situation by asking if I'm sure I need more, now that I've gotten through the performance, while I try to justify my actions by telling myself it's a reasonable amount, just enough to last me through another hour or so of this party. For the first time all evening, I realize he hasn't been indulging himself.

"Thanks," I tell him.

He's adjusting his tie and trying to smooth the wrinkles in his suit coat. "Don't mention it, if you know what I mean. It's just business, like keeping a car running and gassed up."

"Yeah, but my tank has a faulty gauge."

"Ha ha, that's pretty good, Dizzy. You kill me, you're a riot. But that's why you're the creative one and I'm the one who pushes pencils. And do me a favor, really, don't mention this. There may be a reporter or two snooping around tonight. The saying, 'There is no such thing as bad publicity,' only applies to rock stars, not guys like me."

"Is there anything left for them to expose about me?" I joke.

The room is rocking at even greater levels when we return, though this might just be the coke and my perception. Whenever I'm sober, everybody else seems sober; when I'm wasted, everybody else seems carefree, exuberant, and crazy in a commiserating way. I swear to God I would have made a great pirate, except for having to perform acts of physical man-to-man violence, and also for not being able to binge on about ten Three Musketeers candy bars whenever I felt like it. Of course, everybody thinks they'd be a great pirate—or medieval knight, or French diplomat, or whatever—but I really would. I can go for months without a woman, I can work hard for months at a time, and then, when a self-imposed work exile is finally over, I can party with the best of them; can even overlook minor atrocities, like rape and pillage, if circumstances are right. For instance, if someone pumps drugs into me. Plus I've always loved heights, which worries Murph halfway back to poverty. I used to climb around in the lighting rafters and catwalks pretty often when we first started playing these big arena venues.

Now everyone yells at me the second my foot hits a ladder rung, though at least Walker's nice about it. They're all convinced I'll either reverse all of the wiring connections and fry the entire power system, or that I'll finally take my headlong plunge. Hell, my apartment even has a loft, which I love hanging out in, pretending the rest of the place is the ocean, or sometimes a valley. My bed is a futon, the only type of mattress worth sleeping on, and I had Pierre, ze famous French carpenter, build me a waist-high platform to mount it on, overlooking the rest of my apartment, with all sorts of drawers and storage spaces underneath, and only a six-inch-high mahogany rail to keep me and whoever is with me from going overboard. Unfortunately, it's usually just my guitar that's with me, especially when Clipper is on one of her love sabbaticals. Hell, I wish I had a crow's nest to watch this goddamn gathering from, although just watching people isn't a game for coke, pot would be more appropriate.

The only option is to charge into the party, aggressive as a used-car salesman; to plunge into it, motherfucker, a swashbuckling mutineer who's forced to walk the plank, then sprints down the board and bags a triple flip with a half turn.

"Hey man, how ya doing?" Jay yells to me. Suprisingly his tone is friendly, like he hasn't seen me in two months, let alone been pissed off at me for almost a year. He's the only one in the room not wearing a shirt.

"Hua, bobba bobba bobba, me-Yow!"

My mouth makes several other noises as well, all in the excitement I can't contain, all in expressive, eager tones, and all in good nature and appreciation. As pissy, irritable, immature, jealous, and underhanded as the guys in the band can be at times, me included, we've also known each other long enough to pick up on one another's nonverbal cues quickly, so I realize, without even thinking about it, that Jay is in a great mood. Let bygones be bygones! Let the world be ours again!

"So?" I ask.

"So the show's over, another day another dollar, nobody got killed, that we know of. The cops have split already, and there's plenty of beer and plenty of babes. What else do you need?"

"The show was all right with you?"

He's already stopped paying attention to me; his gaze follows several of the younger women (*follow me to heaven on the leash stretching from hell...*). He's practically yelling. "The show was fine. Some of the endings got fucked up, but so what? Hey, do me a favor! My voice is feeling kind of ragged out, so if you hear me shouting or singing too much tonight, remind me to shut up. Just don't let anyone see you."

"Yeah, sure, no problem." I'm quick to agree, not wanting to destroy his sudden goodwill. I wonder if he's forgiven me for past conflicts, or just forgotten about them momentarily.

82

He disappears just as quickly as he popped up, following a couple of groupies toward the small bar the catering staff has set up. Several people are standing close enough to congratulate me on the show or to nod hello, but who stands out is a lovely brunette wearing one of the evening's skimpier dresses. She obviously came in as part of the record company's entourage, though nobody's hovering over her right now, and while she's holding a glass of wine, she seems more than a bit self-conscious about how dressed up she is. She's exactly my height, so I notice her wonderful, understanding blue eyes first.

"Do I know you?" I ask. Down in L.A., this would mean either, "How famous are you?" or "What can you do for my career?"

"I don't think so. Hi, I'm Katherine. And you're David Zimmerman, right?" She smiles and offers her hand, which I accept.

"I guess I must be. Katherine, that's a downright sensible-sounding name, especially in this crowd. Is it usually shortened to Kathy?"

"Kate, if anything."

"Even better."

It's her eyes that have me believing she understands every nuance, subtlety, and undercurrent of what I'm saying—along with her smile—but even realizing how this illusion works can't prevent me from falling for her instantly. The simple fact that she didn't reel off a list of every acting production she's ever been in when I asked if I knew her makes me hope she's enough of a nobody that I can actually pick her up, as opposed to the truly talented and powerful Hollywood-type beauties, who laugh at me these days, instead of with me, even when they get whatever pointed jokes I'm making. I wish I'd taken a shower when we got off stage, instead of standing here stinking, and that I'd brushed my teeth, as well. The cocaine coursing through my capillaries is the only reason I have any confidence at all, but what confidence it is—like Thor, like Genghis Khan, like Churchill.

One of the Cali Coptors walks by—scrawny, unconfident, intimidated, clutching a beer as a security blanket, but apparently pleased with their performance—and my immediate urge is to grab him by the ears and scream into his face, "Keep on rockin', baby, or it'll eat you ALIVE!" Wisely, I resist.

"Did you enjoy the show?" I ask Katherine.

She touches my forearm casually. "You were, uh . . . pretty theatrical."

"Well, as they say, the fans are the people who matter most. It's a cliché, but it's true."

"Most clichés are true, aren't they?"

"Yes, but now you're just trying to come up with an aphorism."

She's grinning in commiseration, luckily not holding her nose. She looked self-conscious before I spoke to her, but now she strikes me as graciously capable and self-confident. Something about her posture lends formality, which has its own rules about romance and class; the way she holds her back reminds me of the old-style Hollywood actresses like Grace Kelly. As does her intricate enunciation. "And how exactly would you define an aphorism?"

"I'm not sure I'd try. I mean, I'm sure I wouldn't try. It's just a word I read on the back of the Who's *Quadrophenia* soundtrack album a few years back, so every now and then I throw it out and try to trick women into thinking I'm really smart."

"Oh, I don't suppose you have to work too hard at that."

Now I'm rolling. "Your best estimate. How many miles is it from here to wherever it is you live?"

"Ninety-three. I'm on Jolsent in San Francisco, close to the park."

"How many of your grandparents are still alive?"

"Only two. Both of my grandmothers."

"How old is the oldest?"

"Eighty-six."

"What's your brother's favorite color?"

She's laughing like I'm the second coming of Robin Williams. So am I. Her hand is practically drawing hieroglyphics on my arm. "How do you know I have a brother?"

"This is America, everybody has a brother."

"Then what's yours? Your brother's favorite color?"

I'm absolutely cracking up. "That bastard? Let's not even start with him! Waiter!"

One of the catering staff brings me a bottle of Sam Adams, and I start to tell Katherine about some of the brew pubs in Boston, my voice still raised high above the racket. But before I know it, one of the record company guys is in my face. He's the type who'll pop into one of our recording sessions for five minutes and exclaim, "Keep up the good work, guys!" right when we're stuck on a technical problem so difficult we're about to throttle one another.

"So how's old Dizzy treating you?" he asks Katherine, with the same sort of personal undertone I'd been aiming for only moments earlier.

"He hasn't bared his fangs quite yet," she says, and smiles.

"Well, that's another victory for pharmaceuticals, right Dizzy?"

Probably a grimace flashes across my facile-yet-translucent

visage, a scowl, a sneer, instead of the appropriately amused, patient grin. Goddamn fucking asshole moron! But my reaction isn't just to his one stupid line, although one of my three rules in life is to never mention drugs to a woman I'm trying to pick up, no matter what I'm on at the time—they know my access, and will hint at it themselves if they're interested. My reaction is to everything I suddenly see coming, a brick fucking wall in front of me; him wanting to protect Katherine from me; him wanting to steal her from me; him destroying any chance I might have tonight, even if he doesn't get her himself. But I'm so pissed off, ready to rip this guy's goddamn heart out with two bony fingers, that I can't manage a snappy comeback.

"Dizzy?"

I still don't reply. I'm thinking too hard.

"Dizzy, hey, are you feeling dizzy, or what?" He gets a decent laugh out of himself at this, because it's not like I've collapsed yet. But he's suddenly made himself the good guy and me the weakling, the sick-guy druggie, which may be true, since I could have avoided this turn easily if I'd stayed clean tonight. Hell, I could even dig myself out of this hole now if I could become instantly straight. "No, seriously, Dizzy, are you all right?"

"I'm fine and you know it." I take four steps away, like I'm about to split, then I wheel back. "All I can say, before I do you the favor of disappearing, is that she had her hand on my arm."

"What the hell is that supposed to mean?"

"It means you're lucky I'm not a goddamn pirate."

"A pirate?"

Katherine has been watching this exchange in utter amazement; we might as well have pulled pistols and challenged each other to a duel. I turn to her and ask, as calmly and politely as possible, "So, Katherine, what's your last name?"

"It's Millis. Why?"

"Never know when I might run for political office."

Hiding in the crowded room is easy enough after that, but

I'm really not in the mood to dance, or to make forced small talk, or to have people watching me at all. Unfortunately, the coke has got me so wired that I could drink all night without passing out. And I know that if I think about Katherine too long, I'll get both pissed off and bummed out. Grover is still dancing on the table, while Jay has his tattooed arms around the pair of groupies now, like he's won the damn Boston Marathon. K Dot is at the buffet table with the same exec who's been supplying me all night, and Alex has disappeared, maybe to sulk, polish off a bottle of whiskey, then call his ex.

It only takes me a minute to spot my next victim, who I— like anyone fitting the *Jeopardy* "Notorious" category—make sure is vulnerable: a babe of nineteen or twenty, leaning against a wall, momentarily alone. She is attractive, but not so obviously sexual that men are hanging over her.

"Hey, I'm Dizzy," I say.

"I know."

"Listen, I'm gonna clear out of here, get my driver to take me back to the bus and hotel, see what's going on there, generally chill out for a while, maybe a beer or two, maybe some music, maybe a quick nap. Any interest in coming along?"

She glances around the room. "Uh, sure, that'd be cool. Just give me a minute to tell my ride not to wait."

I never ask if the ride was a guy or a girlfriend. And I certainly don't look back to see if Katherine is watching me. What would I do if she was, not take off with the girl? I'm already hustling out to find Tubbs. *I'm gonna blow your mind . . . I'll take you from behind . . .*

10 | The Last Seduction

E RIDE BACK TO THE HOTEL IN THE LIMO. SHE TELLS ME HER name, which I forget immediately—it'll be an absolute miracle if I don't slip and start calling her Clipper, or Katherine—but she doesn't seem to harbor any illusions about me being a super-nice guy or about the two of us going anywhere but where we can be alone. No party back in someone's room, no sing-along with Dizzy and Alex strumming on acoustics, no circle of friends holding hands to watch the sun come up. I kiss her once or twice right when we pile into the limo, sweet young wine breath, no cigarette stench, me reaching for her elbow, of all body parts, not her breasts or her crotch, jiggling her arm like a marionette part, making sure she's real, an actual warm, intelligent being next to me, pressing against me. Then I grab a bottle of water from the mini-bar and collapse deep into the plush leather seat.

"Can I drink some of this?" she asks. She's pulled a bottle of Stolichnaya from the bar.

"Sure. There, use a glass. One of those tumblers. And add some ice. You should always use plenty of ice. Vodka tastes better when it's cold. That's why they drink it in Russia and tequila in Mexico."

"Really? Should I mix it with anything?"

"You can if you want, but you don't have to. The reason most people mix in Coke or something is that they want to suck it down like it was a soda. Just take your time and take small sips."

"Hey, that's not bad."

Neither of us says anything else for several minutes. The only sound is the limo whooshing along the highway. Despite how easily this is all going, I start to feel self-conscious, like I should say something to justify the trust she's placed in me.

"So, did you dig the show tonight?" I ask.

"Oh yeah, it was great. The way you guys jammed on 'Moby Box Culture' was great. It was just like . . . I could close my eyes and feel what each of you were all thinking."

88

"Really? And what was that?"

"I don't know . . . just how much you loved playing it, like maybe if you weren't getting paid to be there, you'd still do it the same way, you love the audience so much. With your eyes closed and totally into the music."

"What other songs did you like?"

" 'Hallelujah Blues' was great. I had my eyes closed through all of it. I swear it's like you wrote it just for me, even though we hadn't even met when you wrote it. God, I didn't even like you guys when you wrote it, I was only like fifteen."

"Help me with the math," I say, knitting my brow.

"What?"

"I mean, which year did we put that out?"

"Nineteen eighty-eight."

"So that makes you . . ."

Her hands, which have been resting on the tops of my hands in my lap, come up and push off of my chest playfully. "Which makes me twenty-two, for your information! I'm no little girl."

"I know that. I was just making sure." Then the old Dizzy kicks in, laying it on thick as Boston clam chowder. "Really, the whole reason I was attracted to you and thought you might want to spend some private time together with me was that even back at the party, you didn't look like you were fooled by all the bullshit that goes on at those events. You looked like you could tell how honest people were being with you just by closing your eyes and picking up their vibe. I mean, you probably noticed some of the guys from our record label, all dressed up in suits. They don't realize that the suits don't fool real people into thinking they're real, too, they just give you something nice to look at before they start talking."

Her mouth is open; her jaw actually moves up and down a couple of times before she gets any words out. "God, you're so right. What do clothes matter, anyhow, we're all naked underneath, aren't we?"

"Absolutely."

"That's right. It's like . . . it's like the better you dress, the more insecure you really are."

"Look at how lawyers dress."

"God, you're so right."

Everybody has beautiful eyes, if you look closely enough, though some are particularly outstanding, blue and twinkling, or dark brown and mysterious; everybody has beautiful eyes, unless they're bloodshot, or swollen shut, or cataracted—I even think a white eye could look all right on a woman, a wolf's eye. For a split second, I think it's Katherine who's in the limo with me. That's how strongly her eyes attracted me. Then, in a weird sort of flashback déjà vu, I remember it's the girl who I'm with. But her eyes are beautiful, as well, an off-turquoise which suck me in in the darkened limo and let me see for a second what some other guy will see five or six years from now, when he realizes he wants to spend his life with her. Her smile is enthusiastic, and if her teeth aren't a bleached Hollywood perfection, who am I to judge? She tosses her head back occasionally to keep her hair out of her face, and the motion, not at all faked or pretentious, makes her beautiful to me as well, far more beautiful than having sculpted Scandinavian cheekbones or a flawless nose, the attributes where,

89

as Paulina Porizkova has pointed out, people pay tons of money to see a genetic difference of two or three millimeters.

The only thing which isn't entirely beautiful about her is that she's with me, and that my intentions are mildly evil, no plans for anything that'll take longer than an hour or two. I can imagine how disappointed all the boys who grew up with her, who spent their high-school years chasing after her and her friends, would be if they could see her now, so easily swayed by a scumbag like me, who by some cosmic accident has ended up rich and popular. And what really kills me is how incredibly sure I am that she wouldn't understand any of this, even if some insane sense of propriety roused me enough that I tried to explain how much of a loser I am to her, to talk her out of sleeping with me. Maybe she would claim she understood it, then do whatever I wanted her to do anyway, because you can't truly learn something like that by hearing it, only by living it, which takes time. Worst of all, I take a perverse pleasure in giving her opportunities to prove I'm right, sick son of a bitch that I am.

"What do you think people should wear?" I ask.

"Well, whatever they want, I guess."

"What does your outfit say about you?"

"What?"

"I mean, and don't take this personally, but isn't it kind of hypocritical that so many of the fans we get at our shows are all dressed alike, or that so many of the guys have long hair, just like the guys in the band do, when one of our messages, if we have any messages at all, is that you don't have to conform?"

She takes a long sip of the vodka. "I guess so. What do you mean?"

"Well, why do you like Blood Cheetah?"

"Because you guys are great."

I don't groan out loud, and I don't tell Tubbs to turn the limo around, but I suspect I should. "Right, but can you tell me why we're great? Be specific."

"Because you understand your fans. Because you understand me."

"But just a few minutes ago, you said you didn't even like us when we first recorded 'Moby Box Culture,' which wasn't even one of our first hits. And it was our first hits that started us down the road to being as popular as we are now, a time at which you're convinced that 'Moby Box Culture' is one of your favorite songs, and that we understand our fans."

"Well, that's different."

My eyes are closed now. "How's it different?"

"I don't know, it just is."

We're both quiet for a minute. This might be my personal record for speaking the least words to someone I'm attracted to but have never met before before getting into an argument with them. Or it might not be. My tone hasn't been downright nasty, but I haven't been flirtatious and animated and teasing, either. I hope she isn't taking me all that seriously; half the problem is just that I'm too exhausted to deal with any of this rationally. But the pendulum of my emotions swings back in her direction just as quickly as it had arced away, and I come to my senses enough to realize I should put some effort into negating the opinion she's probably forming of me.

"I'm sorry," I say. "It's just that there's been a lot of pressure on the band lately, and I'm pretty bushed right now. It's good to find someone I can talk to about actual issues, though."

She takes my hands in hers again, strokes them like she'd massage a person's temples. "That's okay."

"In this business, you never know who to trust."

No response.

"But I can trust you, can't I?"

She laughs out loud. I've obviously crossed the threshold into being totally ridiculous. Her eyes flash as she takes another large sip of the vodka. "I haven't lied to you yet, have I?"

"I knew there was a reason I liked you." I rouse myself enough to give her a kiss on the cheek.

* * *

Tubbs pulls up at the hotel, but he only waits ten minutes before he comes back to tap lightly at the window. He bows his head and speaks apologetically; he obviously doesn't want to ruin anything for me.

"Sorry, Mac, but Mr. Murphy wanted me to bring the car back as soon as I could, so you all will have to either get out or come back with me. You can bet your sweet ass they'll have me running back and forth all night long. Sorry."

"Oh, that's all right."

The girl and I climb out. Tubbs looks disappointed that she doesn't even have to adjust a shoulder strap.

"You'll be all right?" he asks, very seriously. "I mean, you'll be able to make it from here?"

"No, you don't have to worry about finding me passed out right on this very spot three hours from now, if that's what you mean. I'm not sure where we're even going, but we'll certainly end up there, won't we?"

He starts back toward the driver's door. "You got your key?"

"Yes, Tubbs, I've got my key."

"Key to what?" the girl asks, practically tugging my arm off. Now that we're standing again, I notice she's at least eight or nine inches shorter than me, which means a total height of no greater than five feet, max, which in turn means—I swear to God I've seen it enough times to know—that discovering music and relating to music and finding bands she can devote herself to is one way of dealing with whatever insecurity her height causes. Maybe she was even standing alone at the party because only moments earlier she had seen me, David Dillinger Zimmerman, not the best-looking guy in the band, let alone in the room, flirting with Katherine, super-babe from the city of San Fran, and had felt inadequate by comparison.

The key Tubbs asked about is the key to the bus, so I have access to my berth. To this day, Murph tries to get me to stay in a hotel room like the other guys, arguing it's for my own safety, but the truth is that he's psychotically paranoid I'll either lose the key, give it away, or trade copies to groupies for drugs and sex. He also made damn sure the key to the door wasn't the same one for the ignition, because we all know that's a rampage waiting to happen. I explain all of this to the girl while we walk a slow, romantic loop around the hotel, imagining ourselves a knight and a lady to its medieval design, its turrets and balconies. Two goofy security guys drive past us once in a golf cart, but wisely don't hassle us; I would have pummeled them with bribes and a disarmingly laid-back attitude. The night air is still comfortable and warm, a relief after the air-conditioned limo, which was getting to be too cold. The only blessings missing are stars in the heavens above, because of the city's glare, and our own sobriety. The girl has at least enough brains to have brought the bottle of vodka along, which I take liberal slugs from, hoping beyond hope to delay my crash, to ignore my slight yet intolerable hangover symptoms. I have no idea what the time is, but it must be something like three in the morning.

"Hey, can we go in a hot tub?" the girl asks.

"I guess so," I groan. "If the hotel has one. Why?"

"I'm just in the mood, that's all."

Several hundred-dollar bribes are required for us to get into the health club at this hour. The bastards; it's not like I've declared my intention to trash one of their rooms. And even at that, one of the chubby security guys hangs around as long as possible, like he wants to watch us have sex in the tub. The girl starts out in her tank top and panties, then grows bolder and gets naked with me. I'm too beat for sex by this point, however, and all we end up doing is cuddling in the water. The best strategy would have been for me to simply sneak her off and have my way with her somewhere at the stadium, then let Tubbs knock me out with a microphone stand and drag me back to my berth; that would've been just as moral as what I have done, plus she'd have known I was a creep right off. But at least she's twenty-two, not eighteen. The extra four years can make a huge difference.

When I can't take the hot, bubbling water for another second, I climb out of the tub and start walking out through doors I think will funnel me outside and toward the bus, still naked, my jeans, T-shirt, and sandals rolled in my arms.

"Where are you going?" the girl yells.

"To bed."

I hear her sloshing out of the water also. "Well?"

" 'Well' what?"

"Do you want me to come with you, or not?"

"You can't. I mean, I can't. We can't. Listen, I'm so tired that if I don't find a bed right this second, I'm gonna keel over. And I hate to be an asshole, but you should probably just go home."

"How?"

We've already reached the bus. She's struggling to pull her clothes onto her wet body. God, I wish Tubbs was around. It takes me about five minutes to get the lock open. "Here, wait a minute, I'll give you some money. Go to the front desk and call a cab. Tell them it's for both of us, if you want. Tell them to meet you right by the bus."

"Do you at least want my phone number?"

"Sure." I fumble back inside for a pen and some paper.

"It's Linda, with a *y*."

This cracks me up. I'm laughing so hard that I'm almost crying. I have to bend over, hands on my knees, and catch my breath. "That doesn't spell Linda, it spells Lindy."

"What?"

"Lindy, like Charles Lindbergh, the flier."

For the first time all night, she seems genuinely pissed off at me. "Why did you have to be such a bastard?"

Maybe I can hear her crying as she walks away, maybe I'm just imagining it. I trip on the top step as I climb back up into the bus, then I crawl down the aisle toward my berth on my hands and knees. Thank you, Lord, for this life and this pain.

94

Part

2

11 | Finished Product

O BE PERFECTLY HONEST, I SHOULD ADMIT THAT A LOT OF the turmoil the band's going through right now has its roots in the past. It's not an easy lifestyle to begin with, and when you mix in a few fragile-yet-sizable egos, the results can be catastrophic. The *Funk & Fugue* album was supposed to be completed by last December at the latest, but at the beginning of January, we still had a month's worth of mixing to do, so the record company was screaming at us.

What I'd love to have happen when the band is in the studio is me shouting out directions with all the authority and deadly ramifications of an air traffic controller, then switch the metaphor back to music and me being Arthur Fiedler, leading Blood Cheetah as smoothly and with as much Einsteinian panache as he led the Boston Symphony, just a nod of my head and K Dot knows I'm about to shift into a radically different key, about to downshift and really take off, screaming, my Stratocaster singeing my fingers on licks neither of us, or Alex, have played before, but which are pouring out magically the first time, formed as perfectly as my ecstatic vision of the song when I came up with the basic melody back in my apartment, strumming one of several twelve-string acoustics there, maybe even the old Maton Rosewood, which has a good full-bodied sound, but still gives me an idea how the music will sound on an electric guitar. The more mature the five of us get musically, the less abrasive we insist on sounding. If I don't die young, maybe I really will be seventh or eighth in line to succeed Sir Arthur.

What actually happens is infinitely more complicated and time-consuming than that. I remember thinking how cool it would be to be nicknamed God for my musical talents, à la Eric Clapton, but I'm not even our group's version of David Koresh. I may make more money from royalties than anyone else—on a typical song we'll end up splitting the dough forty percent to me, fifteen percent to each of the others, although I could argue for a higher cut if I really wanted to—but once we're laying down tracks for a new song, everybody contributes, even if it takes us a while to remember that Alex explains ideas he's passionate and opinionated about in an understated, mellow way, then just starts playing the way he thinks we should sound. We each devoted dozens of hours to the simplest songs any of our albums contain, and literally hundreds of hours to some of the material on *Funk & Fugue*. All before we even started to rehearse for this tour.

By mid-January, however, the band had completed all the work we could in terms of the various ways each of us performed our parts on all the songs, individually and as a band, instrumentally and vocally. We'd made recordings, literally, of every variation on a theme. At this point, the songs were adopted by whoever we'd chosen as producer, engineer, or mixer. With us, all three of these titles essentially refer to the same job. The job is simple: telling us, Blood Cheetah, when our music sucks. Then our producers try to steer us in the right direction, maybe make a few pointed suggestions, coach us along. Most groups hire people to do this on an album-by-album basis, but we prefer to work song by song, no matter how much more time-consuming and expensive it may be. The first reason for this is that new ideas get introduced to our albums on a much faster basis; the second is, nobody outside the group ends up with an inordinate influence over any one of our discs. The other Blood Cheetah members and I are there to provide continuity, but the mixing process—exactly which drum take mixed with which guitar lead, etcetera—is under scrutiny from a variety of authorities.

Ironically, on *Funk & Fugue*, one of the problems we spent the most time on was making the music sound unrehearsed and spontaneous, which becomes tougher the more intricate a piece is. Overproduction can ruin tracks every bit as easily as not being technically proficient enough with your instruments. Just look at what too much studio time did to Michael Jackson. "Scream," arguably the most important single of his career, in terms of continuing his reign over the pop world, ended up sounding like some techno-dweeb producer was hypnotized by all the neat noise tricks he could cram into it. Likewise, Blood Cheetah's "Living Meals" may be incredibly over-the-top (*the living eat the dead ate the live all is life* . . .), but at least the wild guitars lend balance and proportion to the way Jay is shouting into the microphone.

On *Funk & Fugue*, the postproduction was so time-consuming, labor-intensive that I ended up doing a lot of it alone, because the other guys couldn't cope. Saturation. The originality was gone, and their ability to think critically wiped out. By the time the album was done, I was working on it pretty much by myself. I can't tell you the rules for making a successful rock 'n' roll song, because there are none. I can't even tell you how I come up with new material. It just happens. But the two things I can absolutely guarantee are that if you don't follow your instincts, if you don't fight for your own artistic vision like you're hanging by your scrotal sac, you're fucked. And if you don't grow with each album, if you're not offering your fans something they haven't heard before, your career is fucked. One of the biggest reasons young bands slump is that they're too busy simultaneously supporting and celebrating their initial hits to allot themselves time to recuperate and learn before their record label starts screaming for new product,

99

which in turn ends up being an attempt to rehash whatever sound they guess made them successful to begin with.

When I was younger, I was so convinced of my own genius that I'd listen to the Stones' "Monkey Man" or the Doors' "Peace Frog" or an entire Pink Floyd album side and think, I'm gonna blow those bloated old fuckers away with my next fucking masterpiece! And the truth is, I still think this way when I'm writing new songs and everything's going well. There were moments when I was working on *Funk & Fugue* that I was so happy I wanted to sprint through the streets screaming, elation times a thousand, a million, the music flowing out of me as I trembled with discovery and self-awareness.

And when it came to the songs I was proudest to have written, like "Remote" or "D.C. Me" or "Time to Go," I wasn't even sure I could claim full credit. I was the one putting the notes and the words down on paper, but they went so well together that the instant I saw them, I knew they'd existed forever, just waiting for me to brush my fingers over the right strings, and presto, what was hidden around us, waiting to be discovered, filled the air. I mean, even people who can remember the exact week John Lennon released "Imagine" find it impossible to conceive of a world without it. I might take credit for creating the beautiful songs that are on this album, but sometimes I feel like a scammer, a phony, a faker; all I've done is sneaked into the museum and turned the lights on, not conceived the Great Sphinx.

So this was the type of pressure I had been under, but also the type of incredible joy I could feel, when I was finally finished with the album. The exact moment was a Friday afternoon in late January. I was alone in the studio. I made all the proper copies, including one to take to a party at Jay's place that night. Then I turned all of the machinery off, dimmed most of the studio's lights, and kicked back in one of the swiveling, flex-backed chairs for a while. I tried to think about what the whole process had meant to me, but not enough time had passed for me to look at the album with any sort of objective eye. *Funk & Fugue* was one of the things we'd all be celebrating at Jay's that night, but for the moment, I was glad to be alone.

Maybe I'm too emotional, and maybe I'm biased, but the other issue that was tied up in my emotions at that point was that I really do love rock music, and true rock artists. I've been listening to music in my apartment and found myself crying because a song moved me so deeply. Or dancing around because the music was jubilant, and I was young, carefree, and happy beyond words. A deejay once told me studies show that people listen to radio stations that reinforce and reflect whatever mood they're already in at the time—raucous, aggressive, rebellious, reflective, contemplative, subdued, whatever—so it's likely I'd have been crying or dancing in these situation anyhow, but so what? While I can loathe Blood Cheetah's fans at times, what their devotion really means is that I've touched them, been their friend, offered comfort and camaraderie, often in difficult times, just as other artists have done for me.

Now the sixth Blood Cheetah album was about to be loosed on the world. Sitting there that afternoon, I almost didn't want to release it, except that there was no way in hell legally I could get away with that. I kept fantasizing what a legend I'd be if all the copies were either lost of destroyed, then I mysteriously disappeared. Rock 'n' roll. Rock 'n fuckin' roll! Friends, Romans, countrymen, a strange thing happened on my drunken way to Cleveland . . . we now have such creatures as rock professors, rock anthologists, and professional rock critics. Groups, whose only goal was to spit in the face of authority figures, have books written about them, and guys, who screeched like howler monkeys that they'd never reunite with their bandmates, get back together and allow beer companies to underwrite their tours.

Thank God for Neil Young! Thank God Sid Vicious died! Thank God Blood Cheetah hasn't hired go-go dancers! Worst of all, I knew I was such a bigmouth insecure intellectual that I'd still talk the whole sordid mess to death myself if I got a chance, my diarrheal mind running on near empty, fueled only by various powders and herbs and honeyed liquors, when what I should have done is simply screamed ROCK AND ROLL IS REBELLION, MOTHERFUCKER! With about thirty exclamation points. Period! End of debate. Then smashed my most expensive guitar right through one of the Mass Statehouse windows.

Everything imposed on a song after it's been released—from magazine reviews to videos to whatever groundswell of support fans provide—has nothing to do with how it got written, except for the distinct possibility that the artist fucked it up by trying to figure out what his critics wanted, instead of trusting his gut instincts and abilities. "My Generation" wasn't Pete Townshend's guess at what the mid-1960s teen market would snap up, it was a gigantic rallying call he made the only way he and The Who knew how. One of the reasons it takes me so long to get my head on straight before I can write new material after a Blood Cheetah tour ends is that I have to clear my mind of all the bullshit that's lurking out there, distorting the picture, like the 3D mall art where you have to relax your stare before you can see the whale. Sometimes all it takes to throw me off for a couple of days is to read that Blood Cheetah is the "voice of our generation," or that we're "in touch with the youth of today," or any of the other bullshit, because that makes me want to write something for my generation, not for myself. Pretty soon I'd be coming out with propaganda, pedantry, Nazi art.

If you have time to think about what you're feeling, it isn't rock anymore. There are even songs which were rock 'n' roll once, but aren't any longer, at least not since "classic rock" became such a huge, fucked-up radio format and Time-Life started selling music by the year it came out, those bastards. Ninety-five percent of what passes for rock 'n' roll is actually pop, including a lot of heavy metal. Sometimes I fantasize that there's a giant rating system which I alone am in charge of, with maybe a magazine printing my gospel truth monthly, maybe a prerecorded telephone message or an enormous purple neon sign on the end of Faneuil Hall, or maybe (preferably) guys just bumping into me on the street and asking, "Hey Dizzy, what do you think of the new Pearl Jam album?" And me answering, casually, as I stroll along toward a movie or a late dinner with Clipper, pulling my jacket tighter, "I give it four Zs. Too purposely murky." Or whatever. But the biggest problem of having rock criticism and smug seriousness and analysis is that all of those opinions come from people besides the guy who wrote the songs.

What brought me to my senses was the question of which type of beer would be the perfect way to begin celebrating. We have to live in this world, after all. The studio we had used for the *Funk & Fugue* sessions was in Cambridge, which is just across the Charles River from Boston proper. It was freezing outside, especially as early evening came on, so instead of heading to my apartment, which is in the North End, I decided to pop in somewhere close by. The place I chose was really more of a restaurant than a bar, which suited me fine, since I was still enjoying being alone, but the proprietors prided themselves on stocking over a hundred imported beers. I had three different Belgian ales, and no beer ever tasted better. They tasted so satisfying I didn't want any more right then. I headed out, grabbed that morning's *Herald* from a streetside vendor, then ducked into a T station.

Two teenagers came down the cement platform. One was in a wheelchair, the other was pushing him. The first thing I noticed was that the boy in the wheelchair was at least mildly retarded. The angle he was holding his head at told me he wasn't a hundred percent there. The other one, who looked like his brother—same combination of pale Irish skin and jet-black hair—seemed tired of pushing him, moving with the irritated, heedless speed of someone who doesn't care how well a job is done, just that it's over.

I probably watched them more closely than I should have, dipping my paper low. The T entrance was up on the street level, and I couldn't remember what accommodations were

103

provided for the handicapped. The boy in the chair noticed me watching them, and, as his brother settled onto the bench fifteen feet down from me, whispered something to him. I lifted my paper back up.

"No," the older boy said. A straightforward, mechanical voice.

More whispering.

"No. I mean it."

The one in the wheelchair started whining. "Puh-lease." I tried not look over, because public attention was probably exactly what the older boy was hoping to avoid.

"All right. Just stay here and be quiet," he instructed, speaking in a lower, sympathetic tone. He stood up and took a few steps toward me. "Uh, excuse me, but do you have the time?"

I could hear the subway train rattling down the tracks, out of the dark underground tunnel. I folded my paper and sat up straight. "No, I really don't. Sorry."

"It's him!" the boy in the wheelchair screeched. His eyes were wide, staring at me. His head bobbed with excitement. "I told you it was him, Mike! That's Dizzy! Hello, Dizzy!"

I couldn't help smiling. "How you doing?"

The older boy buttoned the top of his coat and took the wheelchair's handles. The train was obviously going to be his escape. It had already come to a halt. "I'm sorry about him, mister."

"Don't be."

"I have all your albums," the retarded boy shouted. "I have all your albums and I know all your songs. That's Dizzy, Mike! Hey, Mike, that's Dizzy!"

"I know, I know . . ."

"Can I have your autograph?" the boy cried.

"Hell, you can have my whole newspaper."

The older brother slapped his pockets, looking for a pen.

"Did you write 'Love Song Number 42' for me and my girl-friend?" the boy in the wheelchair asked. His brow furrowed with the possibility. His eyes were so moist he looked like he was crying. "I always tell her you wrote that song just for us.

Hey, do you have another album coming out? My mom tells me it might be a long time, but I know it won't. Did you write "Love Song Number 42 for me and my girlfriend?"

"You know, I just might have," I said. I scribbled the first thing that came into my head on the top of the newspaper: *Always read the good news first—Dizzy Zimmerman.* "Does he really have a girlfriend?" I asked his brother, as I handed them the paper.

The train doors opened. The first of the early evening commuters were hustling aboard. The older boy pointed the wheelchair across the cold cement. He tapped his finger against his temple. "He thinks he does, so I guess that's good enough."

"I do!" the boy in the chair insisted. He was craning his neck around to see me. "I do, I do, I do! Thanks for the paper, Dizzy!"

They were gone before I had time to remember it was my train as well. But the retarded boy's enthusiasm reminded me that not all our fans are tough young punks with fists raised like führer salutes. (*Blood Cheetah, über Alles . . .*) Or for that matter, like the guys who started the brawl in Reno. Most are unobtrusive; you wouldn't know they were fans unless they mentioned it. And coming at that moment, the encounter only strengthened my satisfaction at having finished *Funk & Fugue.*

The kid made me proud. I was incredibly glad I wasn't drunk right then, no matter what might happen when I got to Jay's. I could picture the retarded boy's family slapping a pair of oversize, seventies-style earphones on him when he finally got the album, to keep the noise level down, but I could also picture how big his smile would be. What I was thinking was that I might not be Mozart yet, but that maybe I'd kicked Salieri's ass.

12 | Parties Large and Small

HE PARTY WAS AN INFORMAL FRIEND-AND-FAMILY-TYPE AF-fair. The only real relation between any of the guys in the band is that Grover is Alex's second cousin, but since we all lived the same neighborhood growing up, we all knew each other's parents and siblings and in-laws pretty well. For instance, when I was nine years old, I broke a window playing baseball at a local church, and it was K Dot's father who both chewed me out for it and then replaced the glass, not because my father wouldn't have done the same thing, but to save him the effort. Jay has a gorgeous house out in Belmont now, the suburbs, and I swear there's just about a Batsignal he projects when he wants the clan to show up. The other amazing thing is that all of our parents always liked the other guys in the band better than they liked their own kid. My mother was convinced Jay was sweet and innocent, while Jay's mother thought K Dot needed to be sheltered from other kids' taunts when he was young, since he was always chubby.

Besides the *Funk & Fugue* disc, the biggest topic of conversation that night was Sully, a guy my cousin Diana had brought. The two of them were already there by the time I showed up, sitting on a leather couch in the spacious living room, so close to each other you could tell it was a defense against gossip. It didn't take me long to realize this was a coming out for them. Until that point, there'd been rumors that a new man was the real reason Diana was divorcing her husband, but nobody had met him yet. And now that they'd met him, they were ignoring him. Not because they liked her husband necessarily, but because she had two very young children who were caught up in the drama. And because it gave them someone to feel superior to.

I had barely gotten in the front door and taken my coat off before Diana called me over. Sully stood up to meet me, shaking my hand. He looked like a pretty rugged guy. His hands felt strong enough to strangle a baboon. Later, I'd find out that he worked for the DPW in Medford.

"You guys are great!" he gushed. "I've bought all of your albums. Some of them twice. Seen a lot of your shows at the Garden, too."

"Then I guess the band owes you at least a couple of beers."

He was holding a glass of Sam Adams in his left hand, from the keg that Jay kept on the back porch. He used this hand to gesture. It was easy to picture him at a Patriots game. "You're the only group I even buy anymore. All the other groups that are out these days suck. It's just noise."

"Who do you mean?" I asked. I could already tell we were headed down the wrong track, but instead of just telling him that *Funk & Fugue* would be out soon, or offering him an advance copy then excusing myself, I wanted to have a little fun with him.

"All of 'em. Grunge rock? What the hell is that? You throw a dirty lumberjack shirt on, let your hair fall into your eyes, and sing crap nobody can understand. Between that shit and all that rap shit, MTV sucks. But at least U2 still puts out some albums."

"Who else do you listen to?"

At this point, he thought I was his buddy, that I cared about his opinion. I did care, but in a different way than he realized.

I already knew there was no way I could change his mind. He chugged some of his beer before he got going again. "I just like good old rock 'n' roll. You know, the groups that meant something: the Stones, the Who, Jimi Hendrix, The Doors, Bruce Springsteen when he was still with the E Street Band, and of course, Zeppelin. Zeppelin was the best rock band ever. Today's music is just noise."

"Is there any chance you just like the older groups because that's what you grew up with?"

"Nah, I don't think so. They were better, that's all."

"Every band you just named was biggest during the seventies, when you were young, so all the guys in those bands are older than you are, right? So naturally you're not going to think someone like Axl Rose or Eddie Vedder has anything to teach you."

"Axl Rose? That whiny little faggot? He sucks worst of all!"

"If you don't like Guns N' Roses, you don't like rock 'n' roll."

"Oh, you're out of your mind! You're nuts!"

Then I really tried to provoke him. For some crazy reason, Jay had the thermostat set at about ninety, and I wanted to see which one of us would wipe the sheen of sweat from our brow first. "Hell, the way I see it, Guns N' Roses could be the Led Zeppelin of the nineties, if they wanted. You know, the heaviest-sounding band that's still talented enough musically and popular enough that they can sell out any stadium, any time, although it already looks like they've decided not to be."

"Musical talent? They suck. If you want musical talent, listen to Pink Floyd, or Todd Rundgren when he was with Utopia."

"You probably don't even like rock 'n' roll," I accused him.

"You're nuts. I love rock."

"If you don't like the song 'You Could Be Mine,' then you don't like rock music. It's out of control, it's just wild."

"It's no 'Jumpin' Jack Flash!' "

" 'Jumpin' Jack Flash' is a cliché. They made a movie out of it starring Whoopi Goldberg, for God's sake!" I nearly shouted. Then, remembering that Diana would be upset with me if a real argument started, I tried to tone it down a notch. "Listen, my point is just that you're saying the exact same things about groups like Guns N' Roses and Pearl Jam that your parents said about the Stones and Led Zeppelin twenty years ago, that's all. Hate to be the one to tell you, but you've become your parents."

"The new groups just don't have the musical talent," Sully repeated. I wondered how much he'd already drunk. Maybe he'd even had a few pops before he and Diana came over. His arms were out to his sides slightly for balance.

"Hell, if you were a couple of years older, you probably wouldn't like U2, R.E.M., or Aerosmith, either, although Aerosmith's gotten so predictable that Mr. Green Jeans probably likes them by now. And talent is overrated. I didn't play guitar nearly as well when our first album came out as I do today, but people still bought it. And I don't even agree that today's bands don't have as much talent. That's like saying baseball players aren't as good today as they used to be."

"What?" Sully cried. He leaned forward like he was ready to scoop up a grounder with his beer glass. "You're not gonna stand there and tell me that Ken Griffey Junior is as good as Willie Mays, are you? Have you ever seen the old footage of Mays catching a fly ball without looking over his shoulder?"

"Sure, I have, but . . ."

I was still sober at this point, which helped me pick up on the vibes the rest of the people present were sending me behind Sully's back—the death ray stares, the wish-I-had-a-voodoo-doll-of-him mutterings, etcetera. What saved me was that Jay's sister Arlene approached me right then. She was having fun playing hostess.

"Hey, Dizzy, how are you doing? Can I get you a drink or anything?"

"Yeah, how about a . . . Does Jay have any brandy lying around?"

"Probably. Let me check."

When she turned to head for the kitchen, I gave her a split-second lead, then called after her, waving the tape I'd brought in. "Oh, wait a second, where's Jay? Sorry, Sully, I'll be back

109

in a minute. We've got a couple of quick business things to talk about before I get involved with too much drinking."

"Nice one," Arlene said under her breath, as we walked away. Though I probably hadn't seen her in a year and a half, she'd known me long enough to get away with being a wise-ass.

Jay and K Dot were both in the kitchen, sampling from a large table of food. It looked like there'd be enough leftovers for Jay to live on for months. The bar was off to the right. Probably five hundred dollars' worth of new bottles were laid out. Both Jay and K Dot were holding mixed drinks.

"So?" Jay asked. He was wearing jeans and a button-down shirt, which was pretty unusual for him. But he seemed happy that I was finally there.

I held up the tape. "So I'll trade you this brand-new tape for a tumbler full of Benedictine and Brandy."

"Deal." He took the tape from me. "You change anything from yesterday?"

"Nope, just tried to clean the background static off of 'Live-wire' a little more. Other than that, that's the finished thing."

"You sure?" K Dot asked.

"Sure I'm sure."

"Cool," Jay said. "You know where the glasses are. *Mi casa es su casa.*"

K Dot stepped to the bar and refilled his drink. "Come on, Jay, we can listen to it upstairs. Thanks, Z."

They disappeared. I poured a healthy amount of B&B into a glass, dropped a couple of ice cubes in, and started sampling the food. The only thing even close to tasting as good as the drink was the shrimp. They were every bit as fresh and crisp as the Belgian ales had been back in Cambridge. But I'd have felt just as comfortable and relaxed without the drink. It was the type of house I could picture myself in if I ever decided to have kids, with big rooms, airy windows, a finished base-ment, and a half-acre backyard. In a way, I think Jay bought it to give himself some semblance of normalcy when he wasn't on the road. His mother came in to reload her plate with shrimp, and I talked with her for a while. She had been an elementary-school teacher when we were young. It seemed like years ago that we'd all kidded Jay he might get stuck in her class. I couldn't figure out now why that had seemed such an embarrassing possibility, but I knew it had.

Two hours later, I still wasn't very drunk. I had eaten so much food that the booze just wasn't getting through, and at this stage, I didn't feel the need to force it. A lot of the older people had left by then, and the stereo was playing loud. Jay cranked the *Funk & Fugue* tape first, and people more or less just sat around listening to it. Blood Cheetah isn't that great a band to dance to in the first place, and when people aren't familiar with a song, it's even harder to get them out cutting the rug. A wide array of compliments and congratulations followed, but for the most part, I stayed out in the kitchen talking to Arlene. I had already spent way too much time thinking about the album, and I wanted to let some time pass before I tried to think about it in any sort of critical manner. Experience it as fresh music, get perspective.

Arlene is three years younger than Jay, with the same blond-ish hair, but at least she's not losing hers. Her nose hooks the same way Jay's does, too, a little to the left. When people meet either of them individually, they assume the nose was broken at some point, but when you see them together, it's obviously a genetic trait. I always considered her more like a sister than like a regular girl. But now that we were talking, I realized that I couldn't remember the last time I'd seen her, let alone the last time we'd really had a conversation.

"Are you still living in the same place?" I asked.

"The same place?" she asked. "Which one are you thinking of?"

I had meant it as a trick question, a way to circumvent the fact I didn't know where she lived. "The apartment there, in Dorchester."

"I haven't lived in Dorchester for five years," she said. "I'm up in Everett now. Didn't you know that?"

"No, I suppose not."

"Well, I guess that's all right. In some ways, I'm not sure I want everyone from the old neighborhood knowing where I am." She gave me an insider's smile. "Besides, if I was still living in Dorchester, I'd probably be dating someone like Sully by now, wouldn't I?"

"Touché," I said, my eyebrows arcing in approval. "So tell me, are you still working at the same place?"

She could see I was joking. She lifted her beer glass and took a good long drink. "I'm sure I haven't worked there for five years, either, wherever you're thinking of. Where were you thinking of?"

The last rumor I could remember about her was that Jay had given her a hundred thousand dollars to buy herself a condo, precisely because she wasn't working. That would've been her place in Everett, now that I thought about it. But mentioning this didn't seem like a wise choice. "I don't know, weren't you a waitress at Roland's Pizzeria for a while?"

"That was back in high school, you idiot."

Diana rushed into the kitchen. "Hey, come on and dance, you guys. We're gonna put on the *Saturday Night Fever* soundtrack. Nothing against the new album, Dizzy."

"Thanks."

I poured myself another B&B as the two of them headed to the other room. Grover was pretty loud in there, yelling with the record. He's always the first one to start dancing, but he gets everyone else going, too. Alex came down from one of the bedrooms, where I presume some sort of drug was in plenitude. From the color of his skin, I'd have guessed heroin. But since I didn't want any myself, I didn't ask. I really do stay a lot straighter when I'm working on new material than when I'm on tour, so I figured it was best for me to avoid things like that for as long as possible. Alex positioned himself about a foot from me and stared me intently in the eye.

"How's the album?" he asked gravely, like he was asking a surgeon if a terminal patient would survive. His brow remained furrowed.

I started laughing at him. "I think it might just pull through."

"Good, I'm going to bed." Without another word, he turned and went back upstairs.

I went out to dance with the crowd. There were probably twenty-five people boogying around, and sure enough, Jay was stripping. That was probably why he had the heat up so high, so he'd have an excuse. He was already down to just a white V-neck undershirt. Arlene came over and danced with me. What I noticed about her now was that she'd whipped her body into excellent shape. Her jeans hugged her ass much tighter than I remembered.

"Have you been working out?" I yelled, over the music.

"Yeah, I've been going to Bally's!"

"It shows."

"Thanks." She beamed. She bounced over to wrap her arms around Jay. A woman would have to be pretty drunk to do that, even a relative. "Jay gave me a lifetime membership!"

"Yee haa!" Jay shouted.

Next she bounced back in my direction and started dancing close to me, dirty dancing, really. None of what I'd said to her that night was supposed to be flirtatious, but I could tell she was attracted to me. I knew she was about the last person I should try to pick up, but before I knew it, she'd given me an erection. I wanted to hide it, but the easiest way to do that was actually to keep dancing close to her, which just made the situation worse. It probably would've been better if I was wasted, because then my body wouldn't have responded quite as eagerly to her, unless the drug was pot.

Half an hour later, I went out to the kitchen to drink some water and crack a window. The time was just past midnight. Arlene followed me out, wiping drops of sweat from her forehead. I couldn't stop looking at her hair. It was the same basic hair as Jay's, but at some point she'd stopped perming it, which made it look better than his. His still looked too much like Farrah Fawcett's when she was in her 1970s prime.

"Done dancing for a while?" she asked.

113

"Yeah, actually, I think I'm going to head out of here pretty quick."

"Mind if I share a cab with you?"

The truth was that I'd have taken the T if I'd been by myself, or maybe even walked the long miles if I was in the right mood. I almost wondered if she wanted to go with me just in the hopes that I'd pay. Not that I would've minded. I still felt a little guilty for all the things I had forgotten about her earlier. "Sure, why don't you call one. I'm just going to go upstairs and make sure Alex is still alive."

One of the best things about parties at Jay's has always been that everyone there knows me so well, they don't care if I ditch without formal good-byes. This is exactly what Arlene and I did. Nobody would care. They'd all wake up the next morning hungover and empty-headed anyhow. A heavy blanket of snow lay on the ground and on Jay's roof, muffling most of the music booming inside, but as I climbed into the cab, I couldn't help wondering how the people next door felt about having a rock star for a neighbor. Well, he'd be gone soon enough, touring for *Funk & Fugue*. Which would mean a quiet summer for them, if nobody else.

13 Dorchester

"So how's Clipper?" Arlene asked. As we passed under streetlights, I could tell she was smiling.

"She's good."

"Is she in town these days?"

The taxi was warm and commodious. I thought about how wonderful it must feel to be a cabbie driving around all night, adjusting the heater perfectly, listening to whatever radio stations you preferred, ruling your own tiny world. Arlene's question sounded like the beginning of a route I'd hoped not to go, knew I shouldn't go, and had made no attempt myself to go, though I could see it stretched out in front of me like a goddamn superhighway of infinite sexual potential. On the other hand, maybe it was an innocent question. I never really know if a woman is interested in me until I make a pass at her. Sometimes a woman I've thought hated me ended up being one of my most uninhibited lovers, while other times, women who I've thought were flirting brazenly with me have rejected me at the last second, a fighter plane shot down a quarter mile from the safety of the flight deck.

Worst of all, not only was Arlene an old friend, and an

immediate family member of someone else in the band, but at that time, my relationship with Clipper was relatively strong. She'd flown from Boston to L.A. two days before Christmas, to be with some friends. The reason she wasn't back yet was that she didn't want to disturb me until *Funk & Fugue* was done, not that we were fighting any more than normal.

"Actually, she's out in California, but she'll probably be back in a week or so," I told Arlene. "She went out for the holidays, then it was just easier for her to stay there while I finished the album. Maybe she'll be back sooner, I don't know."

"You guys have been seeing each other for a long time, haven't you?"

"Too long, probably," I said, then immediately regretted it. Way too much of an open door. "I mean, yeah, it's been a long time."

116 Neither of us said anything else until we were pulling back into the North End. It's probably the coolest place to live in Boston, unless you're willing to spend the extra money for a high, isolated luxury apartment building, where you're protected from the street noise. But I could never live in a tower. I like to know my neighborhood, take long walks; the entire area is zigzagged with brick alleyways and cobblestones and narrow side streets, where I can hang out for hours, amazed at the enormous array of wild characters hustling past.

"What's the fare so far?" I asked the cabbie, as I climbed out.

He rolled his window down. "Fifteen fifty."

"I assume thirty would get her up to Everett, too."

"Yeah, sure."

Arlene started to protest. "You don't have to do that, Dizzy."

"Gimme a break," I said. "Of course I do. Hell, I probably ate thirty bucks worth of Jay's shrimp tonight."

She stuck one foot out into the snowy road. For the first time all night, I realized she was wearing black clogs. This surprised me and threw me off guard, because I myself was wearing a pair of sandals, and thought I was the only one to be that crazy in the middle of winter. I hadn't even noticed the clogs while we were dancing.

"I'm not sure I want to go home yet," she said, climbing completely out of the cab. "I just didn't want to be around Jay's anymore. Can't we have a drink somewhere? It isn't even close to last call."

The cabdriver laughed at us. He looked at Arlene, and then up at me. "I'll go with her if you won't."

"That's all right. You still get the thirty, though, for being a good sport."

His wheels spun as he pulled away, but he still had his window down and tried to get off one last good line. "Thanks, Bud. A couple of more fares like that and maybe I'll *buy* myself a woman tonight."

"Scumbag!" Arlene yelled after him.

This cracked me up. I couldn't stop laughing. I nearly top- ¹¹⁷
pled over into a snowbank. The temperature was just about perfect for more snow to fall, and in a way, I wished it would. A clean, peaceful dusting as we hurried into the building would've been the perfect New England end to the day I finished one of Blood Cheetah's albums. I was with a woman, which was great, even if it took some effort to remind myself she wasn't Clipper. I knew the best thing to do would be to find another cab, pay Arlene's fare, then run away before either of us had time for second thoughts. But this was not what happened.

"So where are we going?" Arlene asked.

"Do you want to come inside for one?"

"I'm not as naïve as all that," she said. But the way she said it was as a joke, making fun of me for sounding like I wanted to pick her up, after she'd been the one to initiate things this far. She grabbed my sleeve and tried to pull me down the street. "Let's go out somewhere. C'mon, it's Friday night."

"No, a night like this, all there is is college kids in the bars around here."

She was already heading down the block. "College kids? Hey, do you think I could meet any big strong football players?"

I gave up. I gave in. I took her to a bar where I knew there'd be nothing but college kids, the type of frat boys and sorority sisters I've always hated for being so cocky, so self-satisfied and self-serving, as if the gods themselves had ordained they'd be born wealthy and good looking. To a number they were clad in jeans, with big fluffy cotton button-downs or their schools sweatshirts—Harvard, BC, BU, MIT, Brandeis, and Northeastern are just a few of the colleges in Boston—and sneakers to die for. I bought a huge round of shots for the first group we ran into. The guys all asked for Cuervo Gold, while the girls wanted Kamikazes or B52s. They knew who I was, but they weren't as enthusiastic about my presence as I might have expected, maybe because they weren't expecting to see me that night, and maybe because my arrival was so low key. No leaping up on a stage to jam with a house band. No banging my head on the bar until the bartender consented to free-pouring upside-down margaritas down my throat, to keep me from bleeding all over the place. And certainly no bevy of beauties following me around.

In a way, it was the fact that I bought the round that really convinced them I was Dizzy Zimmerman. I hate to say it, but Arlene isn't all that beautiful, at least not the beauty a bunch of idiot frat boys could recognize. The lines in her face, which represent knowledge, and should have made them wonder if she knew tricks in bed that none of their coed girlfriends even dreamed of yet, actually hurt her case. The broken-looking nose didn't help, either. She couldn't compete with the perfect skin and pert breasts the college girls offered, even if she had trimmed her ass down at Bally's.

"Hey, Dizzy finished the album today!" she yelled. Then she raised a glass of Harpoon ale and yelled it again. "Hey, Dizzy finished the album today. Let's have a drink."

I couldn't help wondering how the frat boys would've responded if I'd strolled in with Clipper on my arm. Probably

118

catcalls followed by drunken propositions and passes. In a way, the biggest reason she and I have been able to stay on-again, off-again for so many years is that she's not a particularly good model—showing up late, or hungover, or trying to strangle a photographer with a pair of pantyhose, or calling the other girls bitches—which makes some people reluctant to work with her. There's as large a difference between the top-flight models and the women who're girl-next-door beautiful as there is between All-Pro quarterbacks and the average college player. But her breasts seem to play peek-a-boo, and her crotch defines the term box. Your hand is drawn toward it as if by gravity.

The weird part was that when I realized I was sitting there thinking about how hot Clipper was, I started to feel guilty. I shouldn't have had to apologize for Arlene not living up to anyone else's standards, especially the college kids'. A couple of them grabbed her and took her out to a small, crowded dance floor when the deejay played "What I Like About You," but that was a joke, a goof—crazy, drunken frivolity, which they'd snicker about in the morning. They had no intention of going home with her, at least not while their buddies were watching, any more than they were going to leave me alone with the girls they'd come in with. And the more fully I understood this, the more it pissed me off. I was tempted to slip one of the guys a hundred-dollar bill to seduce Arlene, except that even if it worked, it was a totally insane idea. On one hand, I was a well known musician, but on the other hand, I was in their element and, for the moment, they weren't willing to cut me any more slack than they would've for any other slimy-looking thirty-five-year-old.

A few of the kids asked questions about *Funk & Fugue*, and one girl kept hinting I should promise tickets for whatever Boston area shows the band scheduled, but in general, they let me sit back, leaning against the bar, getting a lot more drunk than I'd wanted to that night. Hell, it had probably been a college bar where I'd first heard "What I Like About You," about fifteen years ago. It was the ultimate moron frat boy song, perfect for making people who couldn't dance want to dance anyhow. But no one could have predicted how god-awfully long the song would last. It was still a classic in both dance clubs and regular bars, plus the ridiculously lucrative car commercials.

The bar closed at two. The lights came on before we were out the door, which probably didn't help Arlene's case for picking someone up. She did give her number to two different guys, scribbling on consecutive cocktail napkins, which cracked me up at the same time it made me wince. If they weren't going to sleep with her tonight, when they'd been drinking, they certainly weren't going to hassle with arranging a date, leaving campus, getting up to Everett, and getting to know Arlene before bedding her.

Out in the street, the air was crisp. I could picture how the front would look on a TV weather map, stretching down from Canada. Arlene took my hand as naturally as if we were a couple who'd been dating for years, leaning against me for support.

"Did you have a good time?" she asked.

"Yeah, it was all right."

"You're not mad, are you?"

"No, why would I be?"

She burped. "Oops, sorry. I don't know. You just didn't seem all that into being there. Like you were bored."

"I was thinking about the album, that's all. Plus I got up pretty early this morning."

"Do you think either of those guys will call me?" she asked. Her voice wavered. She already knew they wouldn't. "Tell the truth."

"Honest truth?"

"Of course honest truth . . ."

"Not a chance."

"Good." Suddenly she started laughing, let go of my hand, and sprinted down the deserted street as best she could, nearly wiping out on the snow and ice in her clogs. "Because I gave them Grover's phone number."

We made ourselves a drink when we got up to my apartment—a mudslide for me and a roasted toasted almond for her—but I knew we wouldn't finish them. I have a decent collection of my favorite movies on video, and for some reason, she insisted on watching *T2: Judgment Day*. Since Guns N' Roses' song "You Could Be Mine" is on the soundtrack, I kept wondering how much of my conversation with Sully she'd overheard back at Jay's party. Was this a subconscious bubble floating toward the surface?

After about fifteen minutes, she slid over toward me on the leather couch. I knew I should leap up right then, mumble good-night, and escape, but I didn't. First she touched my thigh, then, for just a second, my chest, before her hand finally came up and stroked my right cheek, pulling me toward her. We kissed for a second and I didn't care about anything; whether this was right, whether it was wrong, whether anyone would find out or not, nothing. The whole process was as nonchalant and unemotional as going out to pick up the morning paper. The only thing that bothered me was the TV. With the rest of the lights in my apartment turned off, it seemed bright as a nuclear reactor. I clicked it off with the remote.

"You don't have to do that," Arlene said. Her hand was already on my crotch, unbuttoning me.

"It was melting my eyes."

"I'm about to melt something else," she whispered.

I chuckled at this. My retinas were still burning from the television. For a minute I could feel her warm body pressing against mine, but I couldn't see her outline. "Are you sure you want to do this? I mean, we don't have to."

"Does that mean you don't want to?"

"I didn't say that."

She leaned forward and took me in her mouth, starting to pull her clothes off at the same time. "This is a gorgeous couch."

"We'd better go up to the loft," I whispered.

"No, I like the leather."

"But upstairs is where I've got the magic bowl of condoms."

This was true, but it was also true that I didn't want to have sex with her on the couch. A leather couch is for someone you're dying to screw, someone you have to fuck or else you'll explode. And with Arlene, the moment wasn't charged with the proper erotic electricity. She was just something that was going to happen. I had already decided I wasn't going to go down on her, which is as big an indicator of how turned on a woman's got me as anything.

I lost my erection as we climbed the steps, but it rejuvenated once we were in my bed and she took me in her mouth again. I slapped a condom on, mounted her, and did my best to please both of us, bracing my torso above her in a near push-up, so that I could watch her face, and so that she could watch my face as I closed my eyes and shuddered and permitted myself, if only for a fraction of a second, to be entirely hers, releasing myself to her and to the eternity an orgasm consumes. But when I withdrew, I discovered that I'd torn the condom. Three-quarters of the material circled the base of my penis, but the rest hung free, wet and leafy and ragged.

My groan was barely audible. "Oh, shit."

"What's the matter?"

"Nothing." I was in control of myself. I swung my legs over the side of the futon and bent down to pick up my T-shirt, which I used to clean myself.

"Did you break it?" she asked.

I was too embarrassed to reply.

She started to get pissed off. "Dizzy, I asked if you broke that thing."

"God, I'm so sorry," I said. "Yes, I did."

She didn't say anything for what felt like an eternity. "It's just an inconvenience, that's all," she finally mumbled.

"I'm sorry," I repeated. I'd hoped to fall into a deep, comfortable sleep after we got each other off, but now I knew I'd be awake for most of the night.

"I'm not on the pill," she informed me.

"The pill isn't what I worry about these days."

"Have you been tested?" she asked.

"Yes, and I'm clean. Have you?"

"I will be now. Give me that T-shirt." I passed it to her, and could feel her weight shifting around as she reached between her legs to mop up. "This really isn't how this was supposed to go, Dizzy. I'm just getting my life together right now."

"There is the day-after pill," I said.

"I know, and that's what I'll have to do," she said, but without much conviction. "Everything will work out. I'm sure it will. It'll just take some time, that's all."

"The finances are there, for whatever might happen," I offered.

"I know, Dizzy. God, why don't you just let me sleep? I'm not worried about anything."

It was good that she wasn't worried about anything, because me, I was suddenly worried about everything. But she was out cold for the rest of the night. In the silence of the apartment, and the silence of the cold, wintry street outside, her snoring sounded like a whale drowning.

14 | Remorse Is Like

WHO HATES HIS HOMETOWN THE MOST? BLACKS RAISED IN the deep Jim Crow South in the fifties? I saw a documentary once in which a famous black author literally refused to cross a set of railroad tracks leading to the white side of town. Coal miners in one of those economically and environmentally kaput cities in the former Soviet Union, where all the buildings are powdered with soot, the rivers are polluted, and the men die of black lung at forty? Or the poor little boy who's orphaned in a small town, molested by an uncle and a priest, beaten by older children, harassed, intimidated, lampooned, pimped around, robbed, and left for dead, before moving to San Francisco or New York, where nobody knows him?

Arlene puked voraciously in the morning, while I sat on the couch lifeless as a hand puppet, watching the tube because I didn't know what else to do. The best situation would've been for her to have gotten sick the night before, right when we got home from the bar, if only because it would have prevented the mistake we'd made. I almost gagged listening to her, but then, I was pretty hung over myself. It had been a long time since I'd drunk that much.

"Hey, could you call me a cab?" she yelled, between heaves.

"Sure."

I slipped her a check for five thousand dollars as she tried to compose herself. Her clothes stunk of cigarettes. I guess it had been smokier in the bar than we'd realized.

"You don't have to give me that," she said.

"Yes I do."

There were dark circles under her eyes and the skin on her face looked like it needed a good sandpaper scrubbing, to remove the dead layer, but her expression told me she understood that I wasn't trying to patronize her, or to shirk my responsibilities.

"Things will be all right." She forced a smile. "The biggest problem I'm worried about right now is that I feel like shit. That's all."

"You sure?"

"Of course I'm sure. Christ, Dizzy, we're all adults here. If I tell you not to worry about things, then don't worry."

"Well, I mean . . . I don't know . . . I don't know how you want to handle things, that's all."

She put one hand on my chest and spoke earnestly. "I'll handle them my own way, if that's all right with you. *You* don't have anything to worry about. I'll take care of the details."

Everybody loves their hometown, in a way, but the ways you can hate it are more immediate and more visceral; despising the kids you grew up with, convinced there's something better in life than what your old man settled for. (*Sonny, take a good look around. This is your hometown . . .*) And for some reason, Arlene really reminded me of Dorchester. Hell, just about everybody who had been at Jay's party grew up in the same neighborhood. In a way, Arlene and I hooking up felt predetermined. If it had happened ten or twelve years ago, just as Blood Cheetah was first hitting it big, I wouldn't have been half as surprised. But now it felt like a particularly dumb mistake, not just because of the possible future ramifications with either Arlene, or Clipper, or the other guys in the band, but simply because it transported me back to Dorchester right when *Funk & Fugue* was finished and I had to start thinking about touring. And also because, while it was in Dorchester and some of the poorer neighborhoods around Boston that I became a rock musician and a human being, I didn't need to be carrying baggage from my early days around. Not then, at any rate. Just seeing Diana and some of my other relatives at the party should've reminded me of that.

Arlene gave me a quick peck on the cheek, and then she was out the door. She turned around once she was in the hallway. "You don't have to call me. Actually, it's probably better if you don't."

"You sure?"

"Dizzy! . . ." She looked like she was about to say something really critical, then her expression softened. "Of course I'm sure. God, just relax about this, will you?"

If the album wasn't finished already, I would've gone over to Cambridge and the studio after she left. I probably should have gone anyhow; picked up a guitar and started playing, maybe writing new material and maybe just thinking about how the songs on *Funk & Fugue* would translate to live performances. But I didn't. The urgency wasn't there any longer. My other option was to call Murph and tell him that I'd Fed-Exed the master tapes to the record company. But now that the pressure was off of me, I wanted to let him sweat a little. He really is a guy you have to be in the proper mood to talk to. It hadn't bothered me one iota that he hadn't shown at Jay's party. Probably off getting his nose hairs clipped, the bastard.

Instead, I went back to the couch. Guilt like a sledgehammer. Remorse to satisfy the pope. Memories flashing back with Oscar-winning cinematography. Dorchester. In my own head, I was a huge star and a great artist a long time before Blood Cheetah was even good enough to lose WBCN's "Battle of the Bands." A seer, a bard, a prophet. I couldn't forget lying out on Revere Beach with Daniella Most (no admitted relation to

Johnny Most, the Celtics' old announcer) when I was twenty-one. It was the closest we ever came to a date. She was the type of gorgeous high-school chick it took me till twenty-one before I was hip enough to hang out with, plus the first girl I ever saw comb sunscreen into her hair, which was a natural dirty blond and gorgeous. Unfortunately, while she was dating some local stud-loser, my popularity and drawing power leapfrogged over hers like Shawn Kemp dunking over Hervé Villechaise, and we never managed the romantic encounter I'd been fantasizing about since the fourth grade. She was the one I should have slept with the night before, if I was going to regress to Dorchester, not Arlene.

"I'd have Roger Daltrey's child if he'd let me," she said, that afternoon at the beach.

"Really?"

She rolled over. The skin on her stomach looked as bronze and appealing to me as pancakes to a hungry lumberjack. "Yes, really."

127

"Do you realize how many extra hours hearing you say that is going to make me practice tonight?" I said. "I wish I had a guitar right here."

At that stage in my life, I probably could have started strumming away on a public beach, Revere Beach, for shit's sake. Now I'd be way too self-conscious. There was a period of probably five years when I could and would and did play anywhere people would let me, anytime. I was so goddamn insecure, wanting to prove myself, that I had no clue what modesty was. Sometimes nowadays, kids will come up and tell me, swear to me, wail to me, that they'd do anything to be as big a star as I am, yet when I ask them exactly what they have done, they stare at me so idiotically I expect drool to land on my toes. Or they turn their heads and mumble, "Well, you know . . ."

I do know, of course, and can commiserate with what it feels like to be a fucked-up, insecure, pissed-off, terrified teenager. But as Arlene had reminded me, your hometown may be the first sacrifice you have to make. Not leaving it, necessarily, but living in it when everyone there thinks you and your bandmates are crazy—you can't play your instruments yet, your lyrics could have been copped from Hallmark rejects, your stage antics are embarrassing, ripped-off poses. Living there and knowing what everybody thinks, hearing the whispers behind your back in school, even knowing how they'll change their tune if you do succeed, how they'll all claim to have been your first fan, your greatest fan; knowing all that and not taking it personally, not letting it distract you from the work you need to do. What the kids who come up to me really want is for me to give them a magical contact, a carpet ride, maybe the name of someone who'll support them, manage them, and guide them until they're proficient enough to make it on their own. My stock reply is, "quit." Guilty for being too terse, I then relent, and add in a nicer tone, "If you can't quit, then wear your guitar twenty-four hours a day, even to bed, never, ever, ever watch television, try not to play cover songs, take every gig you can possibly find, and wait five years. If you're still not making any money, try to quit again."

128

This advice is as good in Dorchester, Mass., right on the fringes of Boston's happening music community, as it is in East Buttfuck, Kentucky, where maybe one kid in the entire town has heard of L.A.'s Roxy and is dying to go there because he thinks it was where Guns N' Roses got their first real break. A ton of people hate good old Axl, the same as Sully had expressed at Jay's party—think he's whiny, offensive, a shrieker, a batterer, cocky enough to deserve a good ass-kicking, obnoxious, mean-spirited, overrated, undertalented. But I've always loved him just for the story about his pilgrimage from Indiana to Los Angeles: nothing in his wallet but four hundred dollars, nothing in his heart but the determination to be a star.

And if living where you grew up can be Captain Nigh on the Impossible, can mean turning into your parents and their parents and diving into all the eternal gravestones (*centuries live in the minutes to come . . . everyone behind you is where you're from . . .*), then stopping back for a visit can be just as painful, whether or not you return triumphant, the demons ostensibly exorcised. Sleeping with Arlene reminded me of that, but it was also a lesson I'd learned dozens of times over the years. For instance, I was still keeping in touch with everybody I had liked in school when our class's ten-year anniversary rolled around—except for one or two who had pulled the giant head-trip of being dead—so that isn't why I went to our reunion. Nor did I go because I thought anybody who'd once known me as that mangy slimeball Dave Zimmerman would really have changed his mind about me, even though I tooled up in a Ferrari, with Clipper in the passenger seat, one of our first real dates, and over six million album sales to Blood Cheetah's credit. If anything, they'd be thinking of me as that lucky, talentless, mangy slimeball Dizzy Zimmerman.

The real reason I went was to prove I wouldn't not go, that I could at least flip over a push for whatever blackjack of maturity and wisdom others my age threw down, although I suppose that if you really want to argue it, neither the Ferrari nor coaxing Clipper into going were signs I'd grown up, so I might as well have strolled in with the biggest fucking doobie of all time hanging from my lip, just as I'd planned. Clipper talked me out of it, thankfully. She also made me buy a sportcoat and tie to go with my Levi's. I did manage to speak with at least a few classmates who were doing interesting things with their lives—one was flying helicopters for the Marines—or who were genuinely interested in which direction Blood Cheetah was headed next, but the odd part was that the people who I got along with best tended to be those I hadn't known very well while we were still in school, the ones I hadn't formed a strong opinion of, one way or the other. It was pretty depressing to see how many of my friends had essentially turned into their parents, but it was satisfying to stand in a corner with K Dot, drinking a Sam Adams and deciding which ex-fucking football players were the fattest and baldest, which women had faced the years most gracefully, and which married couples were already doomed (never mentioning Alex and his future ex, of course). The bond I felt with K Dot that night was incredible, because I realized, without him having to say it, that while he'd had the same fears about coming back as I did, there was nothing I could conceivably do that night, short of mass murder, which he wouldn't forgive me for and stand by me through.

By the end of the night I was incredibly drunk. Clipper had turned on, flirted with, or annoyed every guy there, some of the women, too, and a couple of fistfights had broken out, which sounds right for Dorchester, but seemed surprising considering how dressed up everybody was. K Dot still claims that we went to a party at Sal Berube's apartment afterward, and that we danced on his third-floor porch until the timbers were creaking, but I don't remember any of that. (*It's hard to skip when you can't find the gate . . .*) Nor do I remember who I danced with the most that night, though it probably wasn't Clipper.

My relationship with her has always been so much of a love-hate affair that even then, on one of our earliest dates, we probably ignored each other all night, didn't speak the entire way home, then ripped each other's clothing off the second we walked in the door. High-school behavior for a high-school event. And we've certainly never cuddled like pandas for hours at a time, the way some couples do; I don't mind public displays of affection, what pisses me off is when the people involved get mad at me for watching.

The longer I thought about it, the less guilty I felt about sleeping with Arlene. Or at least the less guilty I tried to make myself feel. There was plenty of precedent for both Clipper and me in terms of having been unfaithful. But this one really did bother me more than most, if only because Arlene and I had been in my apartment, where Clipper and I had made love hundreds of times over the years. Boston is usually the one town where I'm able to control myself, especially when I'm in a phase where I'm producing music. Usually I just have my little flings when I'm on the road and know I'll never see the girl again. Or never have sex with her to begin with, like Lindy. In a way, I wished Clipper had flown in to surprise me the night before, and caught me and Arlene in the act. Not only would it have given me a pretty good excuse for never calling Arlene back—which I was considering even though she'd told me not to—but it also would've saved me from having to keep the encounter a secret, or worse yet, having to lie about it. The biggest problem with lying once is that it turns you into a liar, which eventually becomes a full-time occupation.

If nothing else, Clipper has taught me a few things about myself, which I suppose I should be grateful for. Despite how much of the time I'm convinced she's an idiot, she has helped me realize how other people see me. We were having an argument once—I couldn't tell you what the hell started it—and she accused me of hating certain friends of hers who were also models. I didn't hate them, I just didn't respect them very much. She accused me of being "an assholey wise-ass," which I countered by claiming I'd never been anything worse than glib. Then she accused me of not being friendly, and this was the one that started to shake my tree.

"How many friends have you made since you got out of high school?" she demanded. The sneer on the words *high school* was supposed to be demeaning.

"Plenty," I claimed.

"Well, I can only think of three or four," she said. "You always make jokes when people ask you questions. Or you refuse to answer. It embarrasses the shit out of me. Just 'cause you're some big rock star, you think you can get away with being an asshole."

Now Sting's song "Still Know Nothing 'Bout Me" may be an accurate enough sentiment for average joes, but what killed me about Clipper's outburst was that three or four was too high an estimate of how many true friends, besides her, I'd made since high school. Also that she was embarrassed when I avoided answering questions people should have had the class not to keep asking after I'd put them off once with a joke. She assumed my celebrity was an excuse for pushing people away, not a basic reason why it was necessary. The qualities which make me successful in a creative field like music are a direct outgrowth of my essential shyness, reservation, and introverted nature, instead of my true nature being a roadblock to success, a fender-scraped, blood-spattered Jersey barrier, a concrete wall bouncing cars back at a hundred miles an hour.

It would make way too much sense for me to have married someone from Dorchester, someone who knew my family and understood not only who I am, but also who I used to be. Most of the things I do in life—the alcohol, the drugs, the wisecracks that fly out of my mouth like I had Tourette's fucking syndrome, the fact I'm thirty-five and have never seriously considered marrying anyone, the long periods when all I want to do is work—probably don't make any sense to a casual observer or reporter, or they get written off with the brisk analysis that I'm crazy. But to me, I'm a puzzle; everybody is. The only way someone can see how very many of my pieces fit together is to have spent mounds of time with me. I'm the only one who's been around for everything that's happened to me, so you can trust me when I say there's definitely a pattern. Which may or may not be why the other guys in the band still put up with me. I have a feeling that touring with me is like learning to ignore the train that roars past your house at two in the morning.

Hell, marrying someone like Arlene at this point would almost look like a public relations trick, a political goddamn gambit, especially since all the women who would have been most eligible are already occupied, and the young, hot ones are way too naïve. How would I cover up their local accents, which can be to people from other parts of New England what a southern hick accent is to anyone from the North? There are quite a few places in this world a person can visit, most of them farther from home than the three-thousand-mile California-dreamin' tour Blood Cheetah is on right now, but you leave them eventually, and your hometown is always the first place you take with you.

15 | The Clipper Ship

THE CRAZIEST PART WAS THAT THE LONGER I SAT AROUND thinking about what Arlene and I had done, the more convinced I was that Clipper would understand. Hell, that she would even be proud of me for being honest and for revealing my shallow self to her, as if a good purge might actually strengthen our relationship. I forgot that my sounding blocks for huge mistakes should always be someone who's going to forgive me, like K Dot, or not even get mad in the first place, just laugh at me, like Grover. My hangover didn't help—the harder I concentrated, the more it seemed like I could get myself over the trough just by thinking the issues through, willing myself back to health.

There was a Celtics game on the tube when I dialed her California number. I remember because the Celtics were winning, a rare occurrence in the last few years.

"Hey, how are you doing?" I greeted her, cheerful as a chipmunk.

"How are *you* doing?" she replied.

My heart froze at the way she stressed the word *you,* a surge of adrenaline as strong as any drug could provide. It was an insider's emphasis, secret code between us. I knew she already knew what had happened, but since there was no way she could know, and especially since she hadn't told me she knew, I had to act like she didn't. A deep breath reset my nerves. Of course she didn't know. I was just being paranoid, a guilty conscience.

Not even twelve hours had passed since I'd had my last drink at the bar, but I wanted one now, if not to steady my nerves, then to loosen my tongue and get whatever argument we were going to have over with quickly. But this was how all my periods of heavy alcohol abuse started, one insignificant incident snowballing into strings of excesses. The *Funk & Fugue* tour wasn't going to start for almost three months, but I could already see how quickly I'd go downhill once it did start, now that the real work, crafting the album, was done. I carried the phone into my kitchen and poured a goodly triple shot of Kahlúa into a wide tumbler, hoping for something sweet, to make up for not eating any breakfast yet. Or any lunch, either.

"I'm doing all right," I said.

"Oh, really?" she asked. Then she didn't say anything else, creating a taut silence. If she was in a good mood, she'd already have been talking a million miles an hour.

"So what are you up to?" I asked. "I'm not interrupting anything, am I?"

"Nope."

"You're just, like, hanging out?"

"Yup."

"Well, I don't know, Clipper, I just felt like calling my babe and seeing how she was doing. But I guess if you're not in the mood to talk, I'll let you go, since you don't seem too talkative today."

"Okay."

I downed the Kahlúa in an enormous gulp. It burned in my throat, with a strong and sticky coffee aftertaste. Then I gave Clipper one last chance to trick me into confessing. "So there's nothing you want to talk about?"

"Nope." Her pause was perfect, her timing so good that maybe she really could make it as an actress someday, instead of being just another pretty face. "Why, is there anything *you* want to talk about?"

"Not really. Hopefully you'll be here in Boston pretty soon. But I did want to say I miss you."

She snorted and guffawed. It sounded like she'd blown enough air through her gorgeous nose to snuff a birthday cake full of candles. "Did you miss me last night?"

Another heart freeze on my part, but not as severe this time, because I was expecting it. "Excuse me?"

"Oh, don't fuck with me, Dizzy."

"Fuck with you about what?"

"Listen, I talked to Jay last night. I called the goddamn party, since that's where you'd said you were going to be, remember? I thought I'd surprise you there. Say hello. But Jay said you'd already taken off. With his sister. What's her name, Marlene? Don't deny it, or I'll hang up right this goddamn second."

I refilled the tumbler, this time with Bailey's Irish Cream, hoping to mellow the Kahlúa taste out a bit, then I went back into the living room. To my great amazement, the Celtics were still winning. I hit the mute button. "Actually, her name's Arlene, not Marlene."

"Did you sleep with her?"

"God, where do you get your information? What makes you ask that? Can't I be friends with women besides you?"

She snorted again. "Friends? That's a good one. Jay certainly didn't seem too happy about it."

"Fuck Jay."

"Fuck Arlene."

Neither of us said anything for probably two minutes. It was a little after noon out in L.A. I could picture her pacing around her apartment in her long silk robe, maybe even hungover herself, her dirty hair falling wildly around her face. It was even possible that she had woken up in bed with someone too, and that the only reason she held the upper hand in this discussion was superior intelligence information.

135

"Does it really matter if I slept with her or not?" I asked.

"Yes."

"Really really?"

"Okay, Dizzy, it doesn't matter. If that's what you want me to say. Does that make you happy?"

"It's not just what I want you to say, it's what I want you to understand."

"Dizzy, I have no idea what the fuck you're talking about. God, you always have to confuse everything so much."

I tried to change the subject. I also tried to trick her into realizing I cared about her, no matter how stupid that might have been. "So when are you coming back to Boston?"

"I don't know if I am," she said. "I mean, I know I'm not, not any time soon. They've offered me a chance to do the Française Louise catalogue, and I think I'm going to take it. Is that all right with you?"

"No, not really."

"Listen, Dizzy, I'm going to go, all right?"

"No, it's not all right."

"*Ciao*," she said.

She waited to see if I'd beg her not to hang up. The truth is that she's a very sexy and alluring woman, the type who can captivate men precisely by not saying anything—nose in the air, ass and attitude to die for. Sometimes she even tries this approach at social gatherings, especially those at which everyone is dressed up. But she gets bored with it once she has a few drinks in her, and winds up flirting like crazy. From ice queen to party girl in fifteen minutes. *Ciao* is one of the catch words she uses when she's in this mode, and now she was using it on me. If we'd been speaking in person, she probably would have flashed a seriously haughty glance, and maybe poked her breasts out, which in turn would have cracked me up.

"When did you decide to take the Française Louise job?" I finally asked.

I heard her open her refrigerator, then I heard her swallowing something. "About two minutes ago."

"Why, because I won't tell you whether I slept with Arlene or not?"

"No, because, as you just said, it shouldn't matter if you did or not."

"Right. And if it shouldn't matter if I did or not, then we should both act like I didn't, right?"

I knew I was skating on thin ice here, but sometimes crazy logic works with her. This time, however, she blew her top. "Fucking-A, Dizzy. What the fuck are you talking about? I'm staying out here and that's all there is to say. I was thinking about it even before the holidays. But this just guarantees it. Even if you hadn't done this, how long would I be there before your next tour starts? A few months, at the longest. What good is that? I'd rather stay out here and model. I need to work. This goddamn job pays really good and I'm gonna to take it. That's all there is to it."

It took every bit of control I could muster not to guffaw myself. She's one of the few women who's funnier when she's mad than when she's trying to be lovable. Then my internal spin control system took over. "So, let me get this straight. I'm the one who called you up because I was concerned that we haven't spent enough time together in the last couple of months and now you're the one who's just brushing me off? All the time I was working on the album and going nuts because of what I knew it was doing to us, and this is how you repay me? Okay, that's fine. But just remember that I was the one who wanted to put effort into working things out, and you were the one who turned a cold shoulder. Don't go around telling all your goddamn model friends how bad I treated you, because when it comes down to it, I'm the one who's willing to make some sacrifices and work things out, not you."

"Dizzy, you're an asshole," she reminded me. She knew everything I'd just said was total bullshit, even if she wasn't clever enough to pick my words apart and explain how it was bullshit. I pictured her pacing around her apartment in agitation, maybe glancing out the back windows, up into the hills, like I was about to come storming down and argue with her face to face.

"Bottom line it for me, Clipper," I said. "Do you want me to fly out there tonight? Is that what it will take to make you happy? I can spare three or four days. I mean, I can't spare three or four days, but I will, if that's what it'll take to get us over this."

"That's a good one, Dizzy, that's beautiful."

"What?"

"Don't give me that," she snapped. "You know exactly what I mean."

"Don't give you what? Christ!"

Neither of us said anything for a moment, and I knew that I'd pushed it too far. I really was being an asshole. Any other woman would have ditched me for good years ago. What I wished was that she was in Boston right then, that I could hug her and the mere physical closeness would reconnect us, heal all our wounds past and present. Eventually the hug would change into caresses, the caresses into kisses, longing, heat, and before we knew it, we'd be making love on the shag carpeting, or on the leather couch, forgiving each other in a never-ending, furious climax.

I sighed audibly. "Okay. What will it take to make you happy?"

"Maybe what would make me happy is if you didn't fly out here tonight," Clipper said. "If we took some time off."

"If we took some time off?"

"At least your ears still work."

I waited a moment before I said anything; I gave her my best meaningful, mournful pause. Then I spoke in a much softer tone. "Well, if that's what you think is best for us as a couple, I guess I can't argue. I can't force you to love me, no matter how much I may love you. My only question is how long you think this might last."

She laughed at me again. "God, you're something Dizzy. How the hell should I know?"

"Well, you are the one who suggested it."

"All right. Why not promise that we won't talk to each other again until the *Funk & Fugue* tour is over?"

I knew she wasn't thinking rationally, she was just lashing out. "Do you have any idea when the tour is scheduled to end?"

"August?" she suggested.

"Try October."

"I can go that long if you can," she claimed, though there wasn't much conviction in her voice. "And if we weren't meant to go that long, then maybe we weren't meant to be together in the first place."

"You'll call me," I said. I was still stupid enough to hope I could turn the conversation into a challenge for her, not me. "You'll be lonely some night and you'll call. But that's all right. I hope you do."

Another lengthy pause.

"Dizzy, I'm gonna go now. I'll talk to you when the tour is over and when you get your shit together." 139

I didn't know what else to say. I was flying pretty high from the Kahlúa and Bailey's already, though I knew I'd have even more when this conversation was over, no matter which way it came out. Mix myself a proper mudslide. I knew I should have made the call clean sober, and also that I should have planned my attack before I got Clipper on the line, but then, I also realized I never should have gone to bed with Arlene in the first place. Well, it was my bed, and now I was lying in it. I took another large swig of the Bailey's. I really didn't honestly believe autumn would arrive before I talked to Clipper again. In a few days, Blood Cheetah would start rehearsing for the tour and things would return to normal.

"All right," I sighed dramatically, like I'd just admitted the Earth was still square. "I'll talk to you later, then."

"*Ciao*, Dizzy."

What I was really pissed off at myself for was that I'd argued my case so badly. If I'd been a lawyer, I'd have had to sue myself for incompetence. I could at least have reminded Clipper she's cheated on me plenty of times in the past. Or worse than just cheating on me—which I picture as a secret liaison, solely for sex—she's gone on dates with other men because she was interested in them as partners, thought they might be the one to save her from me, just as I'd been the one to save her from the mechanic she was dating when she first started modeling. That was one lucky son of a bitch, for the two months she'd stayed with him. Randy his name was. He had absolutely no redeeming qualities or possibility of making money, but since her battered Chevy broke down on the freeway on one of her first mornings in L.A., he was the first guy Clipper met when she moved there. She basically lived off of him for a couple of months, until she could afford her own apartment.

For all I knew, she had slept with someone herself the night before, too, and was being so aggressively pissed-off at me as a way to compensate, not wanting to give me the opportunity to figure out the score. Her favorite club in L.A., is the Raven. She claims this is because a lot of her friends hang there, but the reason her friends hang there is that they're all models as well, or model-wannabees, or model-actress wannabees, or singer-actress-model wannabees, and the Raven is one of the few clubs that still plays the old game of selecting patrons from a long waiting line out front. Since Clipper and her friends are all gorgeous, they walk in with the aplomb of an Emperor penguin waddling into the Arctic Ocean. It makes them feel fabulous about themselves, the bitches. Hell, for all I really knew, she might've been climbing back into bed with someone she'd met there the night before, even as I was stalking around my apartment and wondering if I should bash the phone to tiny bits with one of my guitars. That would've made her feel great. That would've made her feel like she was proving to both herself and whoever the guy was that she was ready to move on to another relationship.

I spent the rest of the day waiting for the phone to ring again. Either Clipper calling me back, or Arlene, or Jay, or K Dot, or even Murph, wondering about *Funk & Fugue*. At eleven o'clock that night I decided to go out for a quick one, though I was already blitzed. The college bar Arlene and I had been at the night before was only the first place I stopped. I can't prove I'm crazy, because Blood Cheetah doesn't employ a band psychologist. I can only present the evidence.

16 | ... Action ...

VIDEO KILLED THE RADIO STAR. ... THE ONLY PROBLEM WITH MTV is that it totally sucks. It doesn't just suck, it sucks a giant fucking elongated, purple, throbbing, erect moose cock. I'd be proud to have thought it up, started it, then sold it in about 1985, right after the Live Aid broadcast, which, as I've said thousands of times before, was a great idea except for Phil Collins flying across the Atlantic, one of the single least humble acts of the twentieth century. But I'd be even prouder to have gotten it started and then blown up all the facilities in 1985.

The next time I saw anyone in Blood Cheetah was almost a week after Jay's party, when we got together to start rehearsing for the tour, and also to shoot footage for the video for "D.C. Me." The idea was that we could kill two birds with one stone. If the director—hereafter referred to as Joe Nouveau Director—felt the footage of the band jamming was his best material, he could use it. If not, he'd use footage of us gesturing to each other and looking either confused, amused, or pissed off. The intercut would be Washington, D.C., of course: monuments, statues, the Capitol, the White House, etcetera.

The basic idea was Alex's, as was the choice of director. I was happy to let him deal with it. Or at least as happy as I could've been, considering my basic philosophical opposition to videos. At the bottom of whatever art crap they may incorporate, they're just advertisements for the songs they're paired with. Plus they're thought up after a song is written, especially if the band wants to stay in business very long. Any time there's a "concept" involved, it means trouble. The final product is usually diametrically opposed to what I was thinking of when I wrote the song. I was sure this would happen with "D.C. Me." It would probably be turned into a polemic against politicians, which wasn't what I'd intended at all. *Your eloquence burns the innocence of the years which you betray . . . We're waiting hoping you won't see how many ways to pay . . .*

Worst of all, Joe Nouveau Director insisted on shooting the footage in Jay's playroom refinished basement, which he claimed was more viewer-friendly than a recording studio or a local concert hall. The scene of the crime. Jay and I got into it almost immediately.

"Well, here he is," he said sarcastically, when I came down the stairs to the basement. The other guys were already there, setting up equipment, while Joe Nouveau Director and several of his helpers were positioning cameras around the room and lugging in other gear from their van. The helpers all looked like college interns.

"Hey, guys, how's it going?" I asked, trying to ignore Jay. The first thing I noticed was that he'd set the heat on about ninety again. It was the middle of winter and he wanted to walk around in a goddamn tank top.

"What's up?" K Dot greeted me.

Grover's drumset was crammed into one corner. He was wedged behind it, tightening down the cymbals. As always, he was laughing at me. "Man, you're in trouble again. Bottom of the ninth, you should've struck out."

I tried to sound as innocent and cheerful as possible. I didn't want the shoot to be a hassle. "Why, what's up?"

"As if you didn't know," Jay chirped.

143

"You've got a problem with me being late?" I asked. "Because I could have been a lot later. The T isn't exactly like driving over here myself."

"I think you know what I've got a problem with."

His eyes narrowed to slits as he tried to give me a manly, intimidating look of death. I really had hoped to come in and have an easy afternoon, but now the choice was between laughing at him and methodically smashing a guitar to bits against his paneled walls, maybe taking out a couple of the overhead lights, too.

"Is it Arlene that you're pissed about?"

"Sure is, Einstein."

"Well, if I'm not mistaken, you're the one who mentioned me and Arlene to Clipper when she called here the night of the party, so I reckon you're not the only one with a reason to be pissed off, are you?"

144

Alex cut in at this point. The video was his baby, so to speak, and he had the greatest interest of any of us in keeping the peace. He was wearing chinos, a nice shirt, and bucks. "C'mon guys, can't this wait until later? These guys are almost ready to go. If we're lucky, we'll be out of here in only an hour or two, then you can argue all you want."

"Fuck the video," Jay said. "This is my house and we'll start when we're all good and ready."

"Any chance of me finding any beer around here?" I asked K Dot.

"Sure, start drinking already," Jay snapped. "Maybe you can take one of the lighting technicians home with you this time. They're all guys, but you aren't too discriminating, are you?"

K Dot glanced at me with his pathetic puppy-dog brown eyes. He already had his bass slung over his shoulder, and he was fingering the strings lightly. "Come on, Jay. Let's just get this over with. Yeah, Z, there's a cooler in the other room."

"You want to have one with me, Jay?" I offered. "Call it a truce?"

"Nope."

Resolution flooded through me. I knew that if I didn't have

a beer then, to help me get over how pissy Jay was being, I'd suck down quite a few later, when I was alone. But that was a sacrifice I was willing to make. "Then I guess I'll chill for now, too. If that's the way we're gonna play it."

Besides my conflict with Jay and my hatred of MTV, the big problem I was having that day was my deep-seated insecurity about my looks. The absolute truth is not only that I never look into mirrors, but that I purposely avoid looking into them, so that if I do see my own reflection, it's an accident, slipshod technique as I'm snorting a line, until the point where I'm so wasted, so far into another goddamn dimension and reality, that I want to stare at myself, watch the parts of my face come apart and be entirely strange and new to me, the way the letters of your own name can be if you stare at them on a printed page long enough.

My nose, the first part of me to touch a woman if she turns away when I try to plant a kiss, is too big—funny how getting it punched in several times when I was younger actually made it grow—much too crooked, and prone to leaking snot without me even noticing. Once every five years is too often for that. My eyes tend to be either bloodshot red or jaundiced yellow, which should mix to form green, but I'm lucky if I get a nice Seattle grey. I wouldn't give either Mick Jagger or Steven Tyler a run for his money in the do-you-have-to-blow-those-up-with-an-air-compressor? contest, but my lips tend to be too thick in the middle and too thin at the corners. And my cheekbones? Vanilla Playdoh!

Everybody thinks bands are being noble or humble or something when they decide not to star in their own videos, but I'm here to tell you, I'm here like a Fenway Park Bleacher Creature; half the time, rock groups aren't in their own videos because of all the back-stabbing that goes on behind the scene, all of the egos and complications and hassles involved. And that's just when the guys are in accord that being on film is a good idea, when they're all convinced they'll look so goddamn attractive that they'll be the ones Paulina Porizkova dumps Ric Ocasek for. It didn't take long at all for Joe Nouveau

145

Director to find out he'd have a tough time trying to align his artistic vision with my basic shyness and insecurity.

"So you don't want the camera on you too much?" he asked me, after only the first few takes. He originally wanted to film some wide-angle shots of the entire band playing, then go back and shoot close-ups of us individually. Apparently I kept turning my face away from the cameras. "You want the focus to be more on Jay singing?"

"Well, I just don't want it on my face for too long, that's all. But I'm not so sure I want it on Jay's face, either." I meant this as a joke, but I guess the humor wasn't so apparent, because nobody else laughed except Grover. Or maybe they just realized how long the afternoon was going to be. Every single video we've ever made took about three times as long as we'd guessed it would.

Joe Nouveau Director pouted and looked patronizingly perplexed. He was already starting to piss me off. His outfit consisted of Doc Martens, wide-wale corduroy pants, and what looked like a chenille pullover. In purple. He paused between words. "Well, what exactly . . . *do* you see . . . as your role in this piece . . . besides the motifs we already have . . . of the city of Washington . . . interspersed with footage of the band playing?"

"Nothing. Absolutely fucking nothing!" I lost control and started laughing like a maniac. Jay immediately used the outburst to show me that he was still pissed off at me. He left his mike stand, stepped through the cameras and lights to the couch on the other side of the basement, plunked down with a sigh, and proceeded to stare at me, waiting. I was yelling already, so I emphasized my point by crouching over my Stratocaster, stabbing it out like a bayonet, and picking a single note back and forth in a frenzy. "I just want this goddamn guitar to be a symbol of everything! A phallus, a giant fucking cock, because I don't have one myself. And a machine gun, a tommy gun, a Gatling goddamn gun, like I'm mowing the audience down, blowing them all to kingdom-fucking-come just because I haven't had enough sex today, motherfucker! Anything besides a lot of time spent on me trying to look pensive or cute!"

Which Joe Nouveau Director, lacking a warped sense of humor about as badly as Jesse Helms, didn't appreciate at all. I kept wondering where Alex had come up with him. Probably met him playing hacky sack in front of Berklee. I also kept wondering if he knew I was the fucking guy who'd written the song in the first place. What I'd really wanted to capture with the song—and who knows whether I had succeeded or not—was the idea of Washington as a city which eats itself, destroying both itself and the people who come there to work, regardless of how good or bad its existence may be for the country as a whole.

"Start the tape again," Joe Nouveau Director snapped at his assistants. He meant the tape we were playing along with. We weren't lip-syncing, exactly, but we were playing without our instruments turned on and without being recorded. Faking it not because we didn't know the song very well yet—although that was indeed the case—but because the soundtrack to be used for the video would be the original studio recording, so that the video would sound exactly like the song did on the album. Standard procedure.

"You sure you want to do it that way?" Alex asked.

"What other options do we have?" Joe Nouveau Director snapped. I couldn't tell whether he was truly clueless, or just didn't want any hassles.

K Dot was sitting on an amplifier, smiling like the Buddha. "Well, we could plug the equipment in."

Joe Nouveau Director wiped his hands on the sides of his chenille pullover in frustration, like his palms were outsweating his armpits. "Why don't we just work on perfecting what we're working on first."

"Yeah, guys, let's get it over with," Jay said. He had come back from the couch and was adjusting the height of his mike stand. This would be his best job of yelling the lyrics in perfect synchronization to the tape yet. "We'll have tons of time to rehearse later."

147

"So, is this considered rehearsing for rehearsal, or faking it for the finalé first?" Grover asked. "And shouldn't I pretend to be wearing headphones either way? That's what all the cool drummers wear in their videos."

"Fuck the headphones," I told him. "This is a song about Washington. You know, politics. So the first thing we should figure out is if Jay should be singing the lyrics from a Teleprompter."

"Doesn't Axl Rose do that?"

Alex started to lose it. You could dress him up but you couldn't take him out. "Guys, why don't we all just shut the fuck up and get this over with? Christ, it's like a bunch of six-year-olds around here."

We calmed down considerably once we got back to work. The truth was that in terms of videos, "D.C. Me" was going to be about as easy as they come. The budget was only fifty grand—including Joe Nouveau Director's trip down to film in Washington—and the time commitment for the band was minimal. Some of our clips have been fucking outrageous. Why should Blood Cheetah be playing on a sheer Utah cliff for our "Energy Moment Sound" video, except to prove we can waste a shitload of money on a helicopter to fly ourselves up there? Jay had already told me he wanted to film a chase scene when we did the video for "Howling" later that spring, but even if we used my Ferrari, or K Dot's Aston Martin, we'd still have to pay the city to close down half the North End for a morning. Or we'd have to shoot it in Hollywood, and that idea certainly didn't appeal to me.

Probably the best idea would be for me to simply stop appearing in Blood Cheetah videos. Use my absence as another layer of metaphor, the same way Pearl Jam's refusal to make videos at all is a symbolic act. I wish I could convince the other Blood Cheetah members that we should stop making videos too, but I'm not sure the music world's fans would provide enough support to carry another Last Righteous Band, especially since Blood Cheetah has already made so many compromises in other areas.

Joe Nouveau Director had us run through "D.C. Me" about ten more times, rearranging the cameras and the lights each time. Why we weren't wearing stage makeup was beyond me, but I didn't say anything. The guys were all doing their best to look like really cool musicians, but Jay was the only one overacting. He looked like he was dying for Joe Nouveau Director to ask him to rip his tank top off as he bounced around the room. Since we didn't have any of our amps turned on, the only people making much noise were Jay and Grover, which sounded weird, just the drums and the vocals washing over the metallic, barely-audible sound of the guitars. On a couple of the takes, I didn't even pretend to play "D.C. Me," except for the leads. One time I strummed the melody to "Howling," but at a much slower clip, while the next time I played the acoustic overture from The Who's *Tommy* album. 149 K Dot is probably the only one who noticed.

"Nice job, Z," he told me with a sly smile, after I played the overture. "You really looked into the camera on that one."

"Well, I'm doing my best."

Once Joe Nouveau Director was satisfied with the material he had shot, we plugged in the amps and ran through the song half a dozen times for real, which is what K Dot and I had thought we should be doing all along. The way the footage would be cut up in the final video, it's not like viewers would've been able tell if we were on measure the entire time or not. I wondered if Joe Nouveau Director would be able to figure out what I'd done when he reviewed the footage later, or if he'd need Alex to point it out for him.

I felt like getting the hell out of there as soon as we were done shooting, but ended up staying almost two more hours. Besides "D.C. Me," we also worked on playing "The Vanguard" and "Crank Squad." No matter how much time we put in on a song when we're in the recording studio, we still have to rehearse it a few times before we're comfortable with how it'll sound when we play live. The comparison Grover always uses is the difference between hitting baseballs in a batting cage and hitting them in a game. Even if the ball is moving at identical speeds, there are a lot more things you're worrying about in the game. And no matter how frustrating our rehearsals are sometimes, plodding through them is necessary. Hell, when the songs are new, sometimes we'll spend an hour or two on them and not even play them in their entirety. But it doesn't matter; the next time we come back to them, they're that much better.

I was pretty relaxed by the time we were ready to wrap things up. Playing a guitar had made me feel good, and the fact we'd covered three songs had given me confidence that we'd be in excellent shape for live performances by the time the *Funk & Fugue* tour rolled around. Best of all, neither Murph nor Annie had shown up. When we're rehearsing, they're just a pain in the ass. The only person we really need to see just toward the end is Walker, to discuss the exact specs we want for various pieces of equipment during the tour. At this point, Murph and Annie were still ironing out the details with the local promoters at all the stadiums we were planning to play.

I glanced at the clock on Jay's wall. Seven o'clock. "Hey, anyone want to grab a burger and a beer with me?"

"I can't, I'm already late picking up my kids," Alex said.

Grover was worming his way out from behind the drums. "Where do you want to go?"

"Hey, Jay," I said. "Do you know an easy place to grab a bite around here?"

"Nope."

"Really?"

He looked me directly in the eye. "Not for you, I don't. Grover, you might like Kennedy's. It's over on Williamson Road, if you remember where that is."

"Wow!" I exclaimed. I was truly astonished. "So this is what it comes to?"

"Ah, forget about him," K Dot said. "He'll get over it. It's not like you popped his mom or anything. C'mon, I'll go with you guys. What we really need to find is an all-you-can-eat buffet. Where did I leave my coat?"

Part of me wanted to stay behind and have a good heart-to-heart with Jay, apologize, apologize, apologize, if that was what he needed, kiss his bleeding ass about how good a singer he was and how much he contributed to Blood Cheetah. On the other hand, I'd done that too many times over the years already. Hell, I'd even come to his house that day with an open mind, willing to forgive him about Clipper if he could forgive me about Arlene, drink a beer with him. So the urge to antagonize him won out.

"By the way, Jay," I called, as I headed up his basement stairs. "Do you remember how old Arlene is?"

He was coiling a microphone wire around his elbow. "What?"

"She's thirty-two. Which is thirty-two years longer than she needs you to tell her how to live." 151

"Get the fuck out of my house!" he yelled after me.

1,001 Arabian Questions

SO I HAD DECIDED THAT SINCE ALL OF THE TRADITIONAL ROCK 'n' roll magazines suck, even *Rolling Stone*, which sucks in a too-professional sort of way, I'd finally consent to being interviewed by one of the men's fashion magazines, the type that hires well-respected writers in the hope that hiply wrangled urban prose will make their readers feel as stylish as when they're looking at Euromodels dressed in expensive clothes. Maybe they really did want to do a piece on me, and maybe they just needed some filler or some controversy. Or maybe the editor who approved the piece owed Annie a favor. Annie arranged the deal as part of the publicity surrounding the release of *Funk & Fugue*.

I should have known better. I momentarily and stupidly confused doing the interview with keeping myself working. There was already tons of evidence of the way I self-destruct when Blood Cheetah moves from the studio to a tour, so maybe accepting the magazine's invitation was just a further acknowledgment of what was to come, a warmup for making an asshole out of myself in front of thousands of people. At least I should have had the common sense to do a television interview, in which my pained, soulful, little-boy's eyes might offset the apparent stupidity of what I was saying.

Liv Ponager, the writer the magazine sent up from New York to talk to me, had apparently written a novel and a book of short stories. We met at the Commonwealth Brewery, not far from Faneuil Hall, at eleven in the morning. The two things that made the interview difficult, besides that it was me she was interviewing, were that she had made enough money from her books to not really care if the piece got published, and that she was newly married, which meant I couldn't flirt with her, not even on an intellectual level.

"What do you think of rap music?" she asked. This was her first question. We weren't even at a table yet, just standing at one of the waist-high wooden barrels that people can use as mini-bars. I had a feeling we wouldn't make it to a table; the way she placed the tape recorder between us told me she already disliked me. She looked like she wanted to wipe her fingerprints off it.

"Is that really the subject you want to start with?" I asked.

"Yes."

"You don't even want to know what my favorite beer is here? You know, something to break the ice?" I signaled to a waitress. "Could I have a porter? It's my favorite."

"I think what you'll find, Mr. Zimmerman, is that we're both pretty intense people, and that I don't intend asking you easy questions."

I started laughing at this, which probably insulted her and turned her into even more of a hard-ass. But if she wanted to show me how intense she was, I could certainly match her efforts. I just didn't realize how bad this would make me look when her article came out. "What was the question again?"

"What do you think of rap?"

"I think it sucks. I think it's a bunch of morons who can't sing, dance like monkeys, and want to shoot people."

"Really?"

"No, not really, but in my brand-new policy of telling the truth about everything, I'll say that it's not just 'cause I'm only five-seven that I'm scared shitless of black people, even ones who're only five-seven themselves, it's 'cause I'm white, and the only time white people aren't scared of blacks is when they outnumber them. And racism is what we're really talking about when it comes to most people's reaction to rap, even blacks'. Whatever music is there usually isn't the rapper's contribution. But if the art form fills a demand, I shouldn't criticize it just because I personally have no demand for it. The white folks who hate rap the most are usually the ones who don't understand it's not for them."

She tried to look me in the eye, be stern. She probably hadn't wanted the conversation to get off to this start, either, but now that it had, she wasn't about to back down. "Do you consider yourself a racist?"

"I consider everybody a racist, it's only some who admit it. For instance, the people who say, 'I don't have anything against them,' are usually too stupid to see that the term *them* is racist. Of course, most blacks, Mexicans, and Asians are prejudiced, too. Any reaction to the color of someone's skin is racism. I mean, affirmative action is racist, but that doesn't mean it's bad."

"How many African-American friends do you have?"

I was starting to get perturbed by this point. Annie had led me to believe the interview would revolve around music, and promoting *Funk & Fugue*. My first swig of the porter emptied half the glass. "Listen, the only guy I've ever met who's told me he'd been anywhere near Africa is a lily-white asshole from our record label who took a trip to Egypt to see the pyramids on money he made selling our discs. But if you want me to prove how many black friends I have, I'll insult the few who I do have by making up lies about ones I don't have, hoping to make you happy."

"Your fans might not take such words lightly," she said.

"Fuck my fans," I said. What I meant was that she was assuming to speak for my fans, and fuck her for doing it, because she was wrong. "The people who are really Blood Cheetah fans understand what I mean. If you die with twenty friends

154

who'll trust you under any circumstance, you're the luckiest man alive. I tip my hat to anyone who'd still say, 'The Menendez brothers are my buddies,' and really mean it."

Neither of us said anything for a moment. I was already done with my beer, and when the waitress wandered by, I signaled for another. Mizz Ponager was frowning. She really did seem disturbed by the direction we'd taken, but she was trying to be in control of the situation. For a second, I thought she was going to apologize. Her outfit for our meeting consisted of a dark two-piece suit, which would have been more appropriate on someone working in a bank, so I started wondering how many of these she had done. She was trying a little too hard to prove herself. I could hear her suck her breath in between her teeth before she posed another question.

"If not rap, what groups do you listen to?" she asked.

"Nobody interesting, and certainly not Blood Cheetah, unless I'm ripping drunk. Very few of the new bands when they're still new. Both their lack of talent and their abundance of talent scares me. It was probably two full years before I could admit how good Pearl Jam and Nirvana were. And, to help redeem my comments from earlier, I'll admit that sometimes I dance in my apartment stark naked to rap or hip-hop songs. I was pretty big on Marky Mark for a while, especially since he's from Dorchester."

"Have you ever met him?"

"Marky Mark? Me? No way, too tough. Crowds like he ran with, maybe my face would have met with their fists, although he's a lot younger than me. I went through high school trying to be invisible."

She looked intrigued but also self-satisfied. Suddenly her demeanor was that of a television detective about to spring the question proving a suspect was lying. "Was it a racially mixed high school?"

"That again? It wasn't mixed enough. The honest truth is that I'd love to live in a neighborhood where I was the only white guy for blocks and blocks. I think it would teach me a lot. But, and here's my racist slant, I'd want it to be one where

155

I felt completely safe. No drive-bys, no crack houses, no robberies."

"You've gone on record as saying drugs should be legal. Do you still believe that? And which drugs?"

I sighed. I knew I was digging my hole deeper and deeper. On the other hand, I didn't care. I just wanted the interview to be over. "I'll probably believe it unless I ever become a parent. Ideally, all drugs could be regulated, which would make them a lot safer. Nobody admits this, even me sometimes, but one of the biggest reasons drugs are so dangerous is that they're illegal. Imagine if you didn't know whether scotch was going to be eighty or a hundred and eighty proof until after you drank it. But you could probably get me to settle for just making pot legal. It's relatively harmless, and it's also an experiment for most kids, which is what they're after."

"What do you mean when you say it's relatively harmless?"

"Please. What the hell am I supposed to mean? If you snort coke, drop acid, shoot heroin, live on eight-balls, Electric Avenues, crystal meth, whatever, you might end up a rock star and make enough money to live the rest of your life, unless you blow all the loot on more drugs. I don't know . . . I mean, pot just isn't all that bad. People wouldn't smoke it if it was painful."

"Have you ever sold drugs?"

"Goddamn, what kind of question is that? I thought we were going to talk about music."

She had been taking notes in addition to the tape recording. Now she tapped her pen impatiently on the brewery's wooden barrel. "As you should be well aware, Mr. Zimmerman, one of the conditions for this interview was that no questions would be out of bounds."

"Well, it's just kind of an irrelevant question, like asking Larry Bird if he ever fouled out of a game. The honest truth is that I try not to, but on occasion it has happened. I have a personal rule to try not to supply anyone but myself with drugs, but there have been occasions when I've hooked up women I wanted to sleep with. But nobody else. I've never made a living by selling drugs, if that's what you mean. I'd always give them to women for free, but believe it or not, sometimes they insist on giving me money, even if they're only guessing at the street value."

"Why is that?"

"Best as I can tell, so they don't feel like they owe me anything."

"Do you feel like they owe you anything?"

"Depends what drugs I'm on myself at the time. I know the best thing for these girls would be to whack me over the head with a frying pan and make a clever escape, but then, maybe it's not so smart to be partying with me in the first place, right?"

"What's the most embarrassing thing you've ever done?" she asked.

"I can't believe this. I'm like Michael goddamn Dukakis, staring across the podium at George Bush in amazement. Have I mentioned that if you can ask any question, I'll expect you to print any answer, like, 'Fuck, fuck, fuck!' Why not at least do your homework and ask, 'Mr. Zimmerman, is it true that on Christmas Eve of 1991, you slid bare-ass down Causeway Street with a tequila bottle in one hand and a bloody reindeer hind leg in the other?' "

Her ears perked up. "Is that a true story?"

"I have absolutely no idea. Could be. Next musical question."

She flipped a page in her notebook. I was done with my second beer by then, and things were falling apart so quickly that I was tempted to step around the barrel and give her a kiss full on the lips. To really be sure whether she hated me, or if she realized everything I was saying was a joke. They didn't look like such bad lips to be kissing, either.

"When did you first feel Blood Cheetah was a success?" she asked, no more warmth in her voice than for any of her previous questions.

"That's a difficult question. We're the biggest bunch of shits and losers known to mankind, in a way. I mean, we're drug addicts, perverts, lazy bastards, borderline psychotics, whatever, but since we make music a lot of parents hate, kids throw fistfuls of money at us, which keeps us out of jail or mental institutions. Paulina Porizkova doesn't think she's particularly attractive, but she thinks Ric Ocasek is handsome enough to marry, so go figure. In Boston there are half a dozen or so musicians you're absolutely not supposed to badmouth, but he looks like a vampire caught on Revere Beach at noon in the middle of August, half his face melted away. One of the few people I could hang out with and never worry about my own looks, except that he's so freaking tall. Steven Tyler's another one you're not supposed to rank on, but Aerosmith's last album sucked. The only halfway decent song was 'Eat the Rich.' The rest was bubble-gum rock, little-girl rock . . . Anyway, I guess Blood Cheetah was a success the first time I ever had a fifty-dollar bill in my hand from playing in public, then the first time we played the Orpheum, then the Garden, all the albums, higher sales, etcetera. Now we're at the point where we have hundreds of people working for us on a tour, but I wish fifty dollars would still buy me food for two weeks. The reason I'm still in the music business is because I love writing songs, not because I need money. If you're just trying to make money, you'll probably end up broke, anyway."

"Which of your songs are you the proudest of?"

"This may sound strange, but in a way, I hate them all. The next ones are always the best. Really, I mean it. Right after we finish an album, I tell myself it might take twenty years to get my head on straight enough to do our next album, but that when I get into it, it'll be my best effort yet. I'm serious when I say I never listen to my own discs except when I'm shit-faced. Maybe one of the reasons I drink so goddamn much is that deep down, I'm pretty shy. The second anyone starts telling me how good my songs are, I feel like barfing on their shoes to distract them and shut them up. Hell, just hearing a question like that is enough to make me want another drink. Waitress! It's like hearing your own voice on a recording, which I still hate, after all these years. Let Jay be the lead singer, for all I care. He likes hearing himself more than he admits, and he admits quite a bit. *I got big tattoos, I wanna show 'em to youse . . ."*

Liv smiled for the first time all morning at this comment. "There's obviously been friction among band members in the past. How well do you get along with one another now?"

"Ooh, that's a really bad question right now. I want to say they all get along better with each other than they do with me, but I know that's probably not true. Or at least they wouldn't admit it. A lot of the time we get on pretty well, especially when we're in the studio and need to get things accomplished, but sometimes we can be really juvenile, especially that bastard Jay. He really is an asshole. We have a few little issues right now. But when we're on tour we tend to take turns playing peacemaker among the scraps and fights the others are having, especially that bastard K Dot. You just get really strung out and tired, especially that bastard Alex. That bastard Grover? Sometimes he'll do some stupid little thing, maybe just a phrase or a facial expression, and you know he's about the best friend a guy ever had, they all are. If I was a bandit in France back when they beheaded people, and Grover was the guy running the guillotine, I'm sure he'd make a joke right before he chopped me that would make me not even mind losing my head."

"Do you ever think about what would happen to Blood Cheetah if one of your bandmates died?"

"Hmm . . . not really, if only because I tend to be everyone's odds-on favorite to check out early. But I can't imagine that the band would go on as Blood Cheetah. More likely we'd split up and pursue other projects, even if that meant joining other bands. It would depend on who kicked, though, and even on how. Jay, K Dot, and Grover all like touring a lot better than Alex and I do, so maybe that's the type of outfit they'd hook up with. But who knows, maybe we'd all open restaurants or bars or whatever other way you can face anonymity. I know I'd go into a serious depression for a long time, maybe emerge only by writing songs about whoever it was that was gone. There is precedent."

159

She glanced down at her notebook again, and kind of tapped her pen on a question she had prepared. "Right now, who do you think are the most important bands?"

"Hands down, U2 and R.E.M. They're in a class by themselves in terms of having seen a lot, having put out a really wide array of great music in the past, and still being able to produce meaningful material. Nobody else is even close. The Stones' songs could be written in eight minutes each these days, so could a lot of Sting's. Guns N' Roses got too busy making money and seeing the world after the *Illusion* albums, Springsteen made his statement as many ways as he'll be able to, and none of the grunge bands have put the time in yet."

"Is there anybody else you'd like to denigrate?"

"Maybe yes, maybe no. If I wasn't being taped, I'd certainly make fun of anyone using the word *denigrate*. Doesn't it mean to free of black women? I guess everyone in every band should be insulted, the fuckers. I just don't have time to hit them all individually. No, that isn't true. The problem is that there are too many good bands out there, not too few. But as I get older, I realize how many of them are just a flash in the pan. People who love music and can make a living out of it without killing themselves should consider themselves really lucky, because there's a shitload of crappy jobs out there. Bands certainly should consider me calling them assholes and morons a challenge, though, and if my big mouth has resulted in a single wrathful song coming out sounding better, then doing this goddamn interview was worthwhile."

"You have a strange way of showing affection, Mr. Zimmerman."

I gave her my best pirate scowl. "Don't even get me started."

"What's the future of rock and roll?"

"Isn't it still Springsteen? I don't know. I don't even know the future of Dizzy. I'd like to say the obnoxious proliferation of seventies music radio stations will end, but it probably won't, and it isn't really rock music to begin with. Eventually we'll get equally shitty eighties-only stations, simply because there's a demand for it, just like there is for rap. It really is a

160

consumer-driven business. Probably there'll be continuing cycles of stagnation and rebellion, which is good. The kids whose parents hate White Zombie now will grow up and hate their own kids' music, etcetera, etcetera, etcetera. I hate it when people say that today's music isn't as good as the music from another era. Most of what's been popular has always been total horseshit, but there's also always been a small percentage that's great and lasts. Everybody thought some sort of musical apocalypse was finally here when punk hit big and the Sex Pistols were puking on fans, but look what came out of punk—groups like U2 and the Police."

She tried another trick question. "What time did you wake up this morning?"

"Whatever time this interview started, but yesterday. I'd love to write a guitar masterpiece which was twenty-four hours long. But most people can't concentrate for more than an hour or two, so the drugs necessary to either listen to it or to play it would kill the average person. An hour's about the maximum clean-and-sober jam length, and even then you think about sex ten thousand times."

Liv caught our waitress's eye and made a little hand signal for the check. "How's your attitude toward answering relationship questions right now?"

"Terrible. I'll categorically refuse. That's another really bad question right now. I might even refuse to remain sitting here. Why fuck up my lovelife more than it's already fucked up?"

"How many women have you slept with?"

"A lot more than I've been in love with, a lot less than I could have if I'd always been sober, ruthless, and totally dedicated to carving notches on my bedpost."

She shut her notebook, obviously trying to end the interview, but the tape recorder was still running. "Are you scared of living your life without ever marrying?"

"No."

"What are you scared of?"

"Honest truth? The only thing I really worry about is losing my hearing, especially my ability to discern subtle sounds and the nuances of certain notes and combinations. I'm already showing a slight amount of hearing loss in each of my ears. I think I'd rather lose my sight than my hearing, but don't quote me on that after I walk into a thornbush and tear up both of my eyes. Everything else in life that's supposed to be frightening I think I can handle. I kind of wish that ten or twelve years ago, I'd taken notes on exactly what decibel levels were comfortable to listen to music at, so I'd have something to compare it with now. In general, I don't think I listen to music as loud as other people do. You'll never see the rubber on my car's tires vibrating and booming. Besides, Boston's a great walking town. Hey, if you want to spend some quality time with me, I'll show you around."

Now she shut off the tape recorder. "I don't think that's an appropriate question, Mr. Zimmerman." She handed our waitress a twenty-dollar bill. "We're all set with that. Thanks."

162

Her notebook and tape recorder went back into her briefcase with the smooth efficiency of a Vegas dealer collecting chips from a losing wager; then she was headed for the door.

"I thought you said that any questions were fair territory," I yelled. The truth was that my offer hadn't been a pickup line. I'd just thought that if she saw me in my natural environment, maybe she'd understand me better. I already realized the article she submitted wasn't going to be a verbatim interview. "Quality time" was a poor choice of terms, though.

Sure enough, the issue came out right as the tour started. The magazine printed an introductory blurb, distancing itself from me by subtly explaining that I'm big with American youth, then describing my physical appearance, schizoid mood swings, impatience, maniacal laugh, and sour disposition. Mizz Ponager's portrait of her own behavior made her sound like a schoolteacher dealing patiently with a miscreant. Murph was thrilled by my comments, of course, as were the other guys in the band, the record company, all sorts of advocacy groups, and two or three of the women I've dated. But I don't think the interview affected sales of the *Funk & Fugue* disc one way or the other. For that I'd have really had to lose it. As it was, I felt lucky that Mizz Ponager didn't bother to report how I tripped and nearly fell as I followed her out of the brewery, though she did get my last comment down: "Really, I'm a nice guy. Try not to make me look like an idiot in your magazine."

Because obviously I could take care of that by myself.

18 | Junky, Drunky, Weezil

"HEY, WHAT'S THIS?" I ASKED K DOT. WE WERE TWELVE years old, walking home from school on trash day. I was holding a half-full bottle of Jack Daniel's. We had been looking for bicycle parts.

"That's whiskey. That's the best kind."

"You wanna drink some?"

"You go first."

"No, you."

"You're the one who found it," he argued.

I fidgeted. "What'll happen?"

"You'll get drunk, you dummy. What are you, chicken?"

The woman living in the house whose trash we were picking yelled out the front window at us, but when we ran, we took the bottle with us, and that was the start of one type of career. This was also about the time I found my first guitar, also in someone's trash, with no strings and a fist-size hole in the body.

Booze and music, the two have always gone together. But hell, the Rolling Stones are still alive, except for Brian Jones, and they consumed more combustibles than just about anybody, including me. One really quick way to mess up your life would be to say, "What would Keith Richards do?" anytime you faced moral or social dilemmas, like whether or not to stay for one last drink. That Brian Jones died so young might have been rock 'n' roll's evil influence, or it might have been, as Mick Jagger has suggested, rock 'n' roll speeding up his natural tendency to destroy himself.

A lot of drunks, junkies, and psychotics roam the ranks of musical genius—which is as different from the music *industry* as Van Gogh slicing off his own ear is from Wall Street—but there's a lot of substance abuse in other artistic fields, too, as well as in America's homeless shelters, maybe just luck of the draw, maybe some infinitely minute difference in brain chemistry determining who becomes a seat-of-the-pants, maniac Olympic downhill ski champion and who's a coke addict suffering heart palpitations. One idea I can even accept is that certain people are headed for addictions from day one, the same way some people are more gifted musically or athletically or whatever. It doesn't matter if this predilection is because of genetics (probably), early childhood experiences (maybe), or teenage hardship (ha!), what's important is realizing that the proper limits for one person are probably wrong for another. There's a chance I couldn't kill myself with alcohol even if I tried, because I'm wired not to and am also wired to not really try, while some Mormon farmboy in Utah is hooked until it kills him the first time somebody slips him a can of Budweiser, forgetting that booze was what did in his uncle Ephram. If scientists haven't mapped out exactly how the brain works yet—and my own warped theory is that brains are so complex nobody could figure all the pathways out and still remember the way home—they certainly can't convince me that most people don't have what amounts to a governor clamped in there someplace. In my case, a governor set at extremely high rpms, but still . . .

165

Arlene called me at about 8 P.M. on the same day I'd done the interview with Liv. I was smoking a fat-ass joint when the phone rang, and I was so baked it took me a minute to re-member to pick up; the temptation was to just stare at the phone, trying to figure out who was on the other end by con-centrating really hard. This was my first pot since mid-September, when I devoted myself to the *Funk & Fugue* album. I'd bought it from . . . well, an old friend, after the in-terview. I told myself it was a reward for having gotten through the interview, as well as the album. But the truth was that it was just another sign of how quickly my life could spiral out of control. A joint is nothing, of course, except that after the first hit I wanted another, then another after that, and I knew I'd probably wake up in the morning remembering how good the last one had tasted the night before. None of which both-ered me at that moment.

"Hello!" I sang into the receiver.

"Dizzy? It's me, Arlene."

"Well, that's certainly good news," I said.

"What? Why?"

"I'm just glad you're not the record company calling to tell me the album sucks." My voice rose and fell spastically, like a cartoon character's, because suddenly everything was very funny to me. There were probably pot fumes wafting out Ar-lene's end of the line.

"They'd actually tell you a Blood Cheetah album sucked?" she asked.

"Not yet, not in so many words. But they usually express 'serious concern that the fan base won't be able to relate.' Or something like that. They get scared every goddamn time we change our sound a little. They're all morons."

"Are you happy with the way the album came out?"

I took a hit off the joint. "I don't know. I probably won't know for years, because we're rehearsing all the songs now, then we'll play them all summer, and I'll need to forget them before I can hear them with a fresh ear. Except now. Maybe I could listen to them right now."

"Why's that?"

"Cause I'm baked out of my fucking skull!" I yelled into the

receiver. Then I roared with laughter for about three minutes.
"Hey, you wanna come over?"

"No."

"I'll turn the heat up as high as Jay does and we can hang
out in bathing suits and smoke a little more weed."

"That's not why I called, Dizzy. Actually . . . well . . . I just
called to tell you you don't have anything to worry about, if
you know what I mean."

I thought about this one for a moment, though I was still
kind of hung up on the idea of getting her into a bathing suit.
My eyes had been closed the entire conversation and I could
feel how easily I'd get a hard-on. "Uh, I guess I'm not following you. Tell me you mean Jay got arrested and now he doesn't
want to rip my head off anymore."

"Dizzy . . ."

"No, okay, I knew that wasn't it."

"Things came around for me," Arlene said. "That time of 167
the month, if I have to be so obvious. You don't have anything
to worry about."

"Cool!"

"That's all you have to say? 'Cool'?"

Luckily, she couldn't see me shrugging my shoulders. I
could imagine her nose, already crooked, crinkling in dismay.
"Uh . . . how about thanks . . ."

"God, no wonder everyone thinks you're such a bastard!"
she exclaimed. "I can't believe I even slept with you in the
first place."

This set me off cackling again. "It was a full moon. We didn't
know what we were doing. We were just kids then. Besides,
you're related to Jay, so you're genetically predisposed to hating me. It's in your blood."

She hung up on me.

Five minutes later the phone rang again.

"Hel-looow . . ." I answered, my best Steve Martin imitation.
If she'd waited an hour, I probably would've gotten desperate
to apologize, and been the one to call her back.

"Listen, Dizzy, you shithead," she started in. "I'm sorry Jay found out about us, I really am. But he's still my big brother, so when he asks me things, I kind of have to tell the truth, or he figures it out anyhow. Like about us going out drinking when we got back to your place last week. So if he's really, really pissed at you, it's because he probably assumes you were getting me drunk on purpose. I guess he can be a little jealous sometimes. I told him about a hundred times that it was my idea."

"Gee, thanks."

"Don't be a smartass."

The conversation had reached the tedious stage where my buzz no longer made everything sound hilarious, but intrusive. I could imagine each of her words coming out of the receiver and wrapping themselves into my ears, like wisps of smoke. I also felt like we were spinning off into some astral void, empty space, not saying anything, because the conversation had been going on forever.

168

"So where are we today, Arlene?" I said. "What's your point?"

"Well, the whole goddamn reason I called was to let you off the hook, remember?" she practically screeched into the line. "Plus this. If you could, try not to talk to anybody about it . . ."

"Hey, I won't if Jay won't. But it's not like it's exactly a state secret."

"The thing is, I'm kind of seeing someone right now, and I know it would ruin it if he found out. He's from Everett. This may be my last chance, if you know what I mean."

I thought I did, but I wasn't sure. She would've had heart palpitations if she knew how close I'd come to mentioning her during the interview with Liv. But that would've just been a stab at Jay. A cheap shot. I could suddenly picture myself as a crotchety old man, scratching my way into senility, yelling at kids in playgrounds, "Shut up, you little bastards, I'm not dead yet!"

"All right," I said. "I won't say anything if you don't. I wouldn't have said anything anyhow. The past is the past, who cares what might have happened? If you're looking for me to promise not to talk about this, sure, whatever, you've got it. Absolute silence. But you've got to make me one promise in return. In a way it's easy, but in a way it might be hard."

"Anything."

I was already starting to chuckle. "You sure?"

"Of course I'm sure."

"Well, if ten or fifteen years down the line, you do tell people we slept together, tell them I was like Tarzan in the sack. Just a goddamn wild ape."

"Dizzy, don't be a loser."

"You promise?"

"Yeah, I promise."

After we hung up, I sat there for what seemed like a long time, although it might have only been five minutes. I was thinking about Arlene and then I was thinking about everything else in my fucked-up life. I could forgive her for anything, including sleeping with me; hell, I already forgave everybody else for everything anyhow, even Jay. I'd barely remembered blowing the condom out on her during our little sexcapade, so I hadn't been particularly worried she might get pregnant, but now that I knew she wasn't, I closed my eyes and rubbed my hand over my own belly. It was almost the same as dreaming I was pregnant myself, and for a split second, I knew that when I went to bed that night, I'd dream I was with Arlene, rubbing her bloated, pregnant belly, until the kick I felt was obviously an alien, and the dream turned to a nightmare.

169

The pot made my emotions feel tangible at first, like I could reach out and grab all the important events not only of the last few weeks, but of the last few years, which in turn would make both those events and my emotions more important; then the pot was holding me back from true insight. A roadblock was erected, arms were lashing against me as I ran through a crowd . . .

The obvious solution was to get out of the apartment, go somewhere, do something, so that the sensations of my body moving would overrule the sensations of the pot, which now resembled a dry-ice fog. I sprinted out of my apartment, ran down to the closest 7-Eleven in just my jeans, long-sleeved T-shirt, and sandals; bought a liter of Mountain Dew, jogged home, mixed half a liter of vodka into the Dew, threw on a sweatshirt, walked back to the 7-Eleven—carrying the bottle of Mountain Dew and vodka—scarfed three chili-cheesedogs, then wandered around for almost an hour, finally settling on Canary Blues, probably the best small club in Boston for catching a live band, even if the bastards wouldn't let me in with my bottle.

After which I guess I'd have trouble convincing anyone I'm not totally self-destructive, except that the next morning, I did wake up with my lucky coin in my pocket. There are still a few brain cells which, if we use an *SS Dizzy* metaphor, haven't mutinied yet, though they may just be in the crow's nest, while the rest of the ship is underwater. Besides, who would organize an intervention for me? Murph? Jay? Someone in my family? And who would come, Alex and K Dot with a keg of Sam Adams? One of my recurring fantasies is that if the other guys in the band ever do try to take a stand with me, I'll see it coming, a free safety reading a pass and intercepting. Then, on the designated day, I'll trick whoever has organized the confrontation into believing I'm watching pigeons from the Prudential Building's observatory floor, and when the crowd converges, I'll sprint screaming through one of the floor-to-ceiling windows. The backpack I'm wearing will blossom, as they gasp at what their stupidity has driven me to do, into a silken parachute emblazoned with the motto SEE YA, SUCKERS!

The rest of the spring followed in about the same vein. What I learned by making *Funk & Fugue*, besides a whole lot more about music, was that I should always have music to work on. What I learned from sleeping with Arlene was that I shouldn't have slept with Arlene. And what I learned from doing the interview with Liv Ponager was that what all the self-righteous geeks in this country have as a hobby is writing snotty, self-indulgent, self-aggrandizingly intellectual letters on their computers, then e-mailing them to magazine editors.

I could already anticipate how a lot of the tour was going to unfold, if not in details, then at least in mood: a flash-forward, perhaps, instead of a flashback. There were other incidents too, of course, but none of them mattered to me, either. I knew it would be at least another year before I got myself straight enough to start working on Blood Cheetah's next disc, but that when I did, I'd feel it was our greatest album yet, just as I had with *Funk & Fugue*. And I also knew that when I was through with it, I wouldn't care what else happened to me, because I'd know I'd worked as hard as I could. What else in life is worth doing?

Part

3

14 | Dale Carnegie's School of

BLOOD CHEETAH PLAYS TWO NIGHTS IN SACRAMENTO, TWO in Oakland, two in Bakersfield, then hits L.A., where we're scheduled to play four indoor shows within a week, because it's the end of August and all the good stadiums are booked for baseball, football, or college soccer, and also because, this being L.A., we're trying to look upscale by playing to ten thousand people instead of fifty thousand, like it was a regular club-and-ballroom tour. Walker and his crew are glad to camp out in one place for a while, especially somewhere they don't have to worry about the one-in-a-hundred threat of rain, so naturally they caravan out toward Sunset and Hollywood, hoping to see some freakier-looking cats than themselves. Me, I'm in about the same shape as I've been in the entire fucking tour. You can't chop a human body in half and expect it to keep growing, like you can with a paramecium, but you'd be amazed how much poison a person can absorb but still recover.

Remember when computers were new and everybody ran around saying how much easier they were going to make our lives, and not just the people who owned stock in software companies? I won't bother explaining the million reasons I'll quit Blood Cheetah the day we go on-line (we're musicians; it's for merchandisers and geeks), but listen, nobody's life got any more relaxing or satisfying, except maybe Bill Gates's, if he'd ease up on his own reins. Clerks still work forty hours a week, shipments still get sent to the wrong drop, and lines still form in grocery stores. Success in a rock band is the same way, an entirely different set of ass-cracking problems than poverty and where your next meal is coming from, sometimes logistical, sometimes legal, and sometimes (rarely) merely moral or ethical.

The first afternoon we're in L.A., Murph throws on a silk sportcoat which I'm sure he paid a lot more for than he would have in Boston, matched with a swank burgundy tie, as if the clothes could turn him into a real businessman, not someone totally full of shit, and he calls a meeting in Jay's hotel room. Which is a joke from the get-go, a Mel Brooks fucking farcical spoof, though I'm the only one who gets the punchline. Everyone in the band is there, plus Annie, and also two lawyers the record company has sent: Bob Gordimer and Ross Elliot.

Jay is standing in the doorway to the bathroom, feet planted, bare-chested, rubbing his tattoos, as if the fact that we're in his room lends him authority, the same attitude he cops when we do stuff at his place back in Belmont. Nobody's gonna take a shit until *this* meeting's over. Annie is sitting at a glass-topped table in the kitchenette with the lawyers, glancing through a small notebook and preparing to take notes, but the real reason she's included is so that when Murph pisses us off, she can calm us down.

"Well, gentlemen," Murph begins, "I suppose the biggest reason it's appropriate for this meeting at this juncture is to talk about business in a general sense, then about some particular business, and finally to see if you guys have any concerns I can help with. Or Annie. You know we're always here for you."

"When you're here at all," Alex quips.

Murph pretends not to hear him. He's strutting around like

a CEO addressing a boardroom full of vice presidents. Maybe having the lawyers here makes him feel even more important than usual. "Let's not forget that this is a business, and we're in business to make money, not lose it. Which is my way of segueing into saying, let's just be blunt, we've got to keep our asses clean from now on. Los Angeles is a pretty wild city, with a lot of things to see, but also a lot more chances to get in trouble, if you know what I mean. Especially since you guys all know the town pretty well, and also because we're gonna be here longer than most of our stops. I'm not gonna make anybody promise me to stay perfectly clean, or any of that bullshit, but for God's sake, use your heads. No drugs on the buses, no drugs in the hotel rooms, that's just stupid. And if you have to start partying with anyone, try not to do anything too stupid. Blood Cheetah certainly doesn't need any more bad publicity right now. If it gets any worse, we're gonna have to donate to some high school's music department or something. Do I make myself clear? We've got to get our shit together."

"Yes, Dad," K Dot says. He's stretched out full length on Jay's bed, tepid gut, soft jawline. He rolls over after he speaks, lying face down, his arms still by his side, such a juvenile and ridiculous way of insulting Murph that I laugh out loud.

Now Annie speaks up. "Well, Murph has got a point . . ."

"And if he wears a hat, nobody'll notice," Alex cracks.

The snickering grows louder now, with only Jay giving Murph any support. Once again I'm amazed that as much as we all argue among ourselves, the other guys and I can circle our wagons instantaneously, even against Murph, who tells anyone who'll listen that he's part of the band, too. But he continues on, talking like we're little kids. "Hey, here's a good dose of medicine for you, and this'll show you what I mean about particular business. Dizzy, there is, as we speak, an arrest out for your warrant in the state of Nevada."

"I assume what you mean is a warrant out for my arrest."

"What did I say?"

"The opposite of that . . ."

Bob Gordimer stands up and takes over at this point. He's probably a year or two younger than I am, but he speaks so seriously he sounds like he's fifty. "Well, apparently enough kids got hurt and enough parents filed complaints after your concert in Reno that the district attorney wants to press charges for disorderly conduct and inciting to riot."

"So, I'm a wanted man?" I ask. I'm already picking up Alex and K Dot's sarcasm. Lawyers make me nervous, but not nearly as nervous as cops do. Being a wise-ass is an easy response. "I was hoping nothing would come of that. I was hoping it would be downgraded to a melee, at best. But I'm such a stupid fuck, I don't even know how to pronounce that word. Is it *me*lay, me*lay*, ma*lee*, or what? No wonder I'm wanted. Makes me wonder if anybody's ever been on MTV's and the FBI's most wanted lists at the same time."

178 "Maybe we should play covers of 'I Fought the Law (and the Law Won).'" Grover pipes in. "Or 'Police and Thieves.' Or 'Tommy Gun.' God, the Clash were fucking hoodlums, weren't they?"

Annie tries to help the lawyers. "Guys, this is pretty serious . . ."

"Well, what's the deal?"

"The deal is this," Bob says. "Ross and I have already saved your ass. We've been out there, and they're ready to make a deal. Here's how it works. The city of Reno isn't going to have you extradited from California or from any other state, but you have to voluntarily turn yourself in when this tour ends. Then you'll be released on fifty thousand dollars cash bail, and wait roughly a week for the lawyers to strike a plea bargain, which'll probably be something like two hundred hours of community service and a ten-thousand-dollar fine. That's all. No biggie. But you can't go back into Nevada until this is taken care of, or you'll be spending a few nights in jail, okay?"

"Well . . ."

"Well what?" Murph snaps. "Jesus Christ!"

I ignore him. "Can I go gambling while I'm out on bail? That would be a riot. There are probably bookies who'd buy me a

Ferrari if I told them I was gonna make an all-out run for the border and that they could have the rights to broadcast the cops chasing me live on pay-per-view. Whoever gave anyone permission to make deals for me, anyhow? Maybe I think it's the stupidest fucking lawsuit I've ever heard, and that I'm totally innocent, and that I really would rather die in a flaming wreck than admit I was guilty of something I didn't do."

"But you are guilty!" Murph shouts.

I spin around. "Fuck you, you weren't even at the show that night, were you? Grover, was he there that night?"

Grover's perched on a stool in the kitchenette, near Annie and the lawyers. He raises his fists and throws an imaginary right jab. "Uh, actually he was. But get 'em, tiger!"

"Yeah, what he said."

"Now, listen, Dizzy . . ." Annie starts.

"Call me Dillinger, I'm an outlaw."

". . . I know as well as anybody how idealistic you can be, but there are a lot of factors we have to consider. First of all, you're not that hard a person to find, especially when you're touring, so getting them to promise not to have you arrested right now is kind of important. Second, they've got about four tapes of you shouting, 'You're gonna die someday, so why not die tonight?' As well as, 'Go crazy!' So it would be pretty easy to convince either a judge or a jury that you were trying to get the crowd riled up. Plus, people did end up in the hospital, which is definitely not the type of press we need right now. Do you realize how much money it'll cost, for both us and them, if this goes to trial?"

"Money's not the point, call Johnny Cochran if you have to. Tell him I'll pay him by the word. No offense to you guys, Bob."

Murph barges back into the conversation. "Jesus Christ, that's the last thing we need. Then everyone will think you're guilty. Just do it the goddamn easy way for once, Dizzy. The record company said they'll take care of the lawyers' fees. All you have to do is show up and shut up, maybe look a teensy bit sorry."

179

"Sounds easy enough to me," Jay says.

K Dot's face is still buried in the mattress. "Yeeee ha! Ride 'em, cowboy, giddy giddy-up! *Arriba.*"

When you're on the road for too long you eventually reach a point where you're so exhausted, both physically and emotionally, no matter how healthy you try to keep yourself—health food, ten hours of sleep every night, no booze—that you start having mini breakdowns stuffed with manic laughter and the knowledge that every single aspect of this world is insane. Right now, Murph trying to talk rationally and professionally is hysterically funny. I start laughing as a reaction to K Dot, but I'm also laughing at Murph, at Annie, and the super serious lawyers of this world, at the idea of jail time for partying too hard at one of our concerts—like getting kicked out of your own birthday party. Hell, at the whole idea of being on tour to begin with.

180

Suddenly I'm not even standing anymore, I'm on my knees, cracking up, losing all control over myself, then I'm rolling on the floor, ready to piss my pants, whole-body convulsions, the laughter where you can't tell if a person's laughing or crying. Murph pokes me in the rib with his shoe after a minute, telling me to get up, but this just makes me laugh harder. I can feel everyone else waiting impatiently for me to shut up, too. Except for K Dot, who's succumbed to the same contagion, and is howling with giggles on the bed. This only lasts for about five minutes, but it feels like an hour. It's all I can do to stop repeating what K Dot said. "Giddy giddy-up, I'm a cowboy! *Arriba.* Giddy giddy-up!"

God, they don't get it, and they never did; don't have the brains to realize I'm useless right now, should be written off and ignored until we go on stage for the first show. Or at least they should have the brains to remember they've all reached this stage themselves at times, and should have learned something from it. Unless Murph has any more important business to cover, like a warrant for me having been issued in Arizona, too, the next state we'll drop like birdshit into, for crimes real or imaginary, we might as well disperse (disband). Or maybe he wants to give me a chance to get serious, get seriously angry, and start ranting.

When I finally calm down, I notice that Bob Gordimer has sat down at the table again with Annie and Ross, the other lawyer, waiting. The expression on his face is a brilliant example of anger checked by patience. No wonder the record company hired him. He understands he's powerless right now; there's no way he could shout at me, or intimidate me, or make me look like an idiot in front of the rest of the band. I'd just go ballistic again. I wonder if they taught him things like that in law school. He might as well be wearing a sharkskin suit, instead of the dark blue he's chosen.

"Do we have a deal?" Ross Elliot asks slowly. This is the only thing he says during the entire meeting.

I let out a huge sigh. "For now we do. I'll let you know if I change my mind."

"Thank you," Bob says. He pulls a few sheets of paper out of his briefcase and jots something down as Murph steps forward again.

"Now, Dizzy aside, do you guys have any other issues you're concerned about?" he asks, like a camp counselor who's hoping nobody has come down with poison oak. Annie probably made him ask this. "I mean, any overwhelming issues?"

Alex snorts. "You don't really mean that, do you? Christ, Walker's the one who solves our problems, not you. It's either something that can be fixed by rewiring a couple of bad connections, or it's something we take a drink and try to ignore, right?" He leaps up from the couch. "I'm out of here!"

"Where the hell are you going?" Jay demands.

"What's it to you? I'm out of here!"

"Me too!" Grover stands up, pulls up the sleeve of his T-shirt, flexes his biceps, and smiles. "If you need me before you need me, I'll be at Muscle Beach in Venice, trying to scam a week's membership. Or I'll be trying to scam lessons from a surf bunny. *Hasta la vista*, Murph. Seventh-inning stretch."

"What?"

181

"What he said!" K Dot calls out as Alex and Grover hurry from the room, then collapses back into another fit of laughter.

I've more or less stopped flopping around on the floor by now, but Jay, Murph, and Annie are cloistered together, having a private discussion about how stupid this meeting was and about how stupid Alex, Grover, K Dot, and I are. In my mind I go over and slug Jay for being such a hypocrite, drop him with one clean punch that doesn't do lasting damage to either his face or my fist, like in *The A Team* episodes, but in reality I just crawl up onto the couch. K Dot is still chuckling on the bed, but more relaxedly, and has rolled back onto his side.

"Hey, Murph," I call out. "If you're really hurt that Alex doesn't want to sit here and bitch about things to your face, I could probably come up with a few good complaints."

"Maybe this isn't the best time," Annie says.

"Well . . ."

Murph relents. "Okay, what is it now?"

"It's everything, really. What else is it ever? It's always everything or nothing. And Alex is right, when it's nothing you take a drink and tell yourself it's nothing, and when it's something, you take a drink, or a hit, and tell yourself it's nothing, which I guess it really is as long as all of us get through this fucking tour without ending up dead or maimed. *Nothing is something, everything is nothing* . . . And that's just for starters."

"What the hell are you talking about?"

"I'm talking about everything and I'm talking about nothing, as if I didn't already say that. Duh. Why the hell didn't we play in San Francisco on this tour? I mean, I know it's only because it was a lot easier to book us into Oakland, and anyone from San Francisco only has to drive over the bridge and hope there's no earthquakes and there they are. But still, I'd rather have played in a tiny little joint that was really, really, really cool than another huge goddamn stadium. Maybe we could have totally changed our set around and played some serious blues numbers, tried to get people dancing, not just jumping up and down and waving their fists. God, our fans can be stiffs sometimes. Maybe we could have freebased our first-ever attempt at covering "I Melt With You," then gone out for a drink at some superhip club until four in the morning. Oakland? Fuck Oakland! And fuck all of Route Five. Why the hell didn't we come down Route One, right along the ocean? When I'm on my deathbed, I'm not gonna say, 'Well, I wish I'd spent more time on major interstates.' Did you ever see the Rolling Rock commercials where they show different cities in different years? One of them is San Francisco in 1975, and that's the one that kills me, because Frisco's such a cool town and because now it's twenty years after 1975 and all the people who were so young and cool, standing around at a very cool party drinking Rolling Rock, are middle-aged fogies now, but hopefully they realized how cool the town they were in was twenty years ago and aren't thinking, Gee, I wish I'd explored more and dated more and done more of the things I wanted to do, because now I've got three kids, a mortgage, a wife who's always nagging me, a boss who's always yelling at me, and I hate my job. There, that's what I think of this whole fucking tour, so there!"

183

Nobody says anything for a minute. Annie's the only one who'll look me in the eye, and if we looked at each other for too long we both might start crying.

"Is there anything else?" Murph finally asks.

"Yeah, I need a whole shitload of new strings. Wanna go with me, K Dot? I'm gonna start out on Rodeo Drive and shop my way down."

"Sure."

"Sound check's at nine," Annie reminds us.

"Yeah, well, we may even be there."

As K Dot and I are leaving, I hear Jay flapping his fat fucking trap. "See, that's exactly what I mean. See what I've been talking about?"

Blah blah blah.

Los Angeles is beautiful because there are so many beautiful and famous residents. I'm almost always ignored, even by the tourists who do recognize me, but who really want to see

Arnold Schwarzenegger or Sharon Stone, or whoever. Maybe some young punks will scream, "Hey, Dizzy!" out their car window if they see me on the Strip, and maybe there are some solid music clubs where I could go and have high-level talks with other guitar players, but I'm not even a producer for a sitcom, so the real pain-in-the-ass I'm-so-hopeful types know I'm not worth begging for career advice and bit parts.

When I first grew my hair long, I imagined being able to go anywhere in the world and not look like a tourist, Japan and China even. Both locals and other tourists would see me sipping tea alone in a café and assume I was either a sophisticated drug runner or a sophisticated religious wanderer. But when K Dot and I decide to start our L.A. spree by drinking on a small, exclusive, elevated terrace bar instead of by wandering into expensive shops to horrify the snobs who work there or by staring into Rolls-Royces until their owners come out and shoo us away, my international messianic style doesn't impress the hostess, who assumes we're from that other L.A. subspecies, the homeless. The only way we manage to get served is to wait until her back is turned, grab ourselves a table, then, when she comes to kick us out, act like she's a waitress, lay a hundred dollar bill on the table, and ask in polite tones for two Chagniene cognacs, a brand which doesn't exist, politely settling for Remy Martin. This is all good old-fashioned obnoxious Dorchester-style fun, but once K Dot and I start drinking we forget about things like pissing off other customers or getting kicked out, and slide into a fairly serious and lengthy conversation about the meeting we've just had with Murph, and about the tour in general.

We decide that getting arrested sucks, that I really will do whatever the lawyers advise—maybe after bitching at them a little more—that everyone should lighten up, this is only rock 'n' fucking roll, that everybody is forgiven for everything they've ever done or not done, even Murph, that K Dot and I both need to get laid by someone we feel happy to wake up with, and, finally, that we'll be best friends forever. We don't actually say this last part, but let's face it, I've hung out with

K Dot for thirty years, and will never know anyone I'm so relaxed around, can say absolutely anything to, unless Santa Claus, the Easter Bunny, and fairy tales are all true and I can find the perfect wife.

Shit, he's such a good buddy that he neither mentions Clipper nor skirts around her when we're talking about women, though her presence is palpable in the conversation, just as she's been looming larger in my mind the whole time the band has been working its way down the state. Besides Katherine, the woman I met after the Sacramento show, I don't think I've spoken more than two sentences to anyone I was truly interested in—as opposed to just lusting after—the entire tour. Which can make a guy pretty lonely. And with Katherine, two sentences was about it.

I can picture K Dot and myself sitting on exactly the same sort of terrace twenty years from now, him doing scores for Hollywood movies, me doing whatever, maybe both of us wearing sportcoats. We'd remind ourselves not to drink more than one or two, then show pictures of our kids, straining to hear each other. And maybe, just maybe, we'd find a way to act even more serious and mature than we've already suddenly become.

We're pretty buzzed by the time we leave, but it's just a head buzz, not real drunkenness, so we grab a cab and head for Hollywood Boulevard, which is a lot farther from Rodeo Drive than it always seems it should be, even when the taxi doesn't take long-cuts and chisel you. We tell ourselves we'll look for Walker and his crew, but since it's getting dark, they've already headed for the sound check.

Mann's Chinese Theatre and the whole Walk of Fame deal are incredibly clichéd and predictable sights to check out, but just the fact that so many tourists make this area one of the highlights of their trip makes it poignant to me. Plus the fact that so many of the stars who're enshrined there are dead now. The great Kinks song, "Celluloid Heroes," is ringing in my head. I am an American, for shit's sake, and if there's anyone Americans love, it's their movie stars.

185

20 | Cadence

HE FIRST SHOW GOES PERFECTLY, EXCEPT FOR ALL THE USUAL fuckups and miscues, the crap aficionados say makes live music superior and interesting and which those nutty Blood Cheetah fans diddle over when they're trading their thirtieth bootleg tape for somebody else's thirty-fifth. I manage not to drink at all before we go on, opting instead to split an enormous couple of joints with K Dot, which puts me in the absolute fucking pocket of highness, like the eight ball dropping in and no game ever went smoother. I swear, as many drugs as I've taken in my life, one of the reasons I've never considered myself an addict is that I get a shitload of pleasure from changing my selections around, switch-hitting, manipulating the batting order. One night coke, another pot. On rare occasions, something even stronger.

The music still sounds better when I'm baked than it does on just about anything else, especially the songs which I have to play a lot of free-form type leads on, plus all the piano stuff. I can literally see the notes, picture them in my mind half a dozen ways; as steps ascending and descending in an indefinite, astral void, or as a woman dancing, moves I can imagine but could never do myself, or as my fingers themselves on the guitar neck, a close-up, or a giant rhythmic chessboard, or any one of a million other ways, each song having its own particular beautiful shape. I can even picture the level monitors lighting up out on Walker's boards, and all of the air molecules in between us, the fans breathing in and out, the arena shaking, pulsing into the atmosphere ever so slightly, tremors that might trigger the Big One, the earthquake of the century, or that may be fooling cows up in Oregon into acting like it's going to rain, plus a few imperceptibly high frequencies, which aliens will detect as radio waves in another galaxy a million years from now.

If I stare at Jay hard enough I can see that he's just a bunch of bones dancing around under his flesh, under his tattoos, a regular "Touch of Gray" video skeleton, especially now that Uncle Jerry is dead and I'm thinking about him more than I would have predicted, especially since I was never more than moderately a fan. But Jerry Garcia wasn't a tragedy. Rock 'n' roll didn't kill him, if anything, it kept him alive. That much at least was in his lyrics. I only hope the people around him choose wisely when they scatter his ashes.

Jay's skull protrudes under his tight, luminous skin, an effect increased by his receding hairline, and if I relax for a minute, the head of my guitar can be a skull as well, with six beady, deep-set eyeballs, spitting out at the audience. When I rake my pick across the guitar's tortured guts like a switchblade, the music spills out of its bowels. Which feels as good to me as it ever has.

Maybe the satisfaction that we've made it to L.A. and that L.A. is a huge milestone on this tour has put me in such a good mood. Suddenly I don't want to be a total waste product. The tour ending abruptly and all of us self-destructing is a lot more likely in L.A. than anywhere else, and therefore more acceptable. Who thinks of Bakersfield as a town that chews people up and spits them out? Just like Heartbreak Hill is where you want to brag about dying to all your buddies if you drop out of the Boston Marathon, which in turn makes it less likely to

187

actually happen there. But of course, true crises are never pre-dictable.

Having at least some knowledge of the area makes me more comfortable than I feel in most other cities, too, though a lot of people would say I've only seen a thin slice of the pie. (*You ain't never been, don't ever come, to the hood . . .*) Familiarity helps me lose the attitude that I can cut people off in traffic, go a week without a shower, or stare at fourteen-year-old girls, just because I'm a stranger in town and don't have any close friends here—so does the fact that we've played this hall before, probably to a lot of these same fans. I promise myself I'll buy a can of spray paint, climb as high into the rafters as I can squirm, and scrawl some cryptic message, like, *Only the Dizzy shall survive!* I've never written any song using plays on my own name or initials, but if I do, it might end up being my first rap: *I'm Dizzy, high as the whole sky, Dizzy, dazzled, razzled, no fool ain't foolin' me, Dizzy, up in your face, moving through space, the D, the D, the Z, so much more is me . . .* With a rhythmic background sample chant of *Hua!*

Being indoors for the next few shows also seems to have stabilized me, though I'm not sure why. It's not like I have an irrational fear of a sniper picking me off from a helicopter which comes zooming suddenly into range. But somehow a weight is lifted. I assume the shows aren't as important to the fans when we play indoors, no matter how stupid this is; that they resemble a casual dinner date, not the biggest, coolest, most-important night of the summer; and that the fans have congregated from local neighborhoods, like me walking over to see a show at the old Boston Garden, not traveling hundreds of miles.

There's definitely a psychological difference between playing to ten thousand fans and playing to fifty thousand, and there's also an acoustic difference between playing inside and playing outside. Unless an outdoor venue was created with big concerts exclusively in mind—say Great Woods, in Mansfield, Mass., instead of sports viewing, say Sullivan Stadium, in Foxboro—the sound ends up being crappy because it washes out over the crowd in strange ways, no matter how cleverly you arrange your speakers. Most seats in a stadium can only hear big, obvious sounds well, nothing too subtle, which is why it's always so tough to figure out what a band's saying in between songs. Unless they're screaming, "You're gonna die someday, so why not die tonight!" Of course, most of the indoor venues we end up playing present difficulties as well, from a booming reverberation that's nearly impossible to detect until someone points it out for you, at which point it becomes nearly impossible to ignore, even on the songs it could conceivably improve, such as "Howling" or "Picasso." It's like having a frat boy singing off key into your ear. But what are we supposed to do, play unplugged in a basketball arena when every kid there is screaming his head off, like he just got laid for the first time? (Think of Mark Hamill in *Corvette Summer*.)

189

One of my favorite touristy places to visit in Boston, when I need a long, contemplative walk, is the Christian Science Museum's "Maporium," a gigantic, perfectly spherical room, maybe thirty feet in diameter, that serves as an immense globe, with the oceans and continents lit up around the viewing public, who cross the inside of the sphere on a catwalk. The globe rebounds sound in fantastically freaky patterns; you might not be able to hear the person standing next to you, but you'll pick up someone whispering fifteen feet down the catwalk. My only problems with the joint are that it closes so early— that is, before 3 A.M.—and that it's always full of high-school kids on field trips. And unfortunately, after a visit or two, nobody I take there remains as enthralled as I am, which leaves me dependent on the high-school kids for voices to listen to the echoes of.

K Dot comes bouncing over about two-thirds of the way through the show. We've both been taking hits from joints between songs, maintaining our buzzes at Himalayan elevations, but we're trying to be subtle about it, not hold them too obviously, only letting the people in the stage wings and maybe the first fifty rows see what we're up to. Other than that, my eyes have been closed for most of the show.

"I'm fucking starving," he yells into my ear.

"So, go get something to eat!"

"What? Where?"

"Fuck the buffet! After this song just dive off the stage, run out to one of the concession stands and grab something! The audience will love it, and Murph will have a fucking coronary!"

"Do you have any money, in case they want me to pay?"

It's the perfect stunt because it was totally unplanned. Everyone with an aisle seat reaches out to touch him as he sprints past, their arms swinging like tentacles. In ten minutes he's scrambling back onto the stage with the aid of a beefy security guard, two cardboard trays cradled in his arms, one holding six beers in plastic cups and the other piled high with hot dogs. "Got 'em all for an autograph!"

190

Alex chows one of the hot dogs, but he's been working on a bottle of whiskey all night, so K Dot and I split the beers, cool and refreshing even though it's shitty Busch keg draft. Jay's too pissed-off at us to even acknowledge the interruption, although I'm sure we'll just about get our balls bitten off for it later, but Grover joins us in a dog. He really does have a better sense of humor than Jay. He tries to impale the wiener lengthwise with one of his drumsticks and eat it like corn on the cob, but it breaks apart.

"Kick it!" he yells, and starts flailing the drums again.

Two loaded hot dogs (most of the load winds up on my jeans) shave the edge off of my next-to-last-dance-with-Mary-Jane cravings, but I don't need any more food than that, because the yeast in the beer starts to expand the dogs. Pretty soon I'm thinking that maybe "one hot dog, one beer, one set of large intestines," is a good rule to keep in mind. But I've made a relatively effective midair, mid-concert switch from pot to alcohol, and while I don't look to Alex for his whiskey, I do signal for a stagehand to fetch more beer when K Dot and I run out, which is about five songs later. One of the nice things about the guitar and the piano both being two-handed instruments is that actually having to play slows my consumption down to about that of your typical war-party Hun. What riles me about the warrant being issued for me in Nevada is that over the last four or five days, I really have been making an effort to chill out, be cool, be calm, not self-destruct, not jump around for hours on end like a mental patient, then collapse and be out cold for ten hours, only to wake to a candy bar breakfast. Is it so wrong of me to suggest that if drugs ever are legalized, Coca-Cola's workforce will benefit, hiring extra people to start mixing cocaine back in? Picture huge vats and snow shovels. What *should* be illegal is for radio stations to play any rock song that's been sold for advertising purposes, say, the Stones' "Start Me Up," at least without a disclaimer, like: 12 MILLION BUCKS AND MICK JAGGER STILL GETS PAID EVERY TIME ONE OF YOU SAPS REQUESTS US ON THE RADIO!!! Bill Gates is so goddamn rich that people would've been happier if he'd paid twenty million to use the Stones tune, the same way tourists would be disappointed on Rodeo Drive if the Cole Haan store's most expensive shoes were only 175 bucks, not eleven hundred, those Nike-owned bastards.

You have to concentrate pretty hard to put on a great show, but I'm not even sure what a great show is anymore, except that the music has to be great. Should it consist of lyric, evocative, and tender renditions? Technically perfect duplications of what's already on our bestselling discs? Headlong speed and furious bombast? Extended solos, where we take turns showing off? Sometimes I'm still freaked out by the essential weirdness of, to misquote the Talking Heads, humans paying money to watch other humans make sounds. And don't even get me started on highway road crews. I rank on them as much as anyone when they're just standing around, but it's fascinating to watch how curiously catlike their attention is when the one guy working down in the hole unearths something interesting, all the other workers shuffling around, craning their necks, trying to get the best angle, blinking in the sun.

191

When I was younger, I thought the obvious solution was to be as physical and theatrical a guitar player as possible, à la Townshend, but now that I'm older I realize you've got to relax and be yourself, dance exactly as much or as little as your natural mood and unnatural buzz inspire. I mean, B. B. King could sit on a stool from now until monkeys play tennis on Pluto and no one would argue that he should be imitating M. C. Hammer. Forcing myself to be animated always backfires; my playing gets worse, not better. Sometimes I prefer to stand in one place for three or four songs in a row, rocking backward and forward, or bobbing up and down, this little rhythmic thing I learned from watching Michael Jackson, of all people. After a while, my self-consciousness fades away, and while I'm still concentrating and focused, the groove I work myself into frees me.

192

It's spooky how close this sensation is to the groove I used to fall into when I was still assembling parts back in my factory days. The only way I could endure that job was by cruising by on autopilot. I was so familiar with where the supply trays were that I worked by touch as much as by sight. The only thing that really breaks me out of it when I'm playing this way is when a fan screams something at exactly the correct wrong moment in the lull between songs, the type of outburst occasionally immortalized on live albums. Other times I'll jam on a song for ten minutes before I can solve a simple math problem.

Tonight what I'm thinking about when the pot and the booze are hitting me just right, before the booze totally overrules my clean, crisp buzz; when the hot dogs fill me perfectly but don't bloat me, and when the music is flowing out of me like life itself, first on guitar and then on the piano, is that I've already forgiven myself for calling Clipper after the show. Why not just admit it's what I want to do? I should be happy with myself whether I get along with her wonderfully or miserably, and in some ways, just understanding this is as satisfying as getting along with her wonderfully. If I've made it from being a useless Dorchester street puke to being a rich-bastard rock star, playing in front of all these goddamn fans, by being true to my own vision, by sheer force of will, not by all the bullshit the people around me would have recommended, then why the hell should I listen to what they'd tell me about relationships, either? To thine own fucking self be true, motherfucker! I've been promising myself for the last six weeks that I wouldn't call her when we got to L.A., the last six months, really, but I've known deep down that my resolution was a lie, a farce, about as realistic as promising to never urinate again.

As the band traveled south through the state, I told myself I'd go to exclusive movie-starish parties while we were in L.A., that I'd freefall into a mature, stable relationship, a woman whose intelligence (not notoriety) equals her beauty, only pulling my ripcord at the last instant, landing serenely. But who the hell wants to hook up with me in the short week that Blood Cheetah's here, me acting the way I always act, no time to really know me, me keeping the hours I always keep when we're on tour. Chances are good that even if I do receive any A-list invites, I'll be too exhausted and wired for any intelligent conversation, compensating with stupid stunts like pulling a Statue of Liberty. (Dip two fingers into a shot of Sambucca, hold them up like a torch, light them on fire, do the shot with your other hand, set the glass down, blow your fingers out.)

Besides, the only option other than calling Clipper is not calling her, and I know that if I don't call her, I'll keep waiting around for her after the shows, hoping she'll simply appear in the dressing room or at our hotel, which would really drive me nuts, especially as the week wore on and she continued to not show. So fuck trying to stay sober and fuck trying to get drunk on purpose. I keep drinking beer at the pace that feels natural. Also fuck Jay and what he thinks of me right now, the rest of the band as well. It'll all pass with time.

I'm not pissed off as we come off the stage, but I am determined. Murph and Annie both try to catch my eye as I brush past them, and Murph asks me some sort of stupid question, maybe hoping to gauge my mood by whether I scream in his

193

face or not, but even if I had time to waste, I'd rather leave them wondering. For all they know, I've had a monklike seizure of remorse, contrition, and need-to-sleep sobriety. I find Tubbs and Earl as quickly as possible. Although we've all come in on the same bus tonight, I insist that Tubbs shuttle me back to the hotel by myself. The others can wait, damn it. And while I do plan to sleep in my berth tonight, I have the hotel's night manager find a room for me, so I can use the phone in private. The hundred-dollar bill I slip him is for promising he'll swear he hasn't seen me.

21 | One, Nine Hundred

"WOULD YOU HAVE ANSWERED IF YOU KNEW IT WAS ME?" I ask.

"What?" Clipper says. "How original is that shit for this time of night? What time is it, anyway? Goddamn, what movie is that from?"

"What?"

Her voice is both hurried and kind of slurred, but the slurring doesn't sound like drunkenness, though I'm fairly drunk myself and am having trouble telling the difference. Probably she's just spaced out from being asleep. "That line's from a movie. Which one? *The Way We Were* or something?"

"I couldn't tell you who was in that, what decade it came out, or what it was about, so what the hell are you talking about?"

"You stole that line . . ."

"No, I didn't, and even if I did, I'm not sure I'd tell you where from. There wouldn't be anything wrong with it. Remember the line from Springsteen about all the movies we would go to?"

"You'll admit it later. You explain everything eventually," she says.

I take a sip of the red wine I've grabbed from the bus's pantry. "This is the hello I get after six months?"

"God, you're insane!"

"What's madness but nobility of soul at odds with circumstance? Someone famous said that—not me. Some other crazy guy."

"What time is it?" she asks.

"Only about one thirty. Not late at all."

I can hear her shuffling around in her bed, getting comfortable. I can imagine her tousled blond hair, always on the verge of becoming a bird's nest, and I can remember how small, smooth, and hand-friendly her buttocks are in the middle of the night. I can even picture how her apartment sits up on a hill above one of the freeways, close but not too close, the easy access making it seem like all of Hollywood is hers to trample over, which it isn't. That she hasn't hung up on me already is encouraging. Most important, it means that she and her great buns probably aren't lying there with some guy.

"So why are you calling me, Dizzy?"

"To see if for once you'd remember to call me Dillinger."

"God, that's so queer," she exclaims. "I can't believe I'm lying here at this time of night having this conversation. I have a shoot tomorrow."

"What do you want me to say? Maybe the quality of someone's life can be measured by how stupid their conversations can afford to be. You know people over in Bosnia right now aren't arguing about how stupid their conversations are, they're arguing about whether it's better to hide in the basement or behind some trees when shells fall."

"Dizzy, what do you want?"

"Duh. I wanna wake you up. I wanna hold your hand. I wanna go sprinting through the mean streets of South Central without getting shot, and then sweep you up in a sprinting-through-the-fields-to-catch-you-up-in-my-arms *Little House on the Prairie*-style reunion. *Is now and ever shall be, World without end . . .*"

There's less perturbation in her voice. "You really are insane."

"So?"

"So why are you calling me? We said we wouldn't until the tour was over."

I may indeed be crazy, and I may be drinking, but I'm not stupid. Clipper needs knuckleballs. I tell myself to keep my verbal wildness under control, because unlike Murph and the other guys in the band, she doesn't have to stand in there. No spitballs, hanging curves, or fastballs to the head, just something she thinks she can keep her eye on. Which is why I'm trying to speak with animation and playfulness in my voice, but not too much. I don't mind getting hung up on, but I want to see it coming, and to have made at least one or two points she'll think about later, instead of just lying in her bed harumphing, like she's gotten the best of me again. This is a conversation I've been thinking about since last winter.

"I called just to see how you are. Say hello, what's up—whatever."

"Okay, you've done that . . ."

"Goddamn, Clipper, why do you have to be such a bitch?" I blurt out. Then add, more gently, "I mean, why do you have to be so obstinate? Hey, did I tell you that they've issued a warrant for me in the state of Nevada?"

"Are you calling me because you're sick of bailing yourself out?"

"Hey, that's pretty good. That's like, I don't know, advanced obstinacy or something. *A,E,I,O,U* . . ."

"Are you going to apologize for calling me a bitch?" she asks.

For once I don't go running off at the mouth, because one of my long, Dizzyesque, rambling, ramshackle lines would just be a way of glossing over my feelings, holding myself aloof from her for another six months, wound me as she might. I go the simple, honest route instead. "Yes, I'm sorry."

"Thanks."

"You're welcome. I wouldn't want to have you bitching about that all night, would I?"

"Aaaaaaaaargh!"

I'm laughing fairly hard at this, and it's an honest laugh, too, not one I'm faking because I know I've actually said something terrible. This is just how things work with Clipper. We've only been talking for two minutes and we're already back to the end of the conversation we had last January. Even ignoring the fact that Blood Cheetah is in L.A. was probably a ploy of hers, whether she came up with it consciously or not.

"You know we're in town now, right?" I ask. "And that we played a show tonight."

"Of course I do. It's been on every radio station for the last two months. Why aren't you off partying with the guys somewhere, and trying to pick up groupies. That Jay, he's a regular Charlie Sheen."

198

"The show was all right and I'm not off with the guys because I'm here talking to you. The show was just averagely great, I guess. I'll have to talk to Walker to find out, he's usually the best judge. I hardly remember any of it now. I swear I still don't know what makes a good show. The concert I enjoyed seeing the most myself was one night in December a bunch of years ago when Alex dragged me out on the spur of the moment to scalp tickets for a Squeeze show at the Orpheum. I was only wearing this big heavy Alpaca sweater, and after the show it started snowing. It wasn't like the band was all that special that night. But I was totally happy as we walked back to my apartment."

"Squeeze always reminds me of INXS," Clipper says. "But I guess their music isn't too much alike."

"Plus the fact that INXS is Australian and Squeeze is British."

"Maybe that's it. Australians always remind me of people from England, except that they're more likely to tell dirty jokes. Isn't Nicole Kidman great?"

"Yeah, she's a regular Emma Thompson."

"Isn't she American?"

"Whatever," I mumble. What I want to say is, "Baby, you've got just about enough brains to hurt yourself."

Neither of us speaks for twenty or thirty seconds, which is a short eternity. We're considering how much honesty and bloodletting we each need, or at least I am. I'm also already wondering if this call was a mistake. Hell, I'm sure it was. But some mistakes have to be made, whether you see them coming or not. I don't really care what her plans are for the next few days, so long as they don't include marrying some hot young movie star, or even some hot old movie star, for that matter.

"So, tell the truth . . ." she starts in.

"Why wouldn't I tell the truth?"

"Because you might lie."

"That's no answer. What kind of answer is that?"

"Well, what was the question?"

"The question was why would I lie?"

Now she's flustered, and starting to get upset. "How the hell should I know why you would lie, you're the one lying. You're always twisting everything I say around. No wonder we always got into fights. Maybe you should be the one to tell me why you'd lie. I'm not the one who called someone up in the middle of the night and started accusing them of lying."

"Neither am I, you're the one who mentioned lying first."

"Oh, goddamn it, Dizzy, next you're gonna accuse me of being the one to mention fighting first, too, right? When you're the one who called me up. Goddamn, you're an asshole sometimes!"

"Hey, didn't I just apologize for calling you a bitch?"

"So?"

"Well . . . ?"

"Oh, so now I have to apologize, too? So that I'm the bad guy and you can say whatever the fuck you want? Well, shit, you can hang up right now if that's what you're looking for."

"I thought you might want to be the one to hang up," I say.

"I wouldn't give you the satisfaction!"

The conversation holds some interest for me again. I'm

smiling from ear to deaf ear at the irony of her resolution, though I make sure not to laugh out loud. I almost could hang up on her right now, and probably should, if only to get her that much more pissed off and emotional and attached to me. Or if not attached to me, at least curious about my next move. I take a large swig of wine.

"So what were you going to ask me?" I say.

"What? When?"

"A minute ago. You were about to ask me something, right before you went flying off on that wild tangent like a wounded duck."

"God, you really are an asshole, aren't you?"

"Maybe, but at least I'm interesting. The worst thing in the world is to be boring. I'd rather be even less attractive physically than I already am, than have people yawning when I talked. Holding chairs up to tame me like an enormous bloodthirsty cheetah or diving for cover is more like it. Having them duct-taping tape recorders to my forehead, because every single motherfucking word I say can be used against me in a court of law, is better than having them think, Oh well, Dizzy's talking now, and I can zone out and think about what color to paint my toenails. So there!"

"I thought you wanted to be called Dillinger."

"*You can call me Pal . . . Call me anytime you're feeling blue* . . . I only want *you* to call me Dillinger. Whew, this wine is making me kind of giggly. We had a band meeting yesterday and I was laughing so hard that if Murph had made me lick his shoes, it would've just cracked me up even more. God, I wish you were here to split this bottle with me."

"That's it!" Clipper squeals. "That's what I was going to ask. How much have you drunk tonight, and have there been any extracurriculars?"

"Now why would I lie about that?"

"Dizzy, don't start with me . . ."

". . . or I'll have to hang up on you."

"You will, not me."

"Right."

"Right. Whatever."

"Don't you know me well enough by now to tell?" I ask. "Maybe I'm just an idiot, but I've always assumed that when people are together for a long time as a couple, they learn to pick up on each other's cues almost instantaneously, like being able to tell just from one another's face if they had a bad day. You should know just by the trembling timbre of my voice that I've got a pretty serious buzz on, but nothing else, certainly no coke or crank or anything, especially since you're probably sober. I got high during the show, but it's gone now. Maybe in another five years you'll be able to tell just from the way I'm talking whether my wine is white, red, or rosé."

A long pause on the other end, a pause equivalent to her frowning at me sadly and disappointedly.

"What did I say?" I ask.

"Five years, Dizzy?"

"So, five years, so what? What about five years?"

"Nothing, never mind."

"What?"

She sighs. "If you really don't know what I'm talking about, then you must be pretty drunk, or else we're both like, totally hopeless."

"Yeah, I know what you mean," I admit, my voice dropping and becoming more intimate, because it really is both of us who have a lot of levels we need to break through. "You mean that I'm saying five years like I automatically assume we'll still be together in five years, or have any sort of relationship at all, which isn't necessarily what you're thinking. Hell, you probably won't want to have anything to do with me in five years."

"I didn't say that, you did."

"But you thought it, didn't you?"

"Do you really want me to answer that?"

I sigh myself, maybe overacting a bit, then I take a huge gulp of wine. Having called her was as big a waste as everything else in my life. "No, you don't have to, although in the

end, it wouldn't matter whether you said yes or no. It's like
. . . well, are you seeing anyone right now?"

"Not really."

"See, it's like that. Maybe you're telling the whole truth and
nothing but the truth, and maybe you're stretching the truth
to spare my drunken feelings. But we both know you would
let yourself fall into another relationship, if you met someone
you liked."

"Oh, all I meet is arrogant asshole photographers and jerks
who think that just because they've got some chest muscles,
they'll be the next Arnold."

"Yeah, but . . . that's not what I mean."

"Don't make yourself crazy over me, Dizzy. It's bad enough
for me when I make myself crazy over you."

"I try not to. But one of my three rules in life, of which I
have about fifty, is that you're always hung up on your last
great love until you find someone else to be more obsessed
with and more in love with."

Clipper chuckles, and instantly the whole conversation ligh-
tens up. "So you're not seeing anyone else either, huh?"

"The only person whose arms I've been in lately was Tubbs,
and he was carrying me."

"You haven't even been on any dates?"

This reminds me of Katherine. I *wish* I'd been on a date with
her. "Who the hell do I meet when I'm touring? Groupies and
eighteen-year-old chicks who're looking more and more like
one of my nieces. None of them would pay any attention to
me if I wasn't in a goddamn band. Probably the next woman
who spends half as much time with me as you have, I'll try to
marry."

"So, is that why you really called me tonight?"

"Yeah, I guess it is. It was easier to call you than to keep
getting totally nervous about whether I'd see you while we
were in town or not. What if you just showed up at one of the
shows with some Hollywood mogul on your arm?"

"I wouldn't do that unless you gave me a reason to."

It kills me when she says things like this. I swear half the reason I've stayed so intrigued by her is that her greatest evil coincides so effortlessly with her greatest naïveté. "Well, just imagine how you'd feel if you were bicycling down the board-walk and saw me strolling on the Santa Monica Pier with my arm wrapped around some babe."

"That would suck."

"So, will I see you at one of the shows?"

"I don't know, I'll have to see how busy I am. You'd be proud of how much I've been working. Can you get me in?"

"Who are you, Madonna's father? Just show up at the em-ployee entrance and tell them who you are. I'll throw a fit, scream at Murph in public, and get the word out. Will you eat with me before?"

Her pause is just long enough to be noticeable. "I'm not sure that would be such a good idea. I'm not even sure what night I'll come, if I come . . ."

She continues to explain about her busy schedule for longer than either of us needs, then I ask if I can call her again in a day or two, though my heart isn't in it anymore. Sometimes the more you drink, the more sober you feel. We're like two cars that have passed on a highway and have no idea how quickly the distance between them is mounting, they only re-member the flash of being next to each other. After we hang up, I can imagine her getting out of bed, using the toilet, then inspecting her face in the vanity mirror for about fifteen minutes. She's lucky I don't call a taxi and head over there. If she's trying to picture me, she probably doesn't guess what I do next, which is to pull as long a drink from the wine bottle as I can endure, finishing all but roughly a third of it. Then I cork it and hurl it violently against the wall, where it smashes into a few large fragments and dozens of smaller shards, the wine staining the white wall in an interesting, Rorschach ink-blot pattern.

Or maybe she could guess that.

22 | Nobody Ever Dies

WAKE UP IN MY BERTH A FEW MINUTES AFTER HIGH NOON, AND stagger up to K Dot's room to grab a shower. K Dot's sitting up in the bed, his back against the wall, with the bedroom door open, a groupie lying under the sheets next to his legs, while Grover is dancing around the kitchenette area with another young woman, waltzing with her to no music. Since he rarely drinks, he usually has the most energy of any of us in the morning. He's in the middle of a heroic tale, shouting to K Dot.

"Well, I'll tell you, I thought having the taxi wait for us was just Cindy's way of telling me I couldn't seduce her right there on the beach, but it turned out to be the best thing that happened, didn't it, honey?"

Grover sees me come in, flashes a wildly overblown Face-of-Astonishment expression, and tries to spin the girl around, into his arms. "There we were, sliding into home base, because without some scoring it's no fun as a game, is it? There we were, and sand flying everywhere, when suddenly, boom! Flashlights all around us, police dogs woofing inches from our faces, and an umpire calling, 'You're out!' Or something to that effect, right, honey? Well, they questioned both of us, frisked both of us. Luckily my only weapon was gone by then. We thought we were going to be busted for indecent exposure, disorderly conduct, and public intoxication all rolled into one. But, and here's the important part, since we had the taxi waiting, the cops had an easy way to get rid of us. They didn't want to bother arresting us, once they realized we weren't going to argue with them, resist arrest, hassle them, try to escape, or even give them fake names. Nothing bums cops out more than when you do everything they say, because then they can't show you what tough guys they are."

The girl tries to kiss Grover on the neck even as he's yelling to K Dot and me. She probably looked better last night than she does right now, but she looks all right now anyhow, is at least thin enough and young enough. Her blond hair gives her the artificial, looks-good-at-fifty-feet sexiness some men lose their heads over, but up close, I'm reminded of my rule that only four women in the whole world look better with dye jobs than their natural color. Unfortunately, nobody knows who they are.

"The one cop," she exclaims, "he was a pig!"

Grover cracks up. "Yeah, this one guy, I swear he wouldn't have accosted us until we were done, if it was up to him. He wanted to watch. He was the type of guy who if they had him out there on patrol alone, he'd get a pair of night vision binoculars so he could watch people screw, then jerk off into the sand."

"Hey, that's gross," the girl chastises.

K Dot's conquest mumbles something as well, but I can't make out her words. She climbs out of the bed on the opposite side, wrapping a sheet around herself as she stands, without letting us get a good look at her, and heads for the bathroom. The suite already looks like K Dot has been living here for a month, with scattered clothes, bottles and plates, magazines, suitcases, shoes, envelopes, drinking glasses, and purses. After a week, it'll look like movie mobsters have ransacked the place.

"Murph's pretty mad at you," K Dot tells me.

"What for now? I didn't do anything."

"For disappearing like that."

"Hey, I'm not the one who almost ended up busted again."

Grover howls with laughter at this. He kisses the girl, then waltzes her over closer to where I'm standing. "We should have a contest to see who can go the longest without getting arrested. How about ten dollars a day, starting right now? You get arrested, you pay up."

"That's no good. After three or four months I'd start to feel the pressure and do something stupid on purpose, just to get it over with. How about a grand, straight up?"

"Okay, and a case of Samuel Adams cream stout. K Dot, you in?"

"Sure."

"Last one to get busted gets the whole pot." Grover kisses his girl. "Then it's settled. Cindy'll be our witness. Let's just hope it doesn't take too long. It could be years. Dizzy's current trouble up in Nevada doesn't count, of course. Let's hope they decide to pin the O. J. murders on K Dot and his secret accomplice."

"Where did you go last night, anyway?" K Dot asks me.

"I just needed some time to myself."

"You called Clipper, didn't you?"

My blush is already spreading. "Yeah, after a while."

"Just think, you could have split a taxi with Alex."

Grover guffaws. "Aw, man, that's cold. That's a called third strike."

K Dot's girl is taking an awfully long time in the bathroom. When we hear the shower turn on, the rest of us know we're in for a haul, so we order burgers, fries, and milkshakes from room service. Expensive hotels are about the best place left to get a shake, because they use real ingredients and they'll usually listen to exactly how you want them concocted, like fifty percent strawberries, fifty percent vanilla ice cream, whipped for the entire time it takes to cook a burger. We turn the television on, but don't pay any attention to it. I feel a little better after we eat, and even better yet when I finally get into the shower. I can already taste how good my shake would have been if it contained fudge, caramel, Kahlúa, and Godiva instead of strawberries. But I know I should I go back to my berth for a nap. Tonight is an off night, no show, so I promise myself that if I get back up in time, I'll have some dinner, then spend a few hours browsing through a late-night bookstore.

As I'm leaving the room, however, K Dot pulls me aside. "Hey, we're going to a party later. If you're in, meet us here around nine. Don't mention it to Jay, Murph, or Annie. Maybe not even to Walker, if you see him."

"Do the girls have any friends?"

"Friends? Shit, it's gonna be tough enough getting rid of the two of them."

K Dot's right, of course, and when I return to his room later, the girls are still hanging around. The one he spent last night with is named Dutch, and, unlike Cindy, she really does qualify as a groupie. I've seen her at dozens of our shows, and am embarrassed not to have recognized her earlier. I've had some pretty long conversations with her in the past, though I don't remember what any of them were about. I don't even remember why we nicknamed her Dutch, maybe for that persistent little bastard Dutch Kincaid, from a *Cheers* episode. I'm probably the only guy in the band she hasn't slept with, and that's just luck of the draw. It's also blind chance that Jay and Alex aren't here, too; our intergroup alliances have shifted again, that's all. Maybe tomorrow night two or three of the guys will be busy excluding me from something. For some reason, Grover has asked Tubbs and Earl the Pearl to come along. We're taking a limo, and I think he likes the sense of security an entourage gives us. *Let's go, let's go, let's go right now . . .*

Both Tubbs and Earl are dressed better than K Dot, Grover, and me, in pressed slacks, shined leather shoes, white dress shirts and ties. As we pile into the limo, I make some remark about them getting into the party easier than we will.

"Aw, you look fine, Mac, at least for you," Tubbs says.

207

This gets a good laugh from everybody, then there are more laughs as Dutch produces a bong and a bag of weed so large a couple sheets of velvet could disguise it as a travel pillow. I'm always amazed at how incredibly quickly some people, especially women, start acting like they've known the guys in the band their whole lives. Cindy's whispering sweet little nothings into Grover's ear the instant we start driving.

The party is in an area K Dot keeps referring to as Hidden Hills, which sounds like a cool name to me, maybe even a good title for a song, especially if you're an Indian, but I've never heard of it. Tubbs keep promising I can look at his atlas later. Our entrance is as awkward and obvious as if K Dot and I had shown up at a football-team-only party back in high school. Right as I go in the door, which is definitely to a house, not to a club or a hall or even an apartment, I turn to K Dot, still holding the twenty-four-ounce mudslide milkshake that I personally had gone to the hotel's kitchen to supervise the alchemy of, and whisper, "Who's throwing this shindig, anyway?"

"Juliette Bracer."

"Who?"

"You know, she's in that sitcom, *The Man with the Itchy Beard.*"

This factoid gives me a sliver of comfort, as does the notion that other celebrities may show up, though hopefully nobody too outrageously legendary. But what helps the most is knowing that to most people, I'm a rock star from whom you can expect outrageous, socially questionable, don't-try-this-at-home behavior, which gives me a whole banana bunch of freedom. I only wish we'd shown up later, say twelve fifteen, because ten o'clock makes it seem like we didn't have anywhere better to start out.

"Where's the girl with the itchy beard?" I yell.

Juliette Bracer is indeed bracing: tan (tantastic!), tall, curvy, smiling, toothy, brunette, with strong and intelligent eyebrows, understanding eyes. As soon as she greets us, I realize she actually is intelligent and understanding. One nice thing about Hollywood is that, despite all the bullshit you hear, any prolonged success requires a fair amount of sophistication. She rebuffs me gently for my itchy beard wisecrack, then points out the general parts of the house—kitchen with food and booze, living room with boring people talking too stuffily, entertainment basement with conspicuously loud music and no dancing yet. The whole scene reminds me a little of Jay's house. Unfortunately, Juliette's paying far more attention to K Dot than to the rest of us. I can't stop wondering how they know each other without him coming bragging to me about it.

I'm still kind of anxious as Juliette goes to greet some new arrivals, and I'm also stuck in the role of Public Dizzy (*I'm coming for your mothers, I'm coming for your kids . . .*), so my brilliant reaction is to grab a bottle of Cuervo and a handful of tumbler glasses from the bar, head for the living room, and start cajoling people into shots. Tequila is not a very good mix with my huge Kahlúa-based milkshake, but these folks need some serious lightening up, so once again I sacrifice myself for the greater good of a party.

"Hey, come on, it's not like you're paying for these!" I shout. "Aren't you Hollywood liberals willing to do your part for NAFTA? I have an uncle named Jose and he's a great guy. It's just water mixed with fermented cactus juice!"

Tubbs and Earl the Pearl volunteer first, followed by a woman named Fiona, Juliette's sitcom sidekick. Then suddenly, spontaneously, all the straitlaced (certainly not PCP-laced) guys in the room start clamoring for a shot of their own, because, say what you will, call me a racist if you have to, nothing goads stiff white-collar white males into false-machismo drinking as quickly as watching a woman they'd love to bed sucking booze back with a couple of big black guys. I have to assume these are primarily network guys, ad men, and executives. To their credit, Tubbs and Earl don't even look like our bus drivers tonight. They could play it cool, tell the other guests they were anything from backup horn players to astronauts, and I wouldn't be the one to fink.

209

"Hey, let me have one of those!"

"Don't take it too easy on me! And one for my friend here."

Proving once again that if you can fix any machine with a pair of vice grips, a roll of duct tape, and a can of WD-40, especially if you're wearing a pair of Chuck Taylors and your name is Walker, you can jumpstart any social gathering with a good sheen of the Mexican joy-juice. Sometimes cocaine works even better, but it can also backfire and get you kicked out of a party, especially if the hostess doesn't know you very well. When Fiona grabs the bottle from me and dubs herself tonight's "serving wench," I'm free to explore the house a little more. Plenty of people have flushed in by now, and when I go down to the cellar, a few are dancing to Montel Jordan (*This Is How We Do It . . .*). I place my milkshake on a fake fireplace mantel, telling myself I should slow down anyhow, then I step out onto the floor and start boogying gently in one spot, not trying any moves too fancy yet.

210

A brunette of maybe twenty-five or twenty-six comes dancing over and shouts in my ear. "It's too bad about the kid!"

"What?"

"I said it's terrible about the kid!"

"What kid?"

"You're David Zimmerman, right?"

"Yeah, sure."

"Hi, I'm Justine Bracer, Juliette's sister." She offers her hand, we shake, then an unpleasant mix of consternation and embarrassment flashes across her face. "Oh God, you haven't heard yet, have you? God, I'm sorry!"

"What in the Sam Hell are you talking about?!" I ask delicately.

She leads me into a corner by the elbow. "You really haven't heard yet? Well, maybe it's nothing, but I heard on the radio today that a kid got killed last night because he wouldn't fork over a pair of Blood Cheetah tickets. Hopefully I'm wrong, though. Hopefully it's a mistake or a hoax or something. My sister's the only person who was here earlier who'd heard anything about it."

"And what did she say?"

"Just that she'd heard a quick news blip on WTTR, and that there was the possibility some sort of ritual was involved."

"I'm sure it's just a sick joke someone's spreading," I assure her. "I mean, that's just crazy. It's a sick rumor."

"It's sick either way."

Luckily, Blood Cheetah has inspired stories like this before, or like the Phil Collins drowning story, even death threats against Jay once. Justine and I slide back onto the floor and start dancing again, casually and haphazardly together, like ducks. How earnestly she believes the tale leaves me certain that her sister, Juliette, who I assume is the older of the pair, is playing a practical joke on her, knowing that K Dot and maybe some of the other guys from Blood Cheetah were coming tonight. I make a mental note to ask Juliette about it later, then promptly space it. If I can't remember a lot of things I actually have done, how the hell can you hold me accountable for things I've only planned to do? Especially with several drinks in me, several bong hits in me, and a woman dancing near me, for shit's sake. *John, I'm Only Dancing . . .*

It kills me that when you meet a woman and think she's attractive, having an even better-looking sister renders her instantly a bowser, way more than just having a gorgeous best friend would. This is the syndrome I'm suffering through now, dancing downstairs with Justine but imagining Juliette upstairs. She's probably up there making radiantly clever jokes, celebrating the end of a good summer. But I know she's also someone I shouldn't get too fixated on, at least not until we've had, say, an actual conversation.

Refined, genetically superior cheekbones appear to be a common denominator in this crowd, and more so by the minute. I wonder how many of them I should recognize from other sitcoms or from movies. The house is furnished well, but not extravagantly, and I realize it isn't all that large, certainly isn't an estate, perhaps proving that it's only the lead cast members in the top, established shows who're raking in dough hand over fist. When I get a chance, I break away from dancing with Justine, showing her my huge mudslide glass and making a joke about raising her sister's bar bill to mortgage levels. Secretly I'm wondering what substance abuse I might find in the bathroom or one of the bedrooms.

Grover is the first person I run into upstairs.

"Hey, how's it going?" I ask.

He's maybe ninety-three on a scale of one hundred for drunkenness, which is rare for him, and he's incredibly wound up. He practically shouts into my ear. "Whew, good. No time to talk, no time to balk. Hey, that's a pretty good rhyme, just in time. K Dot's in a killer pickle, and I'm loving watching it. Apparently he thinks he can bag our illustrious hostess, so he flirts with her whenever he gets a chance, as does a guy in the corner in the blue blazer, don't look now. None of which is making Miss Dutch happy. But K Dot keeps getting madder and madder at me, because apparently I was supposed to assist him in a big double ditch of Dutch and Cindy earlier. Whew!"

"That sucks!"

"And you know what else? I'm glad. Hell, I'm not even sick of Cindy yet. She's in the bathroom right now. Why pull your pitcher if he's still throwing strikes? Only in this case, he's a she. God, am I drunk! I gotta go dance for a while, see ya."

It's been longer since I really partied with Grover than I realized. He's turning back into a rookie. I'm happy the only music upstairs is what's echoing up from downstairs, since one of my pet peeves in life is constantly not being able to understand what people are saying, but pretending I can anyhow. A few of the folks in the living room nod in my direction, or say hello as I pass, but the graft of a conversation doesn't take with any of them, so I head for the kitchen, thinking maybe a little food would be wise before another drink. And who should be standing there, talking with Juliette and K Dot, and Dutch, but Clipper.

"And here he is," Juliette announces.

"Holy shit, what the fuck are you doing here," I say.

"That's some greeting."

"And that's some hairdo."

"The shoot only ended a little while ago." Clipper leans over to kiss me on the cheek. "I didn't even know if I should come over, because I'm exhausted. But I thought, well, I probably better, just in case the Brace has been guaranteeing people I'll show."

Juliette punches her on the arm. "Don't call me that!"

"How do you two know each other?"

Now Clipper punches me on the arm, which I don't feel. Mike Tyson could be hitting me and I'd barely notice it, I'm so surprised. "Don't you remember? She used to work for the Jareau Agency also. Before she got her show. I swear I introduced you years ago. God, you're forgetful!"

"Oh," I mumble. "Yeah. The Jareau Agency, the twenty-four hour ATM of modeling. They should just call it Girl Bank."

"Dizzy . . ."

Someone calls Juliette from the other room, then Dutch does me the jumbo favor of asking if anyone needs another drink, dragging a reluctant K Dot with her. His ability to watch other people's awkward moments without feeling at all awkward himself is truly world class.

I hand Dutch my glass. "As big a mudslide as you can manage without running everybody else out. K Dot knows what ratios I like."

"Yeah, less milk than a mother mole's tit."

When we're alone, Clipper says, "You don't seem as happy to see me as I thought you would."

"Well, it's a shock, more than anything, that's all."

"Didn't you want to see me? Isn't that what you said last night?"

"Last night I knew you'd say no."

"What? What the hell kind of sense does that make?"

She looks gorgeous, in a pair of old Levi's that hang around her ass and crotch just right, good leather shoes, and a beautifully oversized patterned silk shirt, her face scrubbed clean

213

of all makeup, her hair falling wherever it will. But I'm not staring at her, I'm already glancing around for that goddamn drink Dutch was going to make me.

"It makes every kind of sense. I called you last night to ask if I could see you. I wanted to make sure I knew whether I would see you or not, and to try to guarantee it wouldn't be a surprise somewhere, like it is here."

"I wasn't even sure you'd be here," she says. "All I told Juliette was that Blood Cheetah was in town and that maybe she should try and contact you guys. I wanted it to be a surprise."

"Honey, a man in my condition, I know this sounds really pathetic, but I don't need any surprises."

Now she's getting frustrated. Both of her fists are clenched and she's leaning forward. "Why the hell not?"

"Because things are so unsettled with us right now. Because if we're both at a party, I want to know whether we're there together and will leave together. Because maybe I'm a jealous bastard and maybe I'm still really fucked up about you. I certainly don't want to stand around watching you talk to other guys all night when I know that at the end of the night, I won't be going home with you."

"What are you accusing me of?" she demands.

"I'm not accusing you of anything. This is all hypothetical."

"Oh, hypothetical this, you asshole!"

If I could James Bond my whole life away, always be as perfectly smooth, imperturbable, and regal as I am when I take her by the arm, guide her through the living room, then out the front door and onto the lawn, life would be cool indeed. Dutch, who's approaching with my drink, hands it to me as we pass, like a quarterback dishing off to a running back.

"I'm gonna leave," I tell Clipper.

"Why?"

"Will you go with me?"

She nearly cackles. "Yeah, when monkeys fly out my butt!"

"What movie is that from?"

"God, you're insane!"

"Either way, I'm out of here."

"Why? Can't you at least tell me that?"

I'm already thirty feet across the perfectly manicured grass, but I turn and give her one last chance, stupidly hoping that just sounding serious and really meaning what I say will make her understand. "Because I can't stay here with you, and I can't stay here without you, and I can't leave here after you do."

"I assume you'll call me."

"Sooner or later, yeah."

Then I turn and jog across the lawn toward the street, holding my drink out to one side so it doesn't slop onto me as it spills over the edges of the glass. Our driver sees me coming, but I'm into the back of the limo before he can even get his door open.

23 | Flight

"WHERE TO, SIR?"

"Any highway." (*Heading Out to the Highway . . .*)

K Dot's going to get pissed at me for stealing so many limos, buses, etcetera, but what I'm thinking right now is fuck K Dot, the fat load probably planned Clipper's appearance. He didn't plan it, of course, and definitely won't end up taking heat for the way things worked out between me and her, but he certainly could have warned me about whose party we were heading to, the dumb shit, and who might show up, which would have decreased the surprise I just got so angry at Clipper for creating. It probably wasn't even stupidity, just an oversight caused by his own insobriety and blinding personal goals, like bagging a working actress. After all these years, I still picture the two of us as buddy-buddy tough guys in an action flick, where the one rule is that no matter how nasty a firefight is going to be, the one dragging them into it describes the danger, tries to dissuade the friend who'd fucking die for him. Listen Dizzy, it'll be a mess in there tonight. Lots of booze, lots of babes trying to look good, and lots of rich, attractive men trying to pick them up, which fucks their

heads up worse than any drug. That psycho bitch Clipper
may even show. You got a gut made of rocks and an ego
made of iron? You got what it takes to stand in there and
not flinch even if she gives some guy a blowjob right in
front of you? The starlet's younger sister, Justine? Hell,
you'll be lucky if you take her younger brother, Chuck,
home. Hell of a kid.

When I was in high school, I'd sit in class fantasizing about
different ways I could suddenly be rich and my life perfect.
The biggest of these was always making it in music, but there
were others as well, like burying myself in sand at Revere
Beach and discovering an ancient gunnysack of gold coins
from a sunken Spanish galleon. Or pegging a rock at a squirrel
and discovering my arm was magically strong enough to pitch
for the Red Sox. After a while, I'd get mad at myself for thinking about the same things over and over again, day in, day
out. I'd try to concentrate on getting my work done as efficiently as possible, saving up whatever surplus mental energy
and ambition I had for the times when it might actually do me
some good, like anywhere but school.

Now, riding along in the limo, I'm going through the same
sort of thing; telling myself not to get angry, though deep
down I'm absolutely furious, and telling myself not to take any
of this personally, though it all revolves around me, the person, the fucking drunk guy who can't stop drinking, who after
thirty-five years on this planet, isn't mature enough to handle
being around a woman he knows he shouldn't glance at with
any more interest than if she were a road map, let alone date.
Goddamn, motherfucker, shit piss fuck! I'm disgusted with the
whole tour, the whole fucking world, and especially with myself. And the worst part is that I can't stop thinking about any
of it, either by just ignoring the situation and counting, I don't
know, padiddles with the limo window down and the wind
in my face, or by hurting myself and making pain a substitute
for the problems I can't face up to; getting dropped in South
Central, taking a swing at a gang-banger, to see whether his
boyz beat the shit out of me until I die, or just until I nearly

die. Or finding a good rough-surfaced cement wall, maybe one of the sewer channels feeding the L.A. River, dry except for January and February, punching the concrete until my fist is a bloody, pulpy, sodden mess, red Jell-O with bone fragments poking out, never able to play guitar again, or requiring ten years to relearn it, leading to even greater triumphs, knowing what I'd lost. It's lucky there are no heights around, no skyscrapers with open-air observation decks, no electrical tower I can dare myself to climb, my hair crackling, no thousand-foot Route 1 cliffs I can tell the driver to pull over and let me tumble from, my body bouncing like a rag doll off the boulders before an endless Pacific plunge.

The problem with drugs isn't just how terrible they are for your body, but that they don't do the job as completely as I'd prefer. They're messy and imprecise, cutting through the sheer fabric of my psyche like a chainsaw, not a laser beam. I don't want something to dull the pain, to make me comfortably numb, like a huge rush of fucking smack would, I want something that'll cause total, instant, unavoidable shutdown of all brainilly functions, rendering me comatose for twenty-four hours, twenty-four days, twenty-four months, my subordinated mind absorbing and dealing with all the emotional bullshit of my last ten years, sorting and filing it, after which I'd wake up totally sober, no hangover at all, optimistic as the first day of spring, the first day when you smell the flowers, birdshit, and warm earth, my bloodstream pure as a babbling brook. But I don't even have any of Dutch's pot, and while limo driver can sometimes be a good cover for a drug connection, I'm not in the mood to ask the stiff up front. Some guys you can just read.

When you're old and decrepit, would you rather have your mind go first or your body? And if your mind goes first, do you want to know it and be able to apologize to people and worry so much that you make yourself even sicker, or be blissfully, painfully unaware, like a fish that doesn't realize the lake is drying up until it's flopping on its side in the mud? If I'm so unhappy, why don't I do something about it? Why the fuck

218

don't I? I've got the legal trouble in Nevada to worry about, to run from, try to avoid, but if I had any balls, I'd have the driver blast me up there right now. I could turn myself in at a state border sheriff's office, hands raised, repentant frown, to face whatever punishment they imposed, to actually beg the judge on my calcified knees for a ten-year sentence of hard labor, *breaking rock in the . . . hot sun . . .* because that's what it would take to straighten me out. Prison would be great. Prison would be an incredible learning experience, which I'd probably ruin by heading straight for a bar the second they released me. The only thing I couldn't handle in jail would be having to date big, burly men. The thought of that makes me cringe worse than an acid trip where it feels like bugs are crawling out of my skin.

I started this band and busted my goddamn ass like no maniac ever has for us to be where we are today, and if I mustered that determination, I should be strong enough to pull myself out of this fucking puke-filled, shit-strewn, piss-sopped mess, motherfucker, to reclaim my life and live happily and never give a shit about what anybody thinks. Fuck the band. There are huge sixty-thousand-seat stadiums out there, with all the fans on their feet chanting your name, the roar a hundred times what was ever heard in Rome in the Coliseum, the sound the most incredible power trip ever imagined; and there are women so hot, so sexual, breasts like pyramids, thighs like silk, willing to fulfill your every fantasy, that you start believing God's training you to take over the Universe someday; and there's so much fucking money that your idea of a good laugh is to test drive a Ferrari, then when the salesman asks if you'll take it, shout, "Hell, I'll take two!" But none of that has a goddamn thing to do with why I want to make music or with the moments I've truly lived for rock 'n' roll. So what if Blood Cheetah breaks up? So what if we never play a single note together again? The public can feel pretty sorry for rockers who aren't stars any more—look at all the Whatever Happened to? programs on VH1—but hopefully most retired superstars are smart enough to not want to be famous anymore. I swear I'd

219

rather play an acoustic set once or twice a week in a bar back in Boston, as long as I had time to write songs and the inspiration to write songs, than ever sign another autograph. Momentary public acclaim isn't the same thing as having a satisfying career.

Truly innovative and original musicians will develop a reputation in due time, just as the bands who everybody knows suck but buy anyhow will fade eventually. This is also why the whole idea of alternative rock is so incredibly, stupendously, monumentally ridiculous; what people usually mean by *alternative* is bands that aren't popular yet. And while I can relate to kids who're so pissed off, lonely, and frustrated that they need to identify with musicians nobody else listens to, I also know that if a band is any good, they'll get popular eventually, no matter how antiestablishment their attitude. It happened to the Stones, it happened to the Sex Pistols, to Pearl Jam. Pete Townshend summed up the whole phenomenon in seven words: *sadly ecstatic that their heroes are news...*

It only takes a fraction of a second for me to make up my mind.

"Hey, driver!" I yell.

His dark glass divider window rolls down with electronic hum. "The phone works as an intercom, sir."

"Yeah, fuck the intercom! Take me to the airport!"

"Glendale or Los Angeles International?"

"L.A.-fucking-X, baby!"

"Yes, sir."

Even Tubbs wasn't this polite when he was in his period of having just been hired and of still being scared to irritate anybody who might remotely influence his being canned.

The glass stays down for a second, until he realizes I'm not going to say—or scream—anything else, at which point it hums back up, leaving me to stare at a distorted black reflection of myself. The shadows on my face make me look a lot healthier than I feel. Immediately I wish he hadn't put the glass up, since it's always nice to talk to somebody and distract yourself when you're about to make a horrendous fucking mistake, especially when that person is in no position to make value judgments, has to sit and listen to you impartially, like a bartender somewhere other than your hometown. But it's too late to say anything now. Once I got busted at a party in Boston, thinking I was playing it super cool when the cops knocked on the door for a simple noise complaint. I totally forgot that I'd woven two fat joints into my hair, making them protrude so that I looked like the devil, and I swear the arresting officers ended up wondering if I was an Internal Affairs stoolie, I asked so many questions about what it was like to be a cop. One of them told me the worst calls were suicide interventions. Now, I'm thinking that limo driver might not be such a bad gig, especially if you're a struggling actor who needs every chance he can get to memorize lines.

When my oversize mudslide is gone, I pop open a bottle of Great Western from the wet bar, telling myself to enjoy it because maybe, just maybe, it'll be the last alcohol I ever drink, especially if it makes me feel really terrible in the morning. I imagine my liver looks like a sopping old decayed log, which disintegrates no matter how gently you try to roll it over, the bubbles from the champagne floating along in my bloodstream, ready to cause an embolism. Hell, I'm hungover already, even while I'm still drinking, so why not keep drinking, delaying the bulk of the aftermath? The doctors always say alcohol is alcohol, one beer equals one glass of wine equals one mixed drink, but I'm here to tell you, the other chemicals in whatever you're drinking affect you, too, so not all buzzes are created equal. The champagne doesn't make me feel nearly as sluggish and lethargic as the mudslide did. The anxiety of having made up my mind also gives me a lot of energy, and pretty soon my right leg is bouncing up and down like I was keeping time.

I can't believe how brightly lit LAX is this late at night, though maybe I'm just accustomed to the limo's darkness. The driver opens the door for me, as if he's planning to help me out, then he subtly yet persuasively stands in my way, and

221

asks if I'm almost done with the champagne. This cracks me up.

"Yeah, yeah, yeah. Half a bottle left. Here, maybe you even need the cork back."

He reaches into the limo and places the bottle back where it was. "Thank you."

I'm still chuckling softly as the two of us walk into the closest terminal together. After logging so many miles on the bus, flying again will seem like an adventure. I keep hoping to see a movie star red-eying in from New York City and maybe a Letterman appearance, or at least some Mafia-looking types, but I'm the only one here who isn't an overtired businessman, so the overtired businessmen shuffling through stare at me absentmindedly. I try to act as sober as possible, though the truth is that I don't know where I'm going yet. The driver follows me obediently but resignedly, a couple of yards off my right shoulder, like he's hoping people won't realize we're together, the asshole. Too bad I don't have any superheavy luggage for him to carry, or any bags at all, besides the black ones under my eyes. Too bad I can't always make everyone happy, the bastards. The driver follows me up to the nearest ticket booth, where I have an asinine conversation with a middle-aged female clerk.

"Where can you send me?"

"Well, where would you like to go?"

"Is that your slogan?"

"Excuse me?"

The driver leans forward. "Sir?"

I'm working so hard to act sober that I don't even turn my head. "When's your next flight to Boston?"

"Let me see . . ." Her fingers dance across her keyboard. "Not until eleven in the morning."

"Well, I didn't want to go there anyhow." Which is true, if only because it's not enough of a halfway, time-out type of escape. What am I going to do, hibernate in my apartment, crying maybe, and wait for either K Dot or Murph to think of calling there? "How about San Francisco?"

"Forty-five minutes. One way?"

I nod.

"That will be one hundred nine dollars and ninety-nine cents."

"Which way to the nearest ATM?"

The driver follows me there as well, which irritates me so much that instead of just tipping him and telling him to go back to the party, I insist on stumbling back out to the limo and finishing off the champagne while I wait to take off. Then I tip him two hundred dollars, make him swear up and down that he'll tell K Dot he dropped me off in front of our hotel, and tell him to go back to the party.

24 The San Fran Blues

AN FRANCISCO IN MY MIND HAS THE REPUTATION OF BEING clean, friendly, and safe, while it's her sister city Oakland that is evil and dirty, although these generalizations are probably as stupid, generalization-wise, as everything else I come up with. I'd hum that sixties flower song about going to San Fran and meeting groovy people, but I can't seem to remember who it was by, the title, or any of the lyrics. Memory lapse like a Florida sinkhole.

The only person I can think to call is Katherine Millis, and that's as crazy as any other part of this little adventure. Although I've been thinking about her off and on for the last week and a half, I really only met her that one time, at the post-concert party back in Sacramento. If nothing else, having a very distraught Dizzy Z call her at 4 A.M. may teach her not to have her number published in the phonebook, even without her address. For some reason, I hope she's a school marm, a first-grade teacher. It only takes her a minute to wake up and understand who she's talking with, but considerably longer to agree to take me in for the night, relenting only when

I beg and insist I've got nowhere else to go, that I'd literally pass out in the gutter without her.

She makes me promise she can handcuff me to the couch if I'm acting too drunk for her. I'm sober enough to translate that to dangerous. The address is on Jolsent, between nineteenth and twentieth. I tell her this is perfect, joking that my other option had been to just show up on her street and start searching door to door, but that I'd remembered the street name as Carson. Mostly I'm exhausted now, nearly falling over on the phone, nearly passing out in the taxi, and only getting a brief jolt of embarrassment-inspired adrenaline when the taxi drops me off. She comes down to let me in through a gated entrance, then leads me up to her second-floor apartment. Early indications are of no boyfriend or other significant other. She's barefoot, wearing jeans and a gray sweatshirt, bespectacled and disheveled, refusing to look me in the eye. She moves her coffee table, pulls her futon away from the living-room wall, slides it down from the couch position to the bed position, then hustles into one of the other rooms for a blanket. I realize that I've been cold for a long time, in just my T-shirt, but have been overlooking the discomfort.

"Want to talk now or tomorrow?" she asks.

"I'm sorry, I really am. God, you don't know. Is tomorrow all right?"

"Fine with me." She pulls a three-foot length of metal dog chain from her sweatshirt's pouch pocket, along with a pair of handcuffs. "All right, I warned you. Give me a wrist."

I'm wise enough not to beg her not to chain me up, and also not to make a crack about her having a tough time finding straight men in this city. She cuffs one of my wrists, loops the chain through the futon's thick wooden frame, and links the ends with the other cuff.

"Can you do me one last favor?" I ask, as she turns the lights out, headed for her room. "Please, please, please, please don't tell anyone I'm here. At least not until I can figure out *why* I'm here."

225

The glow from a streetlight illuminates her gentle smile. "Yeah, sure."

"Thanks."

After she closes her door, I use my free hand to remove my sandals and jeans, pull my shirt off except for my handcuffed wrist, and wrap myself up in the blanket. For the first night in a long time, I cry myself to sleep.

It only seems like a couple of hours later when Katherine gets up and showers. I have difficulty remembering how I got here, and little understanding of what I've done, except that it's serious this time. My bladder is so full I'm about to explode, and my mouth feels as dry and sticky as sandpaper. Just before she leaves for work, she unlocks the handcuffs.

"You'd better be here when I get back," she warns. "And if not, you'd better never pull this again."

"I'll be here."

When I return to the futon, mine is the restless, uneasy sleep of the viciously hungover, though having used the bathroom and then gulping down some orange juice helps. Katherine, Katherine, Katherine, what a beautiful and balanced name. I'm glad I remembered it. She returns a little after four in the afternoon, carrying a large satchel in one hand and a pizza box in the other, moving with the bustle of a competent young professional. She's dressed in brown silk pants, a white top, and a matching brown vest; kicks her shoes off at the door, looking incredibly vibrant and alive. Though her hair is pulled back into a ponytail, I notice it matches the color of her outfit perfectly. Her eyes are so blue that they probably match the sky, as well. They remind me of Don Henley, whose eyes are so puppy-dog soulful you want to smack him.

"Well, you're on the borderline of going from famous to infamous," she calls out as she puts her satchel away.

"For what?"

"For pulling your disappearing act, if that's what this is. Want something to eat?"

"Sure."

I'm already pulling on my jeans and my shirt; then she helps me fold the futon back into its couch position, pulls her coffee table back to the middle of the room, and opens the pizza box. The pizza smells as good as any food ever has, topped with peppers, onions, and sausage.

"Do you want to go first, or do you want to hear what I've heard?" she asks.

"Just for kicks, what have you heard?"

We're both sitting on the futon. She tucks one foot under her lovely ass, and turns at an angle toward me, a slice in her hands. "I do freelance work for several magazines, and I was at one of their offices today, re-editing an article for about the hundredth time, when WRVO, which is one of the cooler stations in the Bay Area, broadcast a news story claiming that WTTR, down in Los Angeles, has been running a story all morning that not only has a fan been killed in a dispute over tickets to one of the Blood Cheetah shows, but that when WTTR managed to talk with Blood Cheetah's manager this morning, he lashed out at the entire band, and at you in particular, saying that he hadn't seen you since you left the stage after Wednesday night's show, but that you'd better turn up in time for tonight's show. So now there are all kinds of rumors circulating about exactly how this kid was murdered, which WTTR is trying to set straight at the same time they're also already running mock commercials for 'Where's Dizzy?' and 'D.Z., Phone Home.' Apparently they have a tape, playing in the background, of your manager screaming at you."

I sink into the couch. "Do you have any milk? That's all I want to ask or really care about right now. The rest of it's so goddamn stupid."

"There's milk in the fridge and glasses up above."

"Want some, too?"

"Please."

"See, isn't that simple? Milk has no conscience, no obligations, and no decisions to make. And neither do I, when I drink it. Okay, did they say anything important, like whether they have any suspects, or what type of weapon was used, or where it happened exactly?"

She shifts uneasily, pulls her leg out from under her butt. "Apparently the wound was from a handgun. But there are two weird parts. He had a friend who was with him all night—and should know who did it. They had been at a party together. And at some point before it happened, he had burned the word *Remote* onto his chest, just like the song title from Blood Cheetah."

"What am I supposed to say to that?"

"What do you want to say?"

I take a large bite of pizza. "Well, because this tastes so good, my first reaction is to say that it's a terrible story. I mean, it really fucking blows. But I also want to say that I'm not responsible. It's not my fault. Hell, even if some kid had called me up personally and threatened to kill everybody in his whole goddamn high school if I didn't fork over some tickets, it still wouldn't be my fault, though I'm sure I would have given him as many as he wanted."

Neither of us says anything for a minute, then I continue.

"I mean, I'm sure that at some point I'll start really thinking about this, especially if the details turn out to be as lurid as they sound, and that I'll get incredibly bummed out about it, probably will write at least one song about it, maybe more. But right now, I just can't. It'll take time to figure it out, like everything else. What kills me is that I've always been a hundred percent against band worship, if that's what you want to call it. It kills me how devoted some kids get to the band, and the stupid things they'll do in our name. I can't tell you how many kids have drawings of cheetahs tattooed on their arms because of me. Or because of Jay. One girl I met had even shaved her head, paid someone to tattoo *Dizzy* on her scalp, then let her hair grow back in. But I've never told anyone how to live his life, or that my songs were answers to whatever questions anybody has about teenage angst, whatever, no matter how much I can relate to all of those problems. If anything, I go out of my way to tell fans not to listen to Blood Cheetah. Look at how much trouble my big mouth got me into in Nevada. They want to arrest me for starting a riot up there, if you haven't heard. It really sucks that all of the incredible and indescribable emotions a few basic guitar chords can magically represent also means that people are going to think they understand you, or that you understand them, when it's really just music, and whatever mood I was in on the day when I wrote the song."

"Is that why you showed up here drunk at four in the morning?"

I start laughing, set my slice of pizza down, rock back and forth a few times, and finally end up groaning. I'm still hungover, but this one's actually moderate compared to some of the coke depression troughs my body has wallowed in over the years. I can imagine the pizza molecules already replenishing my cells, buoying me.

229

"Argh! No, naturally another kicker is that this is only the second time I've heard about the kid getting killed, and the first time was just at a party last night. I thought someone was playing a trick on me, or really on the person who told me about the kid. Juliette Bracer, from that show *The Man with the Itchy Beard*. We were at her place down in L.A., and her kid sister told me about the rumors. God, that's not even the beginning of why I was drunk, or why I bolted, but I guess I'm glad I came here, instead of Boston, which was my other option, or even Seattle, though I'm not sure who I would have stayed with up there."

Katherine chuckles at this, but good-naturedly, her eyes flirtatious. "What, there's nobody up there who you've known for a total of ten minutes, gotten really embarrassed in front of, then blatantly picked someone else up in front of?"

"Excuse me?"

"Don't think I didn't watch you go over and whisper in that girl's ear at the party that night in Sacramento. Not that I'm judgmental. I had just hoped you'd stay and talk a little longer first. Hal really got you flustered."

"Hal?"

"Yeah, Hal, the marketing guy from your label."

"God, this'll sound terrible, but I really don't remember why I walked away, I only remember being furious that I had to. Hal? What kind of a guy has a name like Hal? Think of Hal Linden. And having said that, now's when you tell me that you're dating him, right?"

"No, I'm not dating him."

Scarce inflection, no emotion, no teasing or vocal flirtation, then our eyes meet. We hold each other's gaze for the briefest instant, to break only because this isn't Hollywood—because we're both old enough to be wary of instant relationships and because she's right, it's pretty crazy that I flew four hundred miles to look her up, totally drunk, after a ten-minute conversation days ago. I could feed her some line of bullshit right now but we'd both know it was bullshit, just like we both know it would be wrong for me to pry and ask if she's dating someone other than Hal. So I just keep talking about why I left Los Angeles, pausing occasionally to chew some pizza. If running away from the band is going to do anything good for me, I should probably start with telling the truth.

"It's not like I was plotting and planning that you'd be the person I dumped my problems on when I got here. I just wanted to be in San Francisco, which is so much cooler a town than L.A., especially since we didn't play here. Then, right as the plane landed, I had a wild insight and your name popped into my head. Though I guess that if it was a subconscious thing, there's also the pseudo-Freudian explanation that I was terminating things with one woman by heading for another. You're probably aware that I've been dating that nutcase Clipper Evans on and off for the past several years."

"I've seen your names linked in certain gossip rags, yes."

"Well, I hadn't really talked to her since right before this tour began, at which point we agreed we should both be on our own for a while, which for me meant playing and traveling with the band, and for her meant modeling as much as she could in L.A., making of course absolutely no mention of the fact that the band would play out here. So boom! We're halfway through the tour, and not only am I trying to deal with all the usual bullshit, hassles, drunkenness, travel exhaustion, etcetera, plus the fact that I'm now a wanted man in the state of Nevada, but I'm also totally neurotic and fucked up about whether I'll see her or not. The short version is that as soon as we were done playing the show Wednesday night, I boogied back to the hotel and called her, because I just wanted to get over the tension of wondering how things stood, not to beg her to see me or anything. She said she'd come to one of the shows, but pretty much killed any idea like a romantic drive up the Pacific Coast Highway. Which was fine with me, no big deal. Then the next night, the very next night, last night as a matter of fact, she showed up at a party which K Dot, Grover, and I were at."

Katherine lifts another slice of the pizza. "Which was at Juliette Bracer's?"

"Right. I mean, I don't know, maybe I'm just a jealous type or something. To me, it was like she had brought a date, whether she had or not. I had to stand there and watch her talk to guys she might date as soon as the Blood Cheetah buses blow out of town, contributing their last fumes to the L.A. smog bank. I don't know . . . Does any of this make any sense to you?"

Her eye catches mine again. "Sure it does. Of course it does. Until a certain age, maybe twenty-seven or twenty-eight, playing around like that is just a big joke. Head games are a way to be amused. But after a while, they're really a pain in the ass."

"Where did you grow up?" I ask.

"Down in Riverside, which is about forty-five miles outside the center of Los Angeles. Why?"

"I don't know, I guess you just have a little bit of the California surfer-dude accent, which, as fucked-up and crazy as this state is, always sounds pretty optimistic to me. Boston is either conceited, aloof, and disdainful, if you're rich; or conceited, aggressive, and ready to flip somebody off in traffic, if you're poor. God, you know what I love about Seattle? You can drive there from Boston. Just jump on the Mass Pike right by South Station, drive three thousand miles west on Route 90, and when the road ends, look to the right, there's Seattle. They should post signs in each city telling the exact distance, like the road signs in *M*A*S*H*."

"Want some more milk?" Katherine asks.

"Sure."

Maybe in ten years it will be easy for me to tell people how this week unfolded, a rehearsed story, one I can tell as a joke in awkward social occasions, but right now, I'm sick of the whole fucking deal, sick of it before it's even close to being over. I'd give almost anything if I could just be back in Boston and not have to worry about anything tougher than choosing Pitary's or Pascuzzi's for dinner, not have to deal with all the coming turmoil from Murph and the guys, which I'm too chickenshit, wishy-washy, and devoted to them to avoid by simply never talking to any of them again, ever, until twenty years have passed and everyone's clamoring for a cheesy Blood Cheetah reunion.

Katherine is being incredibly great about me showing up, and about not lecturing me on my responsibilities. Clipper would already have told me about a hundred things I should do, especially if my breakdown was interfering with her plans to, say, file her nails, but none of them would be to simply follow my own instincts, which is what Katherine's giving me by advising nothing. I'm already prepared to let her chain me up again if that's what it will take for another night's refuge.

It's getting to be late afternoon, and my image of Murph, Annie, and maybe a couple of the guys in the band going nuts, worrying whether I'll make tonight's show, is pretty funny. Maybe one or two of them, Grover perhaps, is acting as re-laxed as possible, wondering what time they'll make the an-nouncement of no concert, and whether he can head out on the town right away, or should wait a deferential few hours, to see if I turn up in the morgue. I'd put my money on K Dot

being the first to comprehend how fucked up and fucking sick
of it all I really must be to have disappeared.

"So, what should I do?" I ask Katherine. She's walking back
across the room with the two glasses of milk.

"What do you mean?"

"I mean, don't take this wrong, but can I stay here again
tonight?"

She frowns slightly. Dimples appear. "Well, yeah, I guess
so. I think it would be pretty cool to hang out, and spend some
time with you, as long as you aren't going back to L.A. tonight.
Shouldn't you call somebody or something?"

"Yeah, I guess I should. Can I use your phone?"

"Sure."

She sets the milks down on the coffee table and goes back
to the kitchen for a cordless phone. I start to dial, then hang
back up, click off the phone, and slide it as far under the Futon
as I can reach.

233

"You know, I'm not really sure what number to try. So I
miss a concert or two, so what? A little mystery will be good
for certain people. It's only a matter of time until the limo
driver spills the fact that he took me to the airport, anyway,
then the manhunt will shift to San Francisco. The band can
either refund the tickets or schedule another date. It's not like
I'm going around selling cars with faulty brakes or anything.
Nobody's going to get hurt because we didn't play, and maybe
canceling a few shows will calm our fans down a little. Hell,
it's a public health contribution I'm making here. For once, I
really might be saving people."

She's smiling as she watches me; seems truly amused and
interested. "You should have been a politician. Or a lawyer,
with that logic."

"Nah, they get fired for doing the things rock stars base
careers on."

"Oh, really?"

"Packwood? A schoolboy writing dirty letters to *Penthouse*
compared to either Jay or Grover. Me? I end up sleeping alone

even when I pick somebody up, like that night in Sacramento, but that's just some glitch in my brain which makes me blow it on purpose the second I'm certain I can have a woman, my own little catch-and-release program. Ted Kennedy? I could drink him under the table with one kidney tied behind my back. Not that I'm proud of it, but still . . ."

We gab on as we finish the pizza, and luckily, the topics get less and less serious, almost a Yeee-ha! school's-out-for-summer mood, an easy rapport. The nuclear meltdown warning shrieks in my inner voice: "Dizzy, you must not fall for this woman! Dizzy, do not fall for this woman! Dizzy, since you're falling for this woman, speak intelligently, make good jokes, and take a shower as soon as possible!" Which I guess is a pretty hip reaction to have to someone, especially someone so attractive.

25 | The San Fran Blues, Part Two

/
/

WHAT I WANT TO DO THAT NIGHT INSTEAD OF FACING ANY responsibilities is check out San Francisco, walk enough that my belly doesn't stay entirely stuffed with the pizza, and give both my mind and my body some time to purify themselves. The further I am from last night and being drunk, the cleaner my bloodstream gets, which in turn makes my perceptions feel fantastically crisp. The lines on all the pastel apartment buildings look sharp, for once my ears aren't ringing, and after I drop a huge, intestine-scouring crap, my gut feels light and relieved. In my heart, I know no drugs can make my body feel as good as my body itself can. ("In my heart I know I'm right, officer.")

San Francisco is a pretty easy town to stroll around in, although from where Katherine lives you have to drive to all the places that are cool to check out on foot, except for Golden Gate Park and the beaches. We drive to the beaches anyhow, in her Volkswagen Jetta, then park on the bluff where they used to have the old public mineral baths, and watch half a dozen wetsuited surfers riding waves in from a rocky shoulder as the sun sets over the Pacific Ocean in a million colors of orange. (*Sunrise, sunset* . . .)

Going to Fisherman's Wharf is about the most touristy thing you can do in the Bay Area, just like the Walk of Fame is in Los Angeles, but that's why I love it. Seeing all the other tourists, who tend to be middle-aged Plains States Americans, leaves me optimistic, the same way I was glad to realize, on my first visit to Vegas, that it's a cheesy family resort town, not a total sleaze hole. Kicking around the Wharf also makes it less likely that anybody's going to recognize me than showing up at a really hip rock club would, like Amber or The Option. I've showered and brushed my teeth; am wearing my jeans and sandals, but have traded my T-shirt for a long-sleeved white linen shirt that Katherine supplies, saying I can keep it because it belonged to a guy she stopped dating several months ago. Then she gives me a plain baseball cap to tuck my hair under.

236

In return, I buy her a huge ornamental African mask decorated with ostrich feathers and lion hair, from a seriously funky World Antiques shop tucked into the third floor of one of the waterfront brick malls. The woman who waits on us is the type of catty bitch who'll just about stare you out of her shop if you're not Andy Warhol or if you look like you're having too much fun. She's in her late twenties, and is obviously used to being the best-looking female in sight, a position which Katherine threatens, especially if attitude counts for anything. Katherine tries to stop me from buying the mask, protesting that it costs as much as her monthly rent.

"So just bring it back and see if they'll rebuy it if you ever have trouble making your rent," I tell her. The clerk's lips are pursed. "I mean, even if they'll only give you half back."

"We have a very strict return policy."

I'm laughing as I pull out the money I withdrew from an ATM only minutes earlier. "We promise to make sure it still looks like an antique. We won't shine it up or straighten out the feathers or anything."

Katherine pokes me in the ribs and makes a face for me to

shut up, but she's holding laughter back, too. "Dizzy . . . Mr. Zimmerman . . ."

"Call me Dave, for now." I turn back to the clerk. "And we promise that if the feathers makes anyone sneeze, we won't even wipe the spittle off. We'll claim it's monkey saliva. Did you know certain types of chimpanzees make obscene gestures with their toes? It's true."

Katherine drags me out of the shop by the elbow at this point, but getting pulled out of somewhere is a nice change from getting thrown out, and we're laughing uproariously. The one way she reminds me of Clipper is how much more confidence being with a beautiful woman gives me about my own looks. My skin feels scrubbed and fresh from the shower, and the shirt she's given me is large enough that it hangs on me like a sheik's robe. All thoughts of not falling for her are gone, replaced by thoughts of not blowing it with her quite yet, and of figuring out as quickly as possible if she's just being nice to me, or grooving on me romantically, so that I don't get worked up over nothing.

"Where next?" she cries.

"Ghirardelli's. If I'm not going to get sugar through booze today, I better find a replacement. Along with no radio and no telephone, let's make it an alcohol-free weekend. I'll even let you pay, and the mask may not seem so expensive, after all."

"You've got it."

Resisting kissing her as we get back into her car is next to impossible. So is resisting kissing her as we dart around through town, two tiny human beings side by side under the towering financial buildings and executive suites, in and out of the rushing, maddening, frantic traffic. She's driving far wilder than is probably normal, reckless in the night, seeming to know every alley and brick sidestreet, hurtling down one hill then torqueing her engine up the next, making me glad she has solid brakes, since enormous hills are one of the biggest differences between San Francisco and Boston. Making a pass at her when she's not expecting it would show me how she'd react when she's not anticipating having to react, and would

237

be a lot smarter than laying one on her at the end of evening, when she might simultaneously be dreading it and hoping for it. But patience is a side benefit of both sobriety and age, and I'm old enough and sober enough not to be forward at all, to wait until Sunday night, if I have to. I've started to think of this whole trip to San Francisco as taking the weekend off from the band, no matter how much it resembles a stop on the underground railroad.

Haight-Ashbury always seems like an area split between tourists who want to see hippies, poking around the ruins for two or three hours, and tourists who want to be hippies, and are willing to live in crappy apartments for two or three years, walking the walk, wearing the threads, sampling pharmaceuticals. By ten thirty, there seem to be a lot of homeless around, varied and interesting enough to put Boston's cold-weather bums, who concentrate mostly on surviving, to shame. Local shops appear incapable of selling anything new. There are used-clothing stores, used-book stores, just about used-coffee shops. A girl approaches me as I paw casually through a pile of old Levi's in a clothing boutique, and asks if she knows me. I simply respond, cracking up an eavesdropping Katherine, two aisles distant, *"No inglés."*

Then I walk away.

We're back at Katherine's apartment in time to catch Jay Leno's monologue, which is a letdown because it's a repeat. NBC's spending millions of dollars a year on this show and they can't afford a guest host for two weeks a year? ("Blood Cheetah's making millions of dollars a year and they can't afford a guest guitar player when Dizzy freaks out?") We hit the sack earlier than I have any night since the tour began, or for a long time before that, probably. About two in the morning, I hear Katherine moving around the apartment, and before I can think about what's happening, she slips into bed on the futon with me, wrapping her arms around me from behind, in the spoon position.

"Do you mind?" she asks.

"Not if you don't mind me being naked and getting an instant erection."

"That's all right. Skin feels pretty good. But maybe you shouldn't get your hopes up too high. Maybe just lying here is a good enough start."

"After you're the one to climb into bed with me?" I tease.

"Well . . ."

"No, it's all right, really. Maybe it's better this way."

"Hmmm . . ."

"And it's definitely better than the handcuffs."

She shifts her weight. One arm is under my neck, while the other is wrapped over my flank, her hand on my stomach, which doesn't do anything to reduce my excitement. She whispers in my ear. "You know, you smell an awful lot better when you're sober than you do when you're drunk."

"Thanks, I guess. Another good reason not to drink."

"You're sure you don't mind me just lying here with you?"

"No, not at all."

"Have you ever heard of couples where neither of them are virgins, but they still wait until they get married to have sex? Some call themselves born-again virgins, but others don't like how militant that sounds, or the religious connotations. I just did a magazine article on it, mostly interviews. I guess it's a pretty big phenomenon these days, especially with AIDS being such a prevalent fear."

I sigh. My fans would never forgive me. "That doesn't sound like all that bad an idea. I mean . . . it just doesn't."

The adventure ends Sunday night, when I finally call the hotel in L.A. to see who I can get in touch with, whose sweaty fingers I can offer the first chance to wrap around my scrawny neck (although just staying sober for a couple of days has helped my skin lose its translucence; now it resembles live chicken flesh, not dead). Katherine and I have hit every attraction which is supposed to be included in a whirlwind tour of San Francisco, from walking out on the Golden Gate Bridge to driving past Robin Williams's house. If I stayed any longer, we'd have to settle into a normalcy routine of which café is best for a fresh breakfast, which one of us got what sections of the *Chronicle* first, etcetera, which in turn would freak us out. I still can't remember the hippie song about San Francisco, and while Katherine does have some Journey in her music collection (and a lot of David Bowie and Madonna), she can't figure out who I'm talking about, either.

The hotel's switchboard operator denies the band is staying there until I tell her who I am, and even then I have to give her K Dot's mother's maiden name, Magoun, which Murph has apparently left as a password that only I'd know without research.

Even the operator chastises me. "Well, you've caused quite a little stir around here. I don't think I've had to fib so many times since Johnny Cash stayed with us."

"Country music is big in L.A.?"

"Oh, it's *very* popular," she assures me.

The order in which I'd like to talk to people is something like K Dot, Grover, Annie, Walker, Alex, my accountant back in Boston, anybody from our record label, Johnny Carson, Johnny Cochran, the Dalai Lama, the pope, an IRS agent, Clipper, Jay, and finally Murph, so naturally the switchboard operator connects me with Murph's suite, which has been transformed into Task Force Find Dizzy. Murph answers the phone, but it's obvious he's not alone. Later on, Walker will tell me that besides Murph, the people present were Murph's girlfriend Geena, his brother-in-law Eddie, Annie, Jay, an executive from the label, a promoter from the L.A. venue where we're playing, Bob Gordimer, the lawyer, and two private detectives, Magnum wannabe's.

"Yeah, hey, it's me, proceed to scream," I say.

They've hooked up a speaker phone, because as soon as I speak, there's a slight echo, and I can hear everybody telling each other to be quiet, the morons.

"Start recording," someone hisses.

"Got it!" Walker yells. I can't tell if it's the excitement of subterfuge making him loud, or if he's being loud on purpose, to tip me off.

"Where the *fuck* are you?" Murph roars.

"Remember not to scare him . . ." Annie begins, then shuts up so suddenly it's obvious someone has gestured for her to be quiet.

I'm shaking my head and grinning at Katherine. "Murph, are you recording this conversation? Murph, don't lie to me, are there some snot-nosed Pinkertons trying to trace this call even as I speak?"

"I'm here," he stammers.

"Well, of course you're there, you dope, where else would you be? What I really want to know is whether or not you're taping and tracing this?"

"Where are you?"

"I'm standing in what's left of a phone booth that's been blown away by repeated drive-bys in the worst part of East Palo Alto, which I once read in *Hustler* was the murder capital of the United States, holding the phone in one hand while a drug dealer's twisting my other arm behind my back, threatening to tear it off and feed it to his pit bull if I don't come up with the money I owe him, pronto. Aaaaaargh!" My voice cracks like Beavis's. "Send some money, Murph! Send some money, ass-wipe!"

"This isn't funny, Dizzy. Are you drunk?"

"Of course it's funny, Murph, especially since you're being such a dick-for. No, I'm not drunk. We've known each other for how many years and you still can't tell the difference between me drunk and me out of my mind on coke? I'm standing on the very edge of the hotel's roof and since I think I can fly, I'm about to jump. Why don't you send some people sprinting up to save me. Or just stick your head out the window and we can chat on my way down."

"I'm dead serious, Dizzy. This is not funny."

"Hey, that's good, dead serious. Well, I'm dead serious, too. I'll hang up this second if you don't calm right the fuck down."

Now he relents, gives me the pity approach and the We-

were-so-worried-about-you routine, which if anything, makes me want to be more obnoxious. I realize I should have figured out what I wanted to say before I called, but now all I want to know, besides how much I can provoke Murph, is what night Blood Cheetah's next definite concert is, so I can show up. Simply canceling the tour and breaking up the band are options I wouldn't refuse discussing with the other guys, but I certainly don't want to be the one to bring the subject up now, if they can either ignore or forgive my weekend Ferris Bueller imitation. My recent sobriety has helped my mood every bit as much as spending time with Katherine, and the combination of the two has turned my outlook on the rest of the tour from me being a slug climbing a heavily greased pole in order to escape a rapidly rising fire to me being a test driver for Ferrari. All I have to do is not make any stupid mistakes and crash.

242

"Dizzy?" Annie asks. "Are you still there?"

"Of course I'm still here. God, what are you people doing, all drinking from the same puddle of delirium-producing backwater?"

"There's no need to be a wise-ass."

"Would you believe me if I told you that once, when I was a kid, my grandmother asked me how I'd like to have my mouth washed out with soap, so I asked how she'd like to see me blow bubbles out my ass?"

"I'd believe anything out of you, Dizzy. Did that really happen?"

"No, actually, it was just part of some comedian's routine, but he wasn't somebody who everybody knows, so I can usually get away with telling it like it was my story."

She doesn't say anything else right away, which makes me feel bad for about a tenth of a second, her old silent, set-upon, disappointed, abandoned Mom role, though I know it's only a role, a good-cop/bad-cop routine she and Murph have perfected over the years without ever discussing the fact that it's a routine. Then Murph jumps back into the fray.

"So, Dizzy," he begins, quietly enough. "Where the *fuck* are you?"

Which sets me off laughing like a maniac. "Hey, Walker, do they have your skinny ass in there, too?"

"Sure do."

"And they're making you tape this, aren't they?"

He hesitates. He really isn't all that good-looking, in his mid-thirties and about as awkward and scrawny as a teenager halfway through puberty. I can picture him glancing around the room nervously, wondering if it's all right to respond now.

"C'mon, Walker!" I shout. "What the hell are they gonna do? How tough do the security people look, anyway?"

"Tougher than me."

"Who isn't?"

"Thanks, Dizzy."

"No, seriously, promise me you'll destroy any tapes you're making of this. Because this is so fucking stupid. This is like, if anyone ever hears how stupid this goddamn conversation is, we'll never sell another disc, and everyone will assume the songs we've already done, we stole from somebody, like I've kidnapped Beethoven's great, great, great, great grandson, and he's doing all the work for me."

Murph blows up again. "Dizzy, would you shut the fuck up for ten seconds! Goddamn, you piss me off sometimes! Where the fuck do you come off? Are you gonna get your shit together or are we gonna fire you from this fucking band? Holy shit, do you have any idea how many goddamn people are looking for you around here? The goddamn radio stations are playing advertisements saying, 'D. Z., phone home!' God, you're a moron!"

"Take it easy," I hear Annie tell him.

"Why don't you take it easy?" Geena says, in the background. "Like you're doing any good here . . . God . . ."

"You can't fire me, Murph! That's like a ballboy trying to fire Roger Clemens. Whether he deserves it or not, that's just not the way things work."

What I've been sensing for the last few moments is everybody dying to shout out their own opinion, to let loose on me for the split second I'd need to hang up on them, but holding back because that's what they've agreed to do, maybe at Murph's request, maybe at the record company's. But suddenly everybody goes ballistic, and for a few seconds, the old image of holding the receiver at arm's length is true. Jay's the one who starts it.

"Yeah, well I can fucking fire you, you punk!" he yells. "I can fucking fire you by never singing any of your goddamn stupid songs again! I don't need you, you asshole! You've been pissing me off for a long goddamn time!"

"Jay, shut up!" Murph snaps.

"Shut up yourself, why the fuck do you think he's pulling this?"

"People, let's not fight amongst ourselves."

244 "Shut up!"

Even Eddie, Murph's brother, kicks in. He's probably threatened and emasculated by the detectives at the same time they make him feel tougher. "We'll find you, Dizzy, you know we will."

"I'm gonna kick your ass!" Jay shouts.

"Shut up!"

Annie again. "Murph, he'll hang up!"

"Maybe we should let him," Geena screeches at her.

"People, people, people!"

Even Walker's got his dander up, cackling wildly in the background. "Go get 'em, Dizzy! Give 'em hell!"

The confusion is even more complete for me because I can't see all these idiots, and because I don't recognize a couple of the voices. If I were there, and Jay was the one who'd pulled a disappearing act, I hope I wouldn't be taking this any more seriously than Walker seems to be. One of my favorite positions in life is the peanut gallery, tossing an occasional monkey wrench.

What finally stops their squabbling is that they realize I haven't spoken for a minute, and wonder if I've hung up. As soon as I speak, everybody on the other end hushes up. "This is probably the wrong time to ask, but could one of you tell me anything about a kid dying down there?"

"Kids die every day!" Jay snorts.

I can picture everyone turning away from him, or glancing down at their feet. Finally Annie speaks. "It happened, Dizzy, if that's what you want to know. That's the other reason you should really tell us where you are, then come back. I don't know what you're heard, but the initial details seem to be that he refused to fork over a pair of tickets to Wednesday night's show, and that at some point in the night someone spelled *Remote* on his chest in motor oil and set it on fire. The police are investigating, of course, but who knows how much they'll turn up."

"Tell me they don't want to talk to me."

"They don't," Murph jumps in. "But we did get a call from our old law enforcement friends up in Nevada, who're pretty nervous you disappeared."

I groan. "Fuck them. Tell 'em not to worry. I'll show. They can wait."

"He better show," Bob Gordimer says, in the background.

"Oh, I better show!" I mock. He's a suit like all the rest, which is like asking Curly, Curly Joe, or Shemp. He's just better at it than some.

"Dizzy . . ."

"Yeah, yeah, yeah, blah, blah, blah!"

"I'm gonna kick his scrawny fucking ass!" Jay bellows.

Then there's bedlam again (*Helter Skelter,* supposedly written by Paul McCartney as the wildest response he could make to a Pete Townshend song). Things get even louder when K Dot and Alex come into the suite. I've been wondering where they were. Naturally, everybody starts telling them what's going on at the same time.

"Shut up!!!" K Dot finally screams. "Everybody just shut the fuck up!!"

The room falls deathly quiet.

"Z, you still alive?"

"Yeah."

"You still have all your fingers?"

"Yes."

"You in jail?"

"No."

"Can we announce that Tuesday night's show is definitely on?"

"Affirmative."

"Good. See ya."

After a brief, violent scraping sound, the line goes dead. Tomorrow I'll learn that what he's done is grabbed the speaker phone, ripped the line out of the wall, heaved the whole mess through a window, and walked out of the room. Sometimes he's smarter than he seems.

26 | Flags

DEPART SAN FRANCISCO EARLY THE NEXT MORNING, AFTER LEAV-
ing it with Katherine that everything's totally crazy, that I'll
call her in a few days, and that when the tour's over, we'll
hook up and see how strange or how sane hanging out together feels. It kills me to think that now, when Clipper is
finally rendered expendable and I'd just as soon forget about
her, she's probably going to be very concerned, doting, and
phone-cally about me; may even want to get together and
make sure I'm all right. Katherine and I have slept in the same
bed three nights running, but we still haven't had sex, so my
trips to the bathroom before turning in aren't just for brushing
my teeth. How's that for being a madman rock 'n' roller?
(*Touch yourself hot, touch yourself high* . . .) The one thing I
keep thinking is that life can be very strange, that life *is* very
strange, sampling a wide array of voices in my head, everyone
from Steven Seagull (ha!) in his tough-guy-philosopher mode
to the Lama-type figure in the Michael Jordan Gatorade commercials: "Life iz a spor-r-r-t," hoping the different accents will
flesh out exactly what I mean and keep it from becoming a
cliché.

I'm crazy to be Jonesing on a relationship with Katherine so soon and so completely, though I know it's partly a psychological trick to help me endure the shit of going back to L.A. and facing the ball-clenching grind of the rest of the tour. Then again, what in this life isn't crazy and surreal and permissible all at the same time? And if I understand that it's crazy to fall for her so quickly, probably setting myself up like an eighty-foot goddamn bowling pin, what can I label as crazier, or craziest of all? What can't I give myself permission to do? Why is it that the only time I have any confidence at all in my own judgment is when I'm high on the outrageous confidence-boosting groove of composing music? If Clipper flipped her lid and asked me to marry her today, I'd say no, because deep down she's neither happy, nor at peace with herself, nor very smart—although intelligence can be overrated as a reason for loving someone—nor an optimistic person, which is a wildly underrated trait. I don't mean to sound too cocky about myself, but I've always believed my biggest strength is my faith in the essential goodness of the universe, despite how much evil and misery and horror a casual observer might point to. Hell, I wouldn't be all that bummed out if my sentence up in Nevada really did turn out to be jail time. Reopen Alcatraz for me. After I went nuts in solitary for a few days, what would save me is writing incredible songs in my head and promising myself I'd survive long enough to record at least one version of them. I wouldn't even have to escape to be happy, I'd just need to figure a way to watch the sun set over the bay maybe once every six months.

My anxiety on the plane is caused mostly by knowing how much of an incredible pain it's going to be to work my way back into everybody's good graces, exacerbated by not having anyone to talk recent events over with while I'm in the air, as well as refusing to take a drink to steady my jittering nerves, no matter how tempting it is. But other than my nerves, my body feels better now than it has in years, which is one of the reasons steering clear of booze is tougher three weeks after your last great binge than three days after. I swear my

248

breathing is easier than it's been in years, too, just from a few days of not being anywhere where people are smoking. What I try to focus on, on the plane, is Katherine. Truth is, if she asked me to marry her today, I'd probably say yes, if only because marriage is always a gamble, and because she took me in on a night when I was absolutely wrecked and desperate. The national average age for men getting married is still something like twenty-three, though this includes all of those deep-woods ruralities where you're as likely to be marrying a farm animal as a woman. On my next birthday I'll be thirty-six. Crazier things have happened, and crazier things have succeeded, like me becoming a rock musician, if only through force of will.

My perfect wife would smile when she was happy to see me, and would always be overjoyed to see me, whether I was coming back from sea as a grim whaling captain or a nouveau-riche pirate, dancing with me in the kitchen. She would blush when I mowed her name into the lawn then let the rest of it go to seed, be touched when I wrote her a love letter, and never ask if a specific song was about her, because she knew that at the end of the day, all my songs were about the strength she gave me. I picture her as someone elated to lie in bed with me late at night talking about the change of seasons and the passing years, the first night of the year in New England when the windows frosted over and suddenly it was Thanksgiving, cold, crisp, exhilarating air. Who's going to stand on the Great Wall of China with me before I die, just K Dot? Or tremble in repulsed, mesmerized fear, seeing wild gila monsters and their foot-long, forked, flickering tongues in the Australian Outback, if I've even got my continents straight. Or sneak off to find a hidden glade to make love in after touring Baron von Big Baron's castle in the Black Forest, imagining ourselves a rogue and his damsel, not overmoneyed, gawking, hoping-even-street-vendors-will-speak-English American tourists.

Boston is a large enough city that I could live there the rest of my life and still want to write songs, any town is, really, but there's a huge country out there and an even larger world

249

Matthew Holland

beyond it, so why not feed my curiosity until my curiosity is sated? I was young, brash, and ignorant when I worked in the factory, probably offended a lot of the old-timers—though I realize now that a lot of the old-timers probably understood where I was coming from better than I myself did. But I always meant it when I justified my decision to quit that job by lashing out that I'd rather die young and happy than work in a dump all my life. A kid died just the other day, indirectly because of me; people die every day, and individually they're not statistics. I can only hope my music offered moments of solace and camaraderie while the kid was still alive. Hell, though the odds are against it, this plane could go down and me die, hopefully in a fiery ground crash, not an ocean splash-down. The tragedy would be good for Blood Cheetah sales for a year or two, but eventually we'd be oldies. We'll be oldies anyhow, so in a way, continuing to record is just a boldly subtle way of delaying this dishonor, disembowelment. No matter how hard I fight to guarantee it'll never happen, it's entirely possible that Blood Cheetah songs will end up on some goddamn Time-Life compilation album, representing a year in the early nineties. Then what can I do, except scream?

The eighties *are* oldies, the kids of today assume the seventies were a time when musicians were fat, because all the stars who were young then are fat now—didn't Meat Loaf have some kind of hit back then? And the sixties are ancient history, might as well have been the Spanish Inquisition—wasn't that when Taco Bell served the first chicken fajita in America? The biggest thing I remember from being forced to read *1984* in high school is how cool it would be to grow up and spend an entire day in bed with a woman, just like the lead character, but George Orwell has obviously been wrong for a long time. Prince's "1999," which is already an oldie, is going to be a historical footnote pretty soon, and I don't mean to jinx him, but Mick Jagger will probably be the most mourned rock star ever if he can manage to still be touring with the Stones when he dies, which doesn't seem like such a bad bet. I can spit on the year 2000 already, can taste it, reach out like a mime and feel it blocking my passage, can flash forward to it, an eerie reversal of the way I flash back to certain bad acid trips.

All of which means more to me than to simply start Christmas shopping early. What I liked best about Katherine this weekend was that she understood these things without us having to talk about any of them. Women who make it into their thirties without being married tend to think there's something wrong with them, but the irony is that they'll be even better at forty; most men just don't catch on to this until they're about sixty, and in the meantime, can't wait.

K Dot meets me in the hotel lobby, pretending to be lounging casually, reading *USA Today*, but maybe having waited impatiently all morning or having called the airport and figured out the most logical flight for me to be coming in on. There are more security guards letting their presence be known near the front of the hotel and around the grounds than I remember, but I'm not certain this has anything to do with Blood Cheetah. K Dot spins me around and marches me out to a waiting rental car with the casual assurance of a Little League coach herding an erring player back to the bench. He's wearing a black sportcoat, black T-shirt, a pair of Levi's, and black leather shoes, for shit's sake. Combined with the white linen shirt Katherine gave me, this probably ties us, as a pair, for the most adult we've ever looked. And he's acting pretty relaxed.

"Can I drive?" I ask.

"You're not going to flip out and drive us off a cliff or anything, are you?"

"Would I do that without the cameras rolling?"

"Let's hope not."

We take the 10 through town and over to the Pacific Coast Highway, which, if we're going to need scenery to help me ignore him and for him to realize the world hasn't ended, just might suffice. But almost immediately he motions for me to turn onto Sunset and head back inland. The only pleasure this brings is that Sunset is a winding race-course type road, though not nearly as daredevil as Route 1 North over the Tobin Bridge in Boston, where the de facto speed limit is whatever G-forces your tires can take. A *Thomas's Guide* sits on the floor by his feet.

"So?" he finally asks.

"K Dot, I swear to God I feel as good right now as I've felt in a long, long, long time. Better than when we finally finished the *Funk & Fugue* disc. Better than when we finished just about any of our discs, because it's not an elation which I have to come down from and say, 'Okay, I'm spent, what's next, a tour?' It's more like, 'Okay, I've been sprinting through life for six months and now I'm gonna take a time-out and catch my breath, and if people don't like it, that's their problem.' Also, from now on, I think I'm just going to jog along. You know what we need? A definite time to get up every morning. A roll call, because if you don't have to be up, it doesn't matter what time you go to bed, and one of my three rules in life is that nothing good ever happens after one A.M."

He guffaws.

"All right, maybe what I mean is that you never *meet* anybody who's good for you after one A.M. And what fun would it be if I didn't have about a hundred of my 'three rules in life?' "

"You had a lot of people wondering if this was it for you," K Dot says. "I mean, Murph swears a lot and compensates for shit he can't control by getting really pissed off, but there was definitely a moment or two when people were wondering if you'd turn up in the morgue."

"K Dot, it's a gorgeous day out. If we were in Boston, this would be about the best day of the summer, so don't turn morbid on me. It won't work. It's not like I injected a giant tube of heroin into my jugular right before I left the party at Juliette's."

"I know, I'm just telling you what other people thought."

"Well . . ."

" 'Well' what?"

"Well, don't bother. I can figure that stuff out for myself."

Neither of us says anything for a minute, and although I'm trying to think of what to say next, I'm not as uncomfortable with him as I'd be with nearly anybody else. The day is indeed gorgeous, though it's a bit too hot for us to be driving around with the windows down instead of the air conditioning on. But I realize that if I'd gotten drunk last night, the heat would be bothering me a lot more. My beavertail hair is so thickly entwined these days that only a few strands whip around in the wind. (*Cut My Hair...*)

Suddenly K Dot laughs. He raises his arms like he's crossing a finish line. "Hey, guess what? I did it! I managed to get Juliette Bracer to go out with me. We ate a really late dinner together after the show was canceled Friday night, so I guess in that way I owe you one. Then we spent most of yesterday together and drove down to visit some old friends of hers who live in Capistrano Beach. Of course, Murph was pissed, like he wanted me to help the detectives he hired sneak into hospitals looking for corpses or something."

"Okay, see, there you go. Life's not so bad after all. Give me the details. Wasn't Dutch in your way at the party?"

"She kind of was, but instead of acting like it was a big deal or trying to sneak away from her, I ignored her and flirted with Juliette anyway, sometimes with my arm right around her. We all decided to leave at about two thirty, so right in front of Dutch I just said, 'Juliette, this has been a great party. Would you like to have dinner before our show tomorrow night, then stay for the concert?' And she actually said, 'Sure, I'd love to.' Neither of us looked at Dutch, but Dutch didn't say anything, either. So I'm dating, if not sleeping with, my first real star. Maybe she isn't a big star, but at least she's starring in something. It makes her a lot more attractive than she already is. And there's no plastic on her. Trust me on that one."

"See, so what's the big deal if I take a couple of days off? Now you've arrived. Why worry about all the small stuff? Isn't this what we dreamed about back when we were kids?"

He frowns, the bastard. "The only problem is, she's pretty smart, and talks pretty fast. It's almost like it's work to keep

253

up. I hope I don't blow it. I'm gonna go on a diet right away, try to lose a little weight for when we finally hit the sack. I'm just a little nervous, that's all."

"I can't believe I'm hearing this!" I shout, then, for emphasis, I lock up the car's brakes and we come screeching to a halt, the traffic behind us swerving out and instantly laying on their horns, the smell of burnt rubber filling the air.

"I cannot believe I'm hearing this. I don't ever want to hear that crap again. You're K Dot and I'm Dizzy, remember? The two guys they would've chosen to play Butch and Sundance, if we'd only been twenty years older."

He tries to keep a straight face and act mad, but I know he isn't. "God, you're fucking insane. Shut the hell up and drive."

I'm chuckling to myself as we pull away, but maybe this is just a way to keep myself from crying, because I'm so emotional about everything that's been happening and I'm so happy to get this good a greeting from K Dot, who really was one of the people I was most worried about having pissed off. I remember an awful lot of nights in high school when we ended up just driving around town in his mother's Datsun, because we had no money for pizza and nowhere else to go. So what if we're both loaded now? Our friendship is still the same, as is the way we relate to one another. As petty and frustrated as we can sometimes be, whenever our energies come together, I think of the final scene in the original *Star Wars*, when Han Solo comes flying in to save Luke Skywalker's ass. That's how much faith I have in K Dot.

He gestures for me to take the 405 off of Sunset, then the 101, and finally the 210, which is fairly far out into the foothills, heading south for only a few miles before we take an exit in Pasadena, at which point he starts consulting the *Thomas's* in depth, flipping from one page rapidly to the next. I know we're on a specific mission now, and he knows I know it, but that doesn't ruin the spell which taking a circuitous route has created; in fact, the circuitous route somehow justifies letting ourselves get into the spell. His directions bring us into a residential neighborhood very quickly.

254

"So?" I ask.

"So, we have two tasks today. One is to go and do an interview at WTTR. That's gonna suck. The other one's gonna suck even more. You've heard about the kid who got killed?"

"Annie filled me in on the basic details."

"Well, it happened Wednesday night, probably not too long before our show started. The funeral was Saturday evening. Nobody from the band went. We can blame it on Bob Gordimer and Ross Elliot not knowing exactly which laws we should worry about, or we can blame it on the fact that we've been busy looking for you, or we could say we didn't want to cause any sort of disruption for the poor kid's family, but what are we going to do, give Annie fifty bucks to send flowers with? The kid was supposedly a devoted Blood Cheetah fan. He died because he wouldn't give up a pair of tickets to one of our concerts. So I figure we've got to go at some point."

"You're right."

"Right?"

I squeeze my fingers tightly around the steering wheel, then consciously release them. "The only thing that'll suck worse than this is doing the radio station right after this."

"Fuck the radio station, we'll go deal with that bullshit tomorrow."

"Do you know what the kid's name was?"

K Dot's already pointing for me to head down a cul-de-sac. "Yeah, it was Martin Ashcroft. They called him Marty."

"Marty Ashcroft?" I weigh the syllables in my mouth. "Sounds English. Sounds like he could have been the most popular guy in Dorchester about two hundred years ago. Well, Marty Ashcroft, here we come."

255

27 | A Tiny but Not Small Woman

THE HOUSE IS A DUPLEX, SO NATURALLY, LIKE DOGS CHASING their own tails, we go to the wrong door, rousting an old Chinese man who's difficult to understand, until he just points to the other side. The woman who answers our knock doesn't look as if she's been crying, which I perhaps wrongly expected; she seems more shocked than anything, staring at K Dot and me as blankly as if we were lampposts. She's maybe forty-two, not so much older than K Dot and me, with brown hair frosted blond, shoulder length. If I bumped into her on the street, I might guess she was a single mother hoping to make herself more attractive before middle age totally decked her. Her eyes, which are green, take a second to focus on us.

"Yes?"

"Mrs. Ashcroft?"

"Yes, that's me."

"Hi. I know we've never met before, but my name is David Zimmerman, and this is Kendra Scayline." I hope K Dot isn't about to tear my head off for using his real name in public.

Never before have I felt so naked and insincere for not having brought someone flowers, or anything, maybe a goddamn pie.

"Who?" she asks.

"The names most people know us by are usually Dizzy Z and K Dot. We play in the band called Blood Cheetah, or just Cheetah for short."

"Oh." Then the light of recognition really flips on. "Oh, I guess you do. I can't tell you how many times I've shouted at Marty to turn down the music when he was listening to one of your albums. He bought all your albums."

"Mrs. Ashcroft," K Dot says, his voice as soothing and lamb-like as possible. "It's your son we've come to talk about."

"Marty's dead," she snaps.

K Dot and I speak simultaneously, which makes us sound like idiots. "We're very sorry."

"No . . . no, I'm the one who should be sorry. I can at least be civil. Would you like to come in?"

"Please."

This is already worse than I'd have predicted, but since it wasn't my son who was murdered, I guess it's relatively easy on me. Whatever trance she was in seems to have broken momentarily, and she offers us seats in a small kitchen over-flowing with flowers, baked goods, and casseroles. All I really know about losing a family member is that it takes a long time to sink in and be dealt with, which might explain a lot here, but I still expect her to break down crying at any moment.

"Please, call me Paulette," she says. "I haven't been a Mrs. for a long time. Do you want something to eat? I have a fruit basket that's just going to rot, all the cake I could ever eat, cookies, brownies, a lasagne to feed an army . . ."

K Dot and I politely decline.

"No, really guys, I insist. It's nice of everybody to bring all this, but what did they bring it for? I can't eat anything." She's already scooping two large servings from the lasagne and heating them in the microwave on a single plate. "You'll have to excuse me, you really will, it's just that . . . I wish people hadn't brought so much food over yesterday. If I got hungry, I'd go out to McDonald's. That would give me something to do. I just . . . I don't know how I'm supposed to act yet. At the funeral I wanted to make jokes, but everybody was crying, which made me sad—then last night all I could do was stare at this."

"Ma'am?"

"I'll be right back. I should call Jimmy, since you guys are here and all. I'll be right back."

K Dot and I give each other a seriously querulous and uncomfortable look as she disappears. Her footsteps are heavy on the stairs. When the microwave's buzzer sounds, we don't know whether it's better to ignore the food and hope she remembers it, or to grab it and start eating. We opt for eating it; K Dot searches her drawers for forks as quietly as a burglar. The lasagne tastes better than I would have imagined, but of course the only other calories I've had today were a couple of airport candy bars.

"He's coming," Mrs. Ashcroft calls out, clomping down the stairs like a little girl. "He said he'll be over in a few minutes. I didn't tell him who you were. I just said someone was here who he'd want to talk to, and I made him promise to get over as quick as he could."

"Who would he want to talk to?" K Dot asks.

"Well, you two, of course. My God, I hope I said it that way. I hope I didn't say someone wanted to talk to him. Lord knows that poor boy's been through enough already. I hope he didn't think I meant the police again. The poor boy's been through it."

"The police?" I ask, then suddenly feel like a moron. Of course the police would be conducting an investigation, even if a suspect was already in custody.

Anxiety crosses her face. I can see enormous banks of emotion roiling under the surface, and once again I expect a cloudburst of tears, but they don't come. This may be the longest I've ever seen a woman go without touching her hair.

She says, "I guess I should start talking about this right now, so that it won't be something I can't talk about later, but the police were here for quite a while and they also talked to Jimmy for a long time. Because it's so rare for this to happen, where one kid escapes and the other . . . I mean . . . I wish I'd been there. I can't hold Jimmy responsible, if I wasn't there myself. I said I'd always be there for Marty, but I guess I wasn't."

Neither K Dot or I say anything. I'm trying to make it look like my mouth isn't stuffed full of lasagne. Then my attention focuses back onto the plate and it's only with the greatest of self-control that I don't make some stupid comment praising the food, or otherwise changing the subject.

She lets us have it at the same time she lets us off the hook. Her voice is barely a whisper. "I don't blame you guys, either."

"I'd like to apologize anyway," I say, "because we are sorry."

"You don't have to do that."

"Yes, I do."

259

"Did you know there was a kid living out here with his mom who would rather get himself shot than miss seeing your concert?"

I don't respond.

"Of course you didn't. And if you had, I'm sure you would have sent out a hundred tickets, for him to just give away to people. When I was his age my best girlfriend and I would hitchhike to rock concerts and people would fall over themselves to give us rides. Not even try to take advantage of us, just being friendly and helping people out. Because that was how rock and roll made them feel. I'm sure you would have sent tickets."

K Dot looks like he's about to start crying. I know I'm about to. I can't force myself to look Mrs. Ashcroft in the face.

"You want to know the truth? Jimmy wasn't just Marty's best friend, he was his only friend. He was the only other kid in their school who didn't make fun of him the second his back was turned. You know the type of crap kids write in each other's yearbooks these days? Well, listen to what Jimmy wrote in Marty's." She searches around the kitchen for the yearbook for a moment, but flips to the page easily. "Here it is. 'Dear Marty—It's been great to know someone who shared my views and experienced many of the same frustrations as me, like girls, being a loser, basic mediocrity, etcetera, but let's face it, you're a great guy. I'm proud to have a friend like you. Your buddy, James.' Not bad for an eighteen-year-old zit factory, huh?"

Tears are rolling down K Dot's face. Mine are close behind. "That's incredible."

"I'm going to go upstairs for a while," Mrs. Ashcroft says, her taut voice cracking. "Please stay. Jimmy will be over any minute."

"Sure."

"You'll stay?"

"Yes."

Once she's out of range, I whisper to K Dot. "God, this really sucks."

"You've got that right."

"Is she, like, a little bit out there right now?"

"She's freaking. I've seen people freaking on drugs before. Hell, I've seen you freaking on acid, and she's twice as far out there. This is seriously spooky."

"Don't even think about blowing, though."

"I know, I know. You're the one who mentioned it. Remember the night we ditched on the Two Ricks?"

We both raise our forks in salute; we'd both still love to shove a fork up either of the Ricks' asses, two of the guys who thought they were toughest and coolest in our old neighborhood, all the cooler for having the same tough, cool name. *On Your Radio.* Cool, cool, coolest . . . (Joe Jackson's rockingest tune ever). They approached us in a Store 24 one night when they wanted to weasel out of helping someone who they'd promised a jumpstart. K Dot and I said we'd take care of it for them, then we walked outside, shrugged at each other because we couldn't stand them, and climbed into K Dot's mother's car, zipping off into the darkness. The stranded driver was a big, rough-looking black guy. He'd probably scared them into helping him, just as they tried to scare us into taking over for them. The threats and intimidation we received the next time we saw them were worth every bit of the laughter we enjoyed for the rest of that night. Hell, all the times we've laughed about that incident over the years, or retold the story to Jay, Grover, and Alex, would have been worth it by now even if they had kicked our asses, the dumb fucks.

The kid who shows up is as bland and unassuming as the house Mrs. Ashcroft lives in. He doesn't own some hot set of wheels, he's pedaled over on a mountain bike. He's wearing black Nike high-tops and baggy rapper-type shorts, but his dark T-shirt is way too tight, too thread-barrenly old, and too . . . I don't know, even my grandmother could tell he's missed the look he's aiming for, which reminds me that however gangster-tough teenage boys dress these days, the vast majority are still nervous and embarrassed, trying to prove themselves even as they figure out exactly what society expects of them. He has a fair amount of acne left—probably worried about it even at his buddy's funeral—crew-cut sandy blond hair, and uneasy, guilty eyes. Though he's six feet tall, and still growing, his upper body is rail-thin, so thin I find myself thinking that if this is what kids can look like in America, land of Big Macs and Whoppers, the guerrilla fighter children in the world's third world countries must be wraiths.

"Hello?" he asks, poking his head inside. His voice is a scared cat's plaintive meow.

"Come on in."

"Uh, thanks."

He squints at us for a second, trying to figure out who these two long-haired dudes sitting at his best friend's kitchen table are, maybe worried that we're undercover cops, then he realizes who we are, and his eyes practically pop out of his head. He only stares at us for a second before he glares down at his feet, like he's been caught watching his own sister undress, then he looks back up at us, still amazed.

"Holy shit!" he exclaims. "I mean, holy cow! Sorry, I didn't mean to swear, it's just . . . God, I can't believe it's really you guys. I expected more cops . . . er, police, that is."

"It's really us," I say.

"God, I can't believe it. I really can't believe it. You guys are beautiful. I don't know what to say."

The kid has lightened our moods immediately and immensely. K Dot decides to have a little fun. "Well, you could do the I'm-not-worthy routine for us."

"What?"

"You know, from *Wayne's World*. 'We're not worthy, we're not worthy!' Like that." K Dot flutters his hands up and down to illustrate.

"Oh God, you're right. I'm such an idiot."

He bends over and is about to embarrass himself, but I stop him. "Hey, no, don't do that. Really, K Dot, what are you gonna make him do next, go around saying 'Not!' to everything? That went out, like, I don't know, ten years ago."

"Not!" K Dot cracks.

I smile at this, but one of us has to stay serious, no matter how easy it would be to forget where we are. "See what I mean? That wasn't cool at all. You're Jimmy, right?"

"Yeah, I'm Jimmy."

"Well, this is K Dot, and as you've probably figured out by now, I'm Dave Zimmerman, though most people just call me Dizzy." I stand and offer my hand, which it takes him a second to accept, because he's still in the age group which doesn't realize there are more formal introductory gestures than high fives. "It's good to meet you. I just wish the circumstances were better."

"God, it's great to meet you." He nods his head. His neck looks long and disjointed. "And you too, Mr. K Dot. We've been fans of yours forever. I can't remember when I didn't like you guys."

"That doesn't say much for your memory," K Dot jokes.

"God, I mean, no, I . . ."

"Do you want to sit down?"

"Maybe I better. Nobody's gonna believe this."

"Want some lasagne?"

"You don't mind?"

"It's not ours, it's Mrs. Ashcroft's."

"Sure, then."

If nothing else, I'll feel better about pumping some food into the poor boy. K Dot gets up, scoops another serving of the lasagne onto the plate we're already using, and puts it back into the microwave.

"I still can't believe I'm sitting here with Blood Cheetah," Jimmy exclaims. "I can't believe I'm gonna eat with you guys. It's like . . . it's like a big dream I'm having."

"But it's not all a good dream," I say. "You know what I mean?"

He doesn't respond, obviously doesn't catch my drift. His gaze keeps ricocheting from me to the microwave to K Dot to his own hands, flopping about in his lap.

"Hey, Jimmy, look at me. Do you get what I'm saying here? Do you dig where I'm coming from?"

K Dot pulls the plate from the microwave and sets it on the table. "What he's trying to say is that there's a reason we've come."

"Well, yeah, but . . ."

"No, you don't have to say anything unless you want to, it's just that maybe we shouldn't be too happy to be meeting this way, that's all."

Jimmy's body goes limp in his seat. All his muscles relax. The expression on his face is instantly as blank and uncomprehending as it must have been the moment he realized Marty was dead, if he really was a witness. Then he breaks into tears and tremendous nasal sobs. I've never seen anyone start crying so fast, and I've seen some pretty bummed-out people in my life. His hands come up to cover his face, his elbows on his knees. Five minutes must pass before he's able to say anything. K Dot and I poke at the lasagne uneasily.

"Marty, oh, Marty, what the fuck? What the fuck? Goddamn! Nothing was supposed to happen. We just went up there because we wanted to have a good time."

263

"What wasn't supposed to happen?"

He cries hard again for another minute before he can answer. "We'd always talked about how cool it would be when we could finally go to one of the keg parties up in the foothills. We made jokes about it, like, I don't know, just to pass the time, or when things got really rough at school. The guys who went up there were really tough. They call them the Go Boys. But when we finally got tickets to a Blood Cheetah show, it was like we belonged. We figured we'd go up to the party for a little while before the show, so everybody could see how cool we were. It was like the tickets finally made us fit in. But in another way, it was also a gag that only me and Marty understood."

Neither K Dot or I say anything as Jimmy breaks down into blubbery sobs again. I hadn't planned to hear any of this, had kind of hoped not to hear it, just to offer my sincere condolences, then leave. But it's obviously too late for that. I feel like one of those goddamn talk show hosts, not only exploiting people who are already fucked up, but probably fucking them up even worse as a result. Any wisecracks I could think of right now would put Jimmy over the edge. The way he speaks and the way he carries himself and is a little spazzy makes me wonder if his high-school M.O. was computer geek. This incident may have just canceled his first year of college. But somehow I feel it's my job to help him finish confessing now, though I know he's already gone through this with the police.

"So you guys were at your first real party, right?" I ask, when he's calmed down a little.

"Yeah."

"Did anything happen there?"

This inspires a whole new round of crying and I think, okay, something did happen there. Long seconds pass.

"Everyone was really drunk. Everyone was there from school. A lot of people hadn't seen each other since the summer started. The Go Boys were showing off, breaking beer bottles, racing to see who could drink a shot of tequila the fastest, trying to impress girls, you know. One Mexican kid was so drunk that he carved the word *white* into his arm with a knife. I don't remember exactly how it started, but all of a sudden Marty was arguing with some really tough guys about music, and bragging that we had the tickets. A few minutes later, he took his shirt off and wrote the word *remote* on his chest with oil, as a dare. I guess they keep the oil up there to start fires with. I know I should have done something, I really do, but I was scared. He had already chugged about four beers. I just wanted to run away. We were already really late for the concert, especially since we were gonna go back to my house and call a cab. It was like they were all laughing with him and saying they were his friends, but if he didn't kiss their asses, they were gonna beat him up really bad.

"Before I knew what happened, one of them reached over with a lighter hidden in his hand, and kind of flicked it real quick. Marty's chest just lit up. I can still smell it. The flame jumped from one side to the other because the letters were all attached. He looked down at it before he started screaming, then he dove down and started rolling on the ground. Nobody even cared. They were all laughing. One of the guys shouted, 'Hey, let's write *fag* on his back,'cause that's what he is. He's a fucking faggot, just like Jimmy. They suck each other's cocks!' The next thing I knew, Marty was running away. A bunch of the guys chased him up the hill, into the brush. I heard one of them yell, 'Gimme the tickets, faggot.' Then there was a shot, right after that. By the time I caught up, most of them were just standing around, staring at him. One of them pulled the tickets out of his pocket, but the way he hesitated, it was like that took more guts than shooting him had. I really don't even know if it was the same guy. Then they saw me and they all ran away, in different directions. The last thing Marty said was, 'They can't touch me now . . . ' He was trying to be funny. That's from the song, 'Remote.' After that he just kept moaning, and crying for his mom."

His momentary lucidity dissolves, and he breaks down again as he finishes the story. "His blood was everywhere, but he didn't die right away. It seemed like he laid there forever.

265

He kept making these wheezing noises . . . I don't know, it was . . . oh, fucking Marty!"

There's nothing K Dot or I can say. I feel guilty for not wanting to cry with him, but that may take months, just as it'll be months or maybe years before I want to write a song sparked by this episode, the whole story is so unbelievable. There are a lot of questions I'd ask if Jimmy was impartial and detached, but the answers are incidental. Besides, I'm sure the police have cross-examined him for all the details. K Dot moves over and puts a hand on Jimmy's shoulders.

"It's okay," he repeats several times, in a low, soothing voice. "You're gonna be all right. It's okay."

I hear a footstep behind me. Mrs. Ashcroft has come back downstairs. She has obviously been crying. Her face is streaked, her eyes bloodshot and luminous, as surreal as gasoline spilled into water. But she seems unaware of Jimmy.

"What am I going to do?" she asks, defeated.

"Is there anything we can do for you?" I offer.

"I don't think so . . ."

"No, really, I mean it, is there anything you need?"

"Where would you start?"

All I can do is shrug my useless fucking shoulders.

"We are going to put that on his grave marker," Mrs. Ashcroft says. She wipes her eyes with her hands, then her hands on her blouse. "That line. To remember him by. You were his favorite band."

K Dot looks up. "Thank you, ma'am."

"You meant a lot to him."

"Can we . . . can we help you out with the gravestone?" I ask, as delicately as possible. "Or with anything that's too much of a burden?"

She shakes her head ever so slightly. "No, I can afford things, for now, if that's what you mean. It's the future I worry about."

"Get in touch with us if you need help," K Dot says.

"I don't think we'll be hearing from each other again. I appreciate you coming, I really do, but maybe you should go now. I'll give Jimmy a ride if he needs one. The police aren't sure if he's safe from repercussions."

"I've got my bike," Jimmy moans.

Mrs. Ashcroft walks us outside. The day is still magnificent, warm and clear. The San Gabriel Mountains stand out with precision.

"Thank you for not showing up in a limo," she says.

K Dot and I each shake her hand before we move toward the car. Then, in a moment of pissant inspiration, I pull the velvet sheath from my coin pocket and offer it to her. The half eagle is solid and reliable in my hand. "Let me give you this. It's brought me good luck for a long time. Put it away for now, but if you ever get into real trouble for money, have a reliable coin store buy it from you. Do something good with it. Think of it as a last present from Marty."

She smiles tight-lipped, but accepts it.

Then K Dot and I are in the car, working our way back toward the highway, one of the two places where everyone in California ends up eventually.

267

28 | Postlude Electric Power Leads

/E DO THE RADIO STATION INTERVIEW AND PROMO THE NEXT day, but I don't remember any of it except being very polite, very cordial, very gracious, and relatively somber, like a goddamn politician, not going nuts the way I usually do and shouting crazy things into the mike and threatening not to boast, "WTTR is *the* station for guitar!" if the deejay doesn't play all the obscurely brilliant tunes I dust off from their stacks, like Boris Grebenshikov or the Reducers. That all five band members are there, plus Annie and Murph, makes it harder for the deejay to notice how subdued I am, or to get into any depth about either the murder or my disappearance (the two might not look coincidental), or even the band's responsibilities (or lack thereof) toward its fans. Which is just as well by me.

K Dot does mention that he and I went to visit Mrs. Ashcroft, but he glosses over the details, which is also fine with me. Most deejays are good people at heart, moral and upstanding, it's just their circumstance and the circumstance of for-profit radio stations that turn them into idiots, robots, and fat middle-class doormen. But how anyone who really cares about rock music should relate to deejays is still belted out best in the Kinks' "Round The Dial," which is about as greatly sophisticatedly rockin' as the Kinks got.

I'd love to have long, analytical conversations with the guys about what bolting to San Francisco really meant, or about music, the philosophically neutral idea that in this branch of the entertainment world especially, image is everything, is art itself. Just the way a band dresses is transformed into feelings and emotional responses every bit as fully as the progressions of musical notes that comprise their songs. But the only one who's had any interest in this sort of bullshit even in the past, when life was innocent and we all got along, was K Dot, and I certainly don't want to snip the tendrils of trust vining between the two of us right now. It's better to just do things together, not talk too much about them.

With the rest of the band, what we'd probably end up discussing very quickly is why the fuck we should even stick together when this tour's over, which might lead to us breaking up, maybe even on the spot, depending on how boiling our temperatures got. Which in turn would lead to a cheesy, ridiculous reunion in ten or twelve years. Blood Cheetah has achieved so much musically that any record company would believe, probably correctly, that even a shit-disc of our worst outtakes and dribble would sell enough copies to turn a profit. As ridiculous a reason for sticking together as that is, it's good enough for me right now, even if Blood Cheetah just becomes a studio band for my material, while the other guys decide to tour solo as they see fit, the bastards. Luckily, everyone besides K Dot is either too pissed off at me, too disgusted, or too involved in his own worries to be speaking to me, to even acknowledge my presence. Which is good. I'd rather be a fly on the goddamn wall than have them sniping at me and being sarcastic and prickling my flesh with sidelong asides, the way they will—especially Jay—in another day or two, once things have cooled off and they start venting.

I'm still pretty gloomy as Tubbs drives us to the hall but it's only the calm before the storm. The concert is where I come alive. No forecast has predicted the storm, though the fact that I've been sober for a record five days and the sheer bulk of bullshit needing to be purged might be like the barometric pressure plummeting. I'm impatient to have the opening band finish up, would rather skip them altogether. But the storm is the music, and as soon as we start playing, as soon as I strap on my Stratocaster and remember how smoothly my fingers slide over the magical strings, I feel the lightning of it crackling through my bloodstream. I know this is actually adrenaline, but I prefer to think of it as lightning because that's how crisp, electric, and surging it feels. Though I'm not on any drugs, I'm as high as any drugs can get me, coke, crystal meth, meta-amphetamine, what have you, the buzz increased by knowing the only hangover will be healthy exhaustion and work satisfaction. Every nerve ending in my body is on Code Red alert, ready to scramble, fly me back into the pocket, the absolute fucking hole of reality, which I've always known exists.

"Kick it!" Grover screams, every time Jay tries to address the audience between songs. K Dot, Alex, and I dive into the next song. "Rock 'n' roll, motherfucker!"

No matter how many times music has gotten me this jacked, I'm always convinced I'm discovering feelings nobody else has ever heard of, let alone experienced. But deep down, I know the whole reason the audience has brought their glowing, infinitely complicated, yearning selves to the show is to re-experience all the things our music has given them in the past; that they do get it, maybe more than I ever will. Tonight I feel honored just knowing it's songs I've written which we're celebrating. The band is called Blood Cheetah, and for a few hours, maybe I am a cheetah; I feel as natural slashing away at my guitar strings as a cheetah must at a full sixty-mile-an-hour sprint, which no other animal understands; as a dolphin must going airborne ten feet above the surf it loves; as a peregrine falcon must tucking its wings in and feeling gravity suck it through the sky's vortex. There are no words to describe such omnipotence, you can never explain perfection except to say what it isn't.

Sometimes when we're on stage, I feel a million miles away from the other guys, that we might as well be on opposite sides of the old Berlin Wall, staring at one another without ever communicating, but tonight, although they're not talking to me, I feel as close to them as I have in a long time. They've been through all the bullshit, the fucking horseshit hassles, and the devastating hype I've been through, especially lately, until we're back to the point where the world is so obviously trying to beat us down that we're a united front, a five-man electrical rockin' army.

They'll get over the insignificant details, the little shit, just like I have. I trust K Dot to keep a perfectly synchronized bass rhythm for me to land on when I take off on a screaming, seat-of-my-pants lead, just as intuitively as a trapeze artist has to trust his catcher when he lets go of the bar and starts somersaulting through midair. And K Dot has every bit as much faith in Grover as I have in him, and as I have in Alex, poor Alex, who I haven't been nearly as friendly with on this tour as I should've. His biggest problem, besides worrying about his ex-wife and his kids, is that he's the only guy I know who drinks more than me—and who knows what else when he goes off on his own and we tell ourselves he's just bummed out. Maybe he's the one who's a single camel-straw from running away next, and maybe he's the one who never would come back, maybe a suicide, joining the infamous Club, knowing that while the band could never replace him, he's the member we'd find it easiest to justify trying to replace.

The particular sounds of well-known musicians' guitars are as distinguishable as a '74 Beetle engine—think of Hendrix, of Clapton, of the Edge, of Eddie Van-Fucking-Halen early in his career—which is a combination of both what instrument they have wired how and how their hands manipulate which strings in what sorts of stylistic, rhythmic, riffmatic ways. At some point the music becomes a personality unto itself, stands for something more than just the notes; all the huge inarticulate passion and fury of living, emotions busting at the seam, exploding, tearing the night apart, physical and rebellious, just

271

as the lyrics become an anthem and represent infinitely more than the song's theme, as does the singer's voice. The truth is, the way we can all play—K Dot's bass throbbing like an underwater reactor, Alex curtly patterning floral chord imprints, me ripping caterwaul leads—or trying to do something like it on the piano—Grover racing straight at the audience, like train tracks and you expect the Orient Express to come crashing through your living room—Jay has it pretty easy. But with his banshee monkey wail, he could sing the lyrics in ancient Egyptian and our fans would still relate.

Midway through the song "Yellow 5," K Dot comes strolling over. I'm boogying in place with my eyes nearly closed, but every few minutes I go through a phase where I leap up and down, still playing, until I run out of breath, or I dance out to my mike stand and sing backup, still dancing. K Dot obviously has something to say. Once again, it's not about the music. A nonsequitur, like football linemen asking each other for recipes at the bottom of a pig-pile tackle.

"What's with you?" he demands. "You got pot you forgot to share?"

"What?"

"Are you high? You seem pretty smiley tonight."

"No, I'm just happy to play for once."

"Well then, rock on, motherfucker!" he roars, his heavy brown eyes flashing. He bounces out in front of Jay as he crosses back to his side of the stage, showing off for the crowd, and though Jay scowls, the crowd goes nuts, the surge in their screams caroming back through the hall.

Maybe the smartest goddamn thing we could do as a band would be to spread our touring schedule out more, always take five or six days between shows, not two or three. The financial costs would be worth how much better we sound. One of the biggest reasons I'm so excited about playing tonight is that it's been almost a week since I had a guitar strapped over my shoulder. As sick as I can get of touring and of playing the same music over and over again, I do love pour-

272

ing my soul out in a song, no matter how much of a goddamn
cliché that is. I've been wearing a guitar at the moments of my
greatest triumphs and have turned to guitars to work myself
out of my worst depressions. If nothing else, I could never
commit suicide because I'd want to write a final masterpiece
about my state of mind right before I offed myself, not just a
quick note. And after I'd composed for an hour or two, the
satisfaction of working hard would change my mood. Musicians make music, period, and though I'm not the first to say
it, the old, desperate, angst-ridden line is true, rock 'n' roll can
save you. It's worked for me thousands of times.

The first two-thirds of the show fly by, the same way you can
drive a hundred miles and not remember any of it, the same
way this entire tour has, really. We're into the tunes where I
have to play piano, and I swear I'm playing most of them
better than I ever have before, even when we were in the
studio recording them. I'm hitting all the real notes cleanly and
on measure, not taking shortcuts. Now it's time for "Remote."
I lean into the microphone, start to speak, and realize that the
crowd is kind of distant this way, spiritually if not physically.
So I get up and walk over to one of the mike stands, right on
the edge of the stage. The crowd is going absolutely fucking
bananas. I try not to focus on any of the individual faces in
the first few rows, but I can tell that every single person is
standing. Out of the corner of my eye, I see Jay turn away,
like he'd rather go wipe sweat off his chest than listen to me.

"Hey, uh, listen, this won't take long, but I just wanted to
say . . . before we play this next song, that a lot of you have
heard news reports and sometimes rumors about everything
that's going on with the band. But don't believe the hype. It's
all bullshit."

The crowd roars at this, maybe because they understand
and maybe just because I swore. Myself, when I'm in the audience at a big show, I can never make out what the musicians
say between songs, then I'm amazed at how clear it sounds

273

later on a recording, but that might only be my crappy hearing versus good taping technology.

"A lot of you have probably heard that one of our fans was killed last week, and while I'm not going to go into detail about it, I will say that, yes, it did happen, and that every member of this band feels like they lost part of their family. Life is way too cool for it to end that way . . ."

My mind is racing now, trying to figure out what to say next. I had almost wanted the audience to give a moment of silence, or to link arms as a sign of unity, or some other ridiculous gesture, but that's obviously impossible. It would take two or three minutes just for the other guys in the band to understand what I was asking for, let alone the drunk fans in the upper bat-and-nosebleed seats, since we hadn't planned anything together, not even an a cappella rendition of "What a Wonderful World." And the other guys might not think a sponta-neous tribute was such a brilliant idea, even if their resistance was just a petty way of shooting down one of my ideas. When I glance around, Alex is already giving me a serious come-on-you-dumb-fuck-and-don't-say-anything-too-stupid look. Jay has just about disappeared into one of the wings, gesturing to a stagehand for something to drink.

"I'm not going to stand up here and give you some huge sermon about it right now, but I will tell you the kid's name. It was Martin Ashcroft. Marty, for short. If you remember one thing from this show tonight, just try to remember that his name was Marty Ashcroft, and that he really loved rock 'n' roll. His name was Marty Ashcroft. This song is for him."

I walk back to the piano bench, pull it in close behind me, and lean into the microphone. "Sing it with us if you know it . . ."

So that's what he gets. I can't promise anyone I'll stay sober for the next hour, let alone the rest of this tour or the rest of my life. And I can't guarantee that the band will ever record a song about Marty, or that we'll even be together tomorrow morning, for that matter. All I can say is that he's immortal in my heart tonight, that's he's touched me as deeply in death as

I could ever have hoped to touch him in life. I hope his death won't have been in vain. My fingers sweep down the piano keys. Ten thousand souls join together. Ten thousand voices break slowly into song. *"Remote, they can't touch me now . . . Remote, they're all past me now . . ."*